THE REDEMPTION OF GEORGE

A SERMONIC TALE FROM ABUNDANCE FALLS

STEVE WALSH

EVANGELIONS

This book is a work of fiction. Names, characters, places, churches, denominations, corporations, and incidents are entirely the product of the author's imagination, or are used fictitiously. Any resemblance to actual events, locals, or persons, living or dead, is entirely coincidental.

Copyright © 2021 by Steve Walsh
All rights reserved.

No part of this publication may be reproduced, distributed, or transmitted in any form or by any means, including photocopying, recording, or other electronic or mechanical methods, without the prior written permission of the publisher, except in the case of brief quotations embodied in critical reviews, and certain other noncommercial uses permitted by copyright law. In accordance with the U.S. Copyright Act of 1976, the scanning, up-loading, and electronic sharing of any part of this book without the permission of the publisher is unlawful piracy and theft of the author's intellectual property. If you would like to use material from this book (other than for review purposes), prior written permission must be obtained by contacting the publisher. Thank you for the support of the author's rights.

EVANGELIONS LLC
17503 La Cantera Parkway Suite 104 - 174
San Antonio, Texas 78257
www.evangelions.org

ISBN: 978-1-7334336-2-4 (eBook)
ISBN: 978-1-7334336-3-1 (Softcover)
Scripture quotations from The World English Bible.
First eBook and printed edition, 2021

My deepest love for my wife and children
who have suffered through my long nights and
early morning bouts of doubts.

Profound thanks to my friends
Joseph, Lyle, and Sterling
who provided important insights
and criticisms which made the story better.

And to Solo and Jackson who always listened.

All opinions, theological positions,
and mistakes are mine.

Soli Deo gloria
Easter, 2021

PROLOGUE

The First Establishment Church was dead.

I was summoned to the Bureau of Church Oversight where the Director hovered over a large scroll intently studying its contents. He didn't bother to look up as I entered.

"There's no other way of saying it," he said, pinching the bridge of his hawkish nose. "They've lost the Spirit. They no longer serve our purpose. They've bound themselves to the dark-side."

His voice elevated with intensity as he spoke. "Like so many others, they've allowed themselves to be seduced by their unmerited wealth. Their hearts are no longer responsive to the Master. They've substituted His love with their own feelings of good will. They've become another cult in the world, lusting for the things of man."

I didn't dare interrupt him. Great bolts of lightening flashed around us as he spoke. He stopped for a moment and looked at me grimly. "This has been a long time coming. They have repeatedly ignored the Master's warnings."

"Are none to be saved?" I asked.

"A few," he answered. "The others you will scatter into the forgottonverse as chaff in the wind."

I nodded silently at his judgement.

"There is one man in particular that we have hopes for. He is to be spared if he can be redeemed."

"How will I know him?" I asked.

"A wound on his face."

I bowed low before the Director. "What are my orders?"

CHAPTER 1
DAY OF MOURNING

6 A.M.
I arrived at the First Establishment Church on a drizzly Saturday morning. The streets were glistening with the tears of angels, and the sky was as gray as their eyes.

I made my way up a narrow staircase leading from the sanctuary to the choir loft were I found an older man leaning over the balcony. His powerful hands gripped the wooden banister like the talons of a hawk as he observed a group of men working below. His hooded eyes scanned their progress. His breath came as wisps that materialized in the chill air, then disappeared. He pulled a pocket watch from his vest.

"Hector, fire up the furnace," he yelled.

A voice instantly responded, "Si' jefe."

Immediately the squeak of a fan-belt signaled the turning of an industrial blower that started pushing warm air into the room.

He looked easily seventy years old. He was small, powerfully built, with broad shoulders, narrow waist, and thick forearms. There was no paunch, no stoop, and no nonsense to his bearing.

He wore a gray flannel shirt, navy cargo pants, six-inch leather boots, a thick padded vest, and a newsboy cap that covered a tangle of snow white hair. He was accessorized with a walkie-talkie, and a cluster of brass keys that dangled from his belt.

He sensed my presence, straightened up, and without turning pointed into the sanctuary.

"This sacred space was built by hand during America's Gilded Age. There were no nail guns, power saws, or electric drills. Nobody had ever heard of plastic pipe, drywall, or prefab trusses. Computers and smart phones were a hundred years away.

"The wood beams were hewn from first growth Oregon forests. The bronze doors were cast in British foundries. The church bells were poured in Germany, and the wrought iron hammered in New Mexico. Those marble columns at the front of the sanctuary took three days to be set upright using ropes and pulleys."

He paused to momentarily scratch the stubble on his cheek. "You're looking at one of America's greatest architectural wonders. No amount of money could duplicate it today."

He was interrupted by the sound of electrical switches snapping below us, followed by bursts of light from massive crystal chandlers hanging from the vaulted ceiling above.

He waved his arm at the stained glass windows surrounding the room. "They're priceless — the work of one of America's greatest artists."

I envisioned the sanctuary on a clear morning when the early rays of light hit them, and the chamber blossomed into a kaleidoscope of colors.

"Look at that pipe organ behind you. That's a one-of-a-kind, five manual, two-hundred-five rank, classic."

The word classic was an understatement. Dozens of

gleaming silver pipes rose like a metal forest thirty feet into the air from behind a playing console that looked like it belonged on the Starship Enterprise.

"The whole sanctuary rumbles when that grand old lady hits its lowest pitch. At her highest, she produces a sound that is barely audible to the human ear."

"They say the angelic choirs burst into song at that frequency," I said, half joking.

He turned towards me and grinned. His face was the color of roasted pecans, and just as wrinkled. He extended a hand, it was as rough as fifty-grit sandpaper.

"Charlie."

"Sandalphon," I replied. "Just call me Sandy."

He looked me up and down as if I was a horse for sale. "No offense, but you're one big hombre. What have they been feeding you?"

Charlie wasn't the first to comment on my size.

"Actually, I'm the runt in my family," I said, congenially.

"Runt? You must be over seven foot tall."

"Seven foot one, and 285 pounds."

"Of solid muscle."

"Actually, I'm quite docile."

"Docile or not, I'm glad you're on my side."

So was I. Charlie was a legend at the Bureau of Church Oversight.

"I've been the custodian of this church for over a century," he said. "Under different circumstances I would tell you that it's a joy working here.

"There was a time when the congregation found God in the worship, inspiration in the hymns, peace in the flicker of a candle, solace in the prayers, and comfort in the golden light streaming through those stained glass windows."

The luster in his eyes dimmed. "But this church has become a nest for the wicked, and a house of abomination."

I nodded, and he motioned for us to sit on a hard oak pew.

"Let me bring you up to speed."

CHARLIE RUBBED HIS HANDS TOGETHER IN THE CHILLED AIR, puffed on them, and began speaking. "The First Establishment Church is a landmark in the city of Abundance Falls. Its sprawling campus is considered to be a religious shrine.

The church sits halfway up Mount Plentitude on seven wooded acres overlooking the civic center. At an altitude of 920 feet, we're required by the FAA to have our famous red strobe lights blinking on our bell towers to warn nearby aircraft."

"They look like Satan's pitchfork waiting to skewer any wayward pilots," I chuckled.

The old man hushed me with a raise of his hand and continued. "Sightseers from all over the world come to take selfies on the steps of our sanctuary. Street artists sell pastel sketches of the building. Collectors plead to inspect our precious furnishings. Painters beg to examine our fine art. Sculptors yearn to caress the marble statues. Organists seek to play this priceless pipe organ."

He drifted off for a moment, then returned. "But the church won't let them."

I arched my eyebrows.

"You're asking why? It began many years ago when the executive council of this baronial house of God voted that the church would only serve as a private spiritual retreat for the prosperous citizens of Abundance Falls."

"Prosperous citizens?"

"Let me explain." He gestured to the room. "The First

Establishment Church is what religious insiders call a big steeple church. This massive structure is the flagship of the Establishment Denomination, and the source of enormous Establishment pride.

To preach from its pulpit is the pinnacle of an Establishment minister's career. It's a privilege granted only to those masterful in telling comforting spiritual messages that appeal to the sensitivities of successful people."

"I thought clergy were supposed to preach from the Bible."

He looked at me sharply. "Don't kid yourself. Most clergy will preach whatever they think will appease the members of their congregation."

"I don't get it."

He looked at me like I was kidding. "They do it for job security, or the money — and this church has the money. Our executive council gloats that they control one of America's largest church endowment funds at over a half-billion dollars."

I gave a low whistle. "B as in billion?"

"That's right. The fund was originally established by the barons of industry, political fat cats, and oil tycoons to shelter their money from taxes. In the past decades the nouveau riche have added even more."

Why? I thought.

"I know what you're thinking," Charlie said. "Here's the reason. Because as a restricted endowment fund, the executive council can control it, invest it, and make even more money from it without having to publicly disclose their investment performance, or pay earnings to any specific charitable activity, or philanthropic work. That means they can use the fund for whatever activities they choose."

"Such as?"

"To begin with, the fund is used to pay for a team of department managers to oversee a staff of nearly sixty employees who cater to the desires of the congregation.

"It covers the salaries of an executive pastor, a senior pastor, three assistant pastors, several youth ministers, four music leaders, an organist, a public relations team, a state of the art computer department, and the staff of a restaurant sized kitchen.

"It also pays the wages for a multitude of low paid workers who serve as office help, groundskeepers, waiters, maids, security, and maintenance employees like you and me."

"That's a small army," I said, astonished. "There must be thousands of people who attend here."

He smiled faintly, looked skyward, pointed a finger upward, wiggled it as if mentally calculating, then said, "Four hundred, give or take. Maybe a hundred more at Christmas and Easter."

"Four hundred?"

"We used to have a few more, but the executive council drove them off."

"Why would they do that?"

"The yearly interest on the fund pays well into the tens of millions, so they are very particular about who gets to enjoy its benefits."

"What benefits?"

"Here's a few. Free sight-seeing excursions, sumptuous prayer breakfasts, mimosa brunches, luxurious patio meals, extravagant country club luncheons, music concerts, celebrity speakers, cruises to Greece and Rome, tours of the Holy Land, mission vacations to foreign countries, summer retreats, private day care, golf tournaments, tennis parties, and lavish gatherings during Christmas, Super Bowl, and

Easter — all completely free. Not to mention the priceless opportunity to rub elbows with four hundred of the most important citizens of the city."

"No wonder they don't evangelize."

"They do in their own way. It's just that they only evangelize to people who feel comfortable driving statement automobiles, talking about financial investments, skiing in the winter, boating in the summer, living in upscale neighborhoods, and seeking the good life without the guilt."

"They only want people who think exactly like themselves."

He placed a finger along side his nose. "Bingo!"

"That's why they don't want Joe Lunchbucket sniffing around," I said.

His eyes lit up like he'd helped me grasp the physics of a spinning-top. "Welcome to the First Establishment Church of Abundance Falls."

"Shouldn't they spend their money on the needy?"

"They do," Charlie snorted. "Only they consider themselves the needy."

My eyes narrowed.

"Don't act surprised. They're no different from thousands of congregations who spend donations caring for themselves. You pass them every day without realizing it."

"Thousands?"

"Yes. There are countless churches who pamper themselves with the donations they receive. Some make bucketloads of money by merchandizing books, newspapers, and other periodicals. Others sell air-time on their private radio and television stations. Some have worldwide satellite links they own. Many run private schools, colleges, and big ticket sports programs. I know of several who sell religious life, health, and property insurance. Some, like this church have a financial scheme for their members to invest in."

I gave a low whistle. "How do they get away with that?"

"Like any non-profit corporation, it's all in how they structure themselves."

"I've always pictured a church like one of those little roadside congregations that struggle to pay a pastor and their utility bills."

Charlie nodded. "Yep. It never occurs to the average person that most churches have plenty of money in the bank. Just because they're always asking for money, doesn't mean they really need it. They just want it to expand their religious empire."

"Amazing."

"Let me give you an example of how it works here. Fifteen years ago I watched our executive council take thirty million dollars from the First Establishment Church Endowment Fund to create a private non-profit investment scheme called the Sacred Name Unity Fund, or SNUF. Its stated mission was to further God's healing love through compassionate community outreach to women."

He stopped for a moment, looked over the railing, and shouted a few orders to the workers. He turned back and resumed speaking.

"What was I saying?"

"Sacred Name Unity Fund."

"SNUF invests in five companies all focused on some aspect of woman's healthcare. One company owns the land they build women's clinics on, another owns the construction company that builds the clinics, a third owns the clinics, a forth manages the personnel who work at the clinics, and a fifth produces the drugs and pills used by women that go to the clinics. The result is that SNUF has seen an average of 23.5% in yearly returns, since its inception."

"I'm not a business whizz, but at 23.5% annual interest a person would be a fool not to invest in SNUF."

Charlie looked at me with the face of wisdom. "You're right, and almost everyone in the congregation has. That's why nobody questions how the money is made, or the decisions of the executive council."

HE MOTIONED ME TO A WINDOW OVERLOOKING THE STREET. "Look down there," he said, cracking it open.

In the early morning light, dozens of news trucks with satellite dishes pointed skyward were setting up. Camera crews were busy selecting visual backdrops for their reporters. Florist trucks were unloading giant sprays of flowers. Men in bib-overalls were wrestling with bulky boxes, and volunteers were setting up temporary seating.

"Big crowd today," Charlie said. "Every luminary in the country has come to mourn the death of Lilith Wendigo, the heiress of the Wendigo Family fortune. You may have heard of her son Peter, the cyber prince."

"Are they members of the First Establishment Church?"

"Heavens no," Charlie laughed, shaking his head emphatically. "They aren't even Christians. She was a member of some weird Hollywood religion, and Peter is an agnostic. George Goodman set this up as a favor."

"Who's Goodman?"

"He owns Bumble's Furniture Store. The two have known each other since college."

"Did they meet in class?"

"Not exactly. In those days Peter wasn't the refined man

you'll see today. He was a skinny, shy, computer nerd who wore thick glasses and spoke with a slight stutter.

"One night Peter drove downtown to grab a pizza, and on the way back to his car he was mugged in the parking lot."

"What happened?"

"What happened is that combat vet George Goodman was passing by and saw a couple of meth-heads robbing a hapless geek at knife point. The next minute one guy went to the hospital with a broken jaw, and the other with multiple fractures."

A ghost of a smile swept over the old man's face.

"Seriously?"

"Then, if you can believe it, the two scumbags sued George for their hospital bills and emotional distress. That's when Peter's mother Lilith stepped in. George had become a hero in the Wendigo family, and she was not about to let him suffer for saving her son.

"She made a few phone calls, hired a big named law firm, and the case was quickly dismissed. It wasn't long afterwards that George was invited to move into the family beach house with Peter, who was more than happy to have the guy who saved him as a room mate.

"In the following years, Peter introduced George a new social class and way of living. Most importantly he introduced George to his future wife, Sarah."

CHARLIE RUBBED HIS FOREARM LIKE HE WAS WORKING OUT some kinks.

"George was raised by middle class parents to be a good boy, and he grew to be a good man. Ask anyone in the congregation and they will tell you that he leads a good life, and has

The Redemption of George | 15

a good family. They'll say that George is good to people, and people are good to him. They'll let you know that he has good friends, lives in a good neighborhood, and has a good job"

I leaned back against the pew, and listened.

"They'll tell you that George belongs to a good country club, has a good handicap, and occasionally volunteers to do a few good deeds.

"Most importantly, they will boast that his "goodest" quality is that he belongs to a compassionate, caring, spirit-filled, grace-infused, enlightened family of flexible faith, just like they do."

Charlie took a breath and nodded once, as if stressing his words.

I looked around the sanctuary. "Why does George attend here?"

Charlie rubbed his chin thoughtfully. "It's the only church he knows. He's comfortable here. His wife likes it here. He feels secure in his salvation here. In some ways he feels superior to people who don't attend here.

"Besides, George likes being around people who are the same color, speak the same language, embrace the same culture, dress the same, vote alike, root for the same sports teams, and show a polite disinterest towards people who attend other churches.

"As a member of the First Establishment Church he's never forced to obey ridged religious doctrines, musty traditions, or dogmatic creeds. He's free to dress as he wishes, come and go as he pleases, and disappear without so much as saying hello, or goodbye.

"His attendance isn't mandatory and he can skip worship without any guilt whenever he has something more interesting to do. Most importantly, there's no requirement to sing in a choir, decorate the sanctuary, clean up after the service, or even attend a banquet in the Great Hall."

"Which are a few of the reasons why I'm guessing this place has died," I noted.

"You got it. Yet the biggest reason it perished is because the executive council embraced the ways of death. They accepted the teachings of the world, and the philosophies of the damned."

"I don't understand," I said.

"Their pastor never preaches anything that ruffles his congregation's feathers, hints that they should change, or demands that they do anything beyond listening to an affirming sermon of self worth, tenderness, and spiritual unity intended to make them all feel good about themselves."

"And the congregation perished from that?"

"That, and something more evil."

I TURNED MY ATTENTION TO THE ACTIVITIES OUTSIDE THE church. Thousands of dollars had been spent improving the look of the area surrounding it. Streets had been power washed, graffiti removed from sidewalks, a billboard for a local bail-bondsman had been covered with a sympathy message for Lilith, and dozens of nearby panhandlers were given fifty dollars, a bus ticket, and told to relocate somewhere else.

Scads more money would be spent hosting a private banquet and elegant reception for invited guests after the service. It was clear that the red carpet had been woven, cleaned, rolled out, and everyone wanted to be seen walking on it.

Around noon, a long line of black limousines began

pulling up to the church's porte-cochere. Each luxury vehicle was greeted by a man conspicuously dressed in tails, black-tie, white gloves, and top hat.

He bowed low and opened their doors. Flashes from the paparazzi sparkled like fireflies as they captured celebrities, singers, musicians, and scores of lesser known friends of Peter, as they made their entrance dressed in outfits ranging from the lavish to the lewd.

Pulling up fashionably late, the Governor arrived in his bullet-proof Cadillac, escorted by motorcycle officers, black sedans, and local police all blaring sirens like he was the second coming.

"Remember," Charlie said, quietly. "People are only here to be seen by Peter, not because they loved his mother — most never met her."

"Seems hypocritical."

"Not in the world of the super elite where people trade on associations that are second or third removed from the actual person. Frankly, I doubt if she had a real friend in the world."

"Why's that?"

"Lilith wasn't the warm matronly type that you will hear about today. Her critics called her the *helferin.*"

"Helferin?"

"It's a German word for *helper*."

"I don't get it."

"The female guards at the Nazi concentration camps were called helferin."

"What's the connection?"

"Lilith was a fierce advocate for population control and abortion."

. . .

18 | STEVE WALSH

Peter's guests streamed into the sanctuary. Even the most poised seemed uncomfortable as they were shown to their seats by security guards masquerading as ushers. They looked awkward and disoriented in a church, uncertain of what to expect, and afraid of being embarrassed.

Some sat nervously twisting their bulletins into spirals of paper. Others cast anxious glances around the room hoping to spot a friend. Most stared straight ahead with their backs straight, as if by doing so they could speed up their punishment and get on with their lives. One buxom lady squirmed around like she might be struck by lightening for sitting in the house of God.

My mouth twisted into a wry smile. *I wished I'd brought some popcorn.*

Charlie gripped my arm and lowered his voice. "That's Peter Wendigo seated in the front row facing the pulpit."

I saw a fifty-something man with thick copper colored hair. His face was suntanned with sharp contours. He was dressed in a hand tailored blue pin-striped suit, a crisp white shirt, and ruby red tie.

Clinging to him was an exotic looking woman wearing a black fitted jacket over a gray blouse and pencil skirt.

"He's had quite a makeover," I said, mildly amused. "No more glasses, and no more pocket protectors."

"That's mostly due to George's influence."

"Who's the woman?"

"That's his latest girlfriend. She's an actress on a popular Japanese soap-opera. To her right is the Governor, Mayor, Congressman, State Senator, and Chief of Police."

"Pretty important line-up."

"They can't afford not to be seen, they all want Peter's

political and financial support. Seated in the row behind them are the five ruling members of the church's executive council.

"From left to right that's retired General Warlocke, Doctor Dinferi, Judge Mors, Professor Laverna, and Mrs. Von Heekate. They control SNUF, and the First Establishment Church Fund."

I saw that the rest of the room was filled with financiers, industrialists, internet kings, media tycoons, and shipping magnets who all did business with one of Peter's companies. I even noticed some consulate officials from Muslim, Hindu and Buddhist countries wearing their traditional robes and head garbs.

"We got permission from the Fire Chief to place overflow seating along the aisles near the windows," Charlie said.

"They look uncomfortable."

"Believe me, they'd rather be sitting on a metal folding chair than to be left out."

"So where's George Goodman?" I asked.

"That's George with his wife Sarah." He pointed to the row behind Peter.

George was a competent looking guy with a gentle face, brownish hair, graying temples, and friendly powder blue eyes. There was nothing remarkable about him except for an ugly scar running from the corner of his left cheek to his left ear.

His wife on the other hand was an exception. She was fashion magazine beautiful. I wondered how man with George's looks could have landed a woman of such extraordinary looks. Admittedly my speciality is not in the psychology of human attraction, but I had to question their pairing.

Turning my attention to the center of the stage, I saw a

brightly polished urn sitting on a long table. I assumed it held the ashes of the late Lilith Wendigo.

"That's Pastor Pendragon seated behind the urn," Charlie said. "Next to him is the Reverend Doctor Guile slumped in the wheelchair. He's the Pastor Emeritus."

At the bottom of the steps leading to the urn, a large oil painting of Lilith captured everyone's eye. The likeness must have been done when she was in the prime of her youth.

She looked radiant, hopeful, and lovely. A floral wreath suitable for the Kentucky Derby sat next to it. Dozens of floral sprays sent from corporations and courtiers were placed around the church as blossoms of tribute.

Someone had gone to great lengths to let us know how deeply she would be remembered. A stringed quartet, hired from the local philharmonic quietly played Satori's, "Time to Say Goodbye."

No expense had been spared.

As the time drew closer, photographers elbowed for their best angle. TV cameras checked their focus, and police in black tactical uniforms took up strategic locations inside and outside the sanctuary. They were dressed in full battle rattle, ready for any reason to launch a ground assault. Their expressionless faces moved slowly from side to side scanning for any terrorists lurking in the church. Occasionally, one would speak into their wrist.

Charlie quietly lifted a finger to his lips, and then dropped it. As if on his command the bells of the First Establishment Church began tolling, and the ushers solemnly swung the heavy double doors of the sanctuary closed. There was an audible thud, and the room rustled to an expectant silence.

Pastor Pendragon sat upon his throne-chair gazing at the crowd with an air of imperiousness often associated with certain men of God. He waited for the jostling to stop and for the sound of the bells to fade.

Dubbed the "praying mantis" by his seminary classmates for his triangular face, wide-set eyes and elongated body, he pushed himself up using the thick arms of the chair. He smoothed the black suit that draped his thin frame and marched forward to the elevated pulpit with an air of spiritual authority.

Each tread squeaked lightly under his weight as he ascended the platform. When he reached the top, he squared his manuscript, and switched on his wireless microphone.

"Can everyone hear me?" he asked, unceremoniously tapping it. There were motions of affirmation throughout the sanctuary.

He glanced down at a small mirror hidden from the congregation's view. He was self conscious about his pock-marked skin, the wisps of hair slicked over a balding scalp, and the sagging neckline he'd promised himself to have surgically tightened.

Pendragon was a calculating pulpiteer who'd politicked his way up the Establishment Denomination's ladder to seize the coveted title of Executive Pastor.

His best selling books on how to get the most out of God, a weekly radio program, and a soothing baritone voice, justified his salary of over a half million dollars a year in the minds of the congregation. More importantly, he was their personal religious celebrity, and they loved to say he was their pastor.

He peered over his reading glasses, took stock of those in

attendance, and evaluated their worthiness to hear his message. He stole another glance at the mirror to make sure his face reflected the proper sadness for the occasion.

He'd never met Lilith Wendigo but that wasn't a problem. Her secretary had provided him with a suitable eulogy to read. Allowing a few beats for dramatic effect, Pendragon lifted his arms, and a respectful silence from the assembly followed.

"I'D LIKE TO WELCOME EACH OF YOU TO THIS CELEBRATION OF life for our dearly departed sister Lilith Wendigo."

He paused for theatrical effect, then continued. "On behalf of her son Peter, thank you for showing your solidarity in his time of grief. Please bow your heads with me, and pray."

After an all encompassing prayer of heartfelt petitions, Pendragon began reading the prepared script that recounted Lilith's birth, early life, education, and the loss of her beloved husband.

Turning the page, he raised his voice and expounded on her extraordinary courage after the suicide of her daughter.

Peter squirmed slightly at the gross exaggeration.

Pendragon scanned the congregation before he continued somberly. "This is a sad time as we remember the life of such a vibrant person. Lilith was a visionary leader who served as a brilliant inspiration for women of all ages in the struggle for female equality. As a young woman she courageously gave her soul in the battle leading to the landmark victory of Roe verses Wade."

He altered his tone to a sober and serious timber. "As a bold crusader and tireless champion of woman's rights, Lilith used her considerable fortune to support women's clinics where troubled women and girls can find low-cost access to healthcare."

He pointed to her urn. "Even in her final years, although ravaged by disease, she found the energy to help elect state and national politicians who continue to fight against those who would deny a woman's freedom of choice."

He smiled at the Governor and the row of politicians. Many nodded their heads in affirmation. He took a scripted sip of water from a crystal goblet, checked his manuscript, and proceeded.

"That's why I am privileged to announce that the Sacred Name Unity Fund is planning the future construction of the Lilith Wendigo Memorial Health Clinic right here in Abundance Falls."

He nodded towards Peter, and clapped his hands together encouraging those present to join him. People throughout the sanctuary stood up, and began applauding him.

Peter waved modestly. He was baffled. This was the first time he'd heard of this.

JUST AS PENDRAGON WAS ABOUT TO CONTINUE, A NEATLY dressed woman seated next to George stood up and began yelling. "Wendigo was a witch! She was evil! She's burning in hell!"

All eyes widened, heads turned, cameras zoomed in, and everyone watching the live stream on the internet gawked in astonishment. Three state troopers reached for their pistols and began running from the shadows to protect the Governor.

Pendragon recognized the small woman. It was Welma Forthwright, a long time member of the church. His pockmarked face went pale. *Great spirit, not now. The last thing I need is a pro-life martyr.*

"Jeremiah one-five! Free the babies!" she yelled. "We don't want an abortion clinic in Abundance Falls."

"This isn't the time for your histrionics Welma," Pendragon shouted into his microphone. "I'm not talking about abortion."

"Lilith Wendigo is the mother of abortion you Judas. How many pieces of silver did her son pay you to say these lies? Lilith was a monster!"

"Security, escort her out," Pendragon yelled from his perch.

Four heavily armed cops marched down the aisle towards her, and Welma yelled all the louder. "Lilith was an atheist, a God hater, a baby killer! Why are you doing her funeral in this church?"

The entire congregation strained to get a better look at the spectacle.

Welma turned to George, latched onto his arm and said, "Help me George." Before he could reply, one of the cops reached over the heads of two people, and grabbed Welma by her hair.

"Let go of her," George said, shoving the cop's arm away. He noticed the name tag — Officer Smith. "Give us a second."

Instead of waiting, Officer Smith continued to bully his way towards them. In his clumsy attempt to get to Welma, his bulky duty belt snagged on men's expensive suits, and mussed the coiffed hairdos of the ladies. The men shouted and the women pushed him away in anger.

Mother of earth, is no one going to stop this madness? Pendragon wondered.

George didn't understand why the cops were in such a rush. Welma wasn't going anywhere, she was no threat. He turned to her. "Let go of me Welma. You can't escape."

The Redemption of George | 25

"I don't want to escape," she replied, clinging to him harder. "I want to save babies."

"Is this how you do it?"

"You do what you can, George. You're never too old to fight against evil." She immediately resumed yelling pro-life slogans, shouting at the top of her lungs.

The leather fingers of Officer Smith's sap gloves reached out and ripped at her shoulders. George spun the small woman away to shield her from harm, but Officer Smith seemed like he was on a personal vendetta.

"Get off her," George ordered.

"You're interfering with the police," Officer Smith growled, his yellowed teeth were bared like a wolf.

"You're off duty fella," George growled back.

"I'm never off duty, you need to move away, or I'll arrest you."

George glanced at Welma. "Enough is enough. Let go of me."

"All right," she said, relaxing. "I guess I made my point."

Without warning, Officer Smith punched George in the face causing him to stagger backward. At the same time, from the opposite end of the pew, his partner plowed her way down a row of shocked dignitaries with her baton outstretched.

Just as she was about to strike George, a black fist the size of a frying pan grabbed her ponytail jerking her backwards out of the pew."

"That's a no-go lady."

Dazed, she lay in the aisle looking up at the face of a giant African American who was grinning at her dangerously. It was the face that many bad actors had seen in the last moments of their lives.

She instinctively reached for her pistol.

"Don't," the muscular man ordered, and he placed his

foot on her arm. She quickly nodded her head in submission dropping the weapon from her hand.

"Thanks Kip," George yelled, releasing his grip on Welma. "I owe you one."

Kip Flintlock was the legendary head of Flintlock Global Military Corporation.

"I've always got your six, brother," he shouted back. The man was dressed in a brilliant purple suit with lavender vest, a light blue shirt, an orange tie, and a matching pocket square.

Seizing the moment of distraction, two cops grabbed Welma and wrestled her to the floor breaking her nose.

"You bastards," George shouted.

"Stay out of this," Officer Smith said, holding up a taser. His partners began dragging Welma to her feet, blood gushing down her face.

"You miserable cowards," George shouted. "I'll have your badges."

Officer Smith laughed. "Wooo, not like we haven't heard that one before."

"You're lucky he just wants your badges," Kip said, menacingly. "I want your scalps.

Officer Smith pointed at George. "Handcuff the organ grinder and his monkey."

Thunderstruck, George looked at Kip then directly at Officer Smith.

"Organ grinder and his monkey?" George's voice was low and dangerous. The muscles in his neck flared, his chest expanded, and his hands clenched into powerful mallets. He and Kip had been called many things in many languages, but this was a first.

Kip was coiled like a black panther ready to strike. He winked at George, and they rushed at Officer Smith who panicked and fired his taser. Its spear shaped prongs barely missed George, and sunk into the wood of Peter's pew. The entire congregation instinctively ducked.

"You missed buckaroo," George said, smiling wide. "Now I'm gonna enjoy breaking your nose for Welma."

Officer Smith and his team reached for their batons. One of them pulled another taser.

"You fire that thing, and I promise I'll break your jaw," Kip said. The cop fired despite the warning, and the darts struck Kip in the chest.

Kip grinned wide and remained standing. The cop did a double take, and checked his taser, unsure if he was dreaming. Kip casually pulled the prongs out of his jacket and threw them on the floor.

"Now you did it," he said. "Now you've forced me to break your face."

The cop, visibly shaken, backed away. Kip scowled at the police officers. "Who's next?"

Without any further provocation Kip and George waded into the cops, who began swinging wildly at them. Within sixty seconds the police were down on the floor with black eyes, bloody lips, dislocated shoulders, missing teeth and a broken jaw from a dozen precision blows.

The congregation stood on their tip-toes hoping to see more action. From the back of the sanctuary six uniformed reinforcements came rushing down the aisle. Suddenly, as if he'd been in a trance watching a nightmare unfold, the Chief of Police awakened, and jumped to his feet shouting. "Everyone stand down! Stand down, now!"

Instantly, all of his underlings obeyed him like trained dobermans.

"Arrest those two men," he bellowed, pointing at George and Kip. "Get that woman and those officers some medical attention."

Several cops carefully approached George and Kip, who allowed themselves to be taken into custody. That was the moment George first tasted the blood in his mouth.

The whole fight seemed to take place in a flash. Pastor Pendragon stood in the pulpit shocked and shaking. "Please everyone," he shouted into the microphone, "let's take a ten minute break so the police can sort this out."

He nodded to the stringed quartet who began playing something soothing. The congregation remained standing, excitedly talking among themselves about the events of the last few minutes.

After things settled down, Pendragon returned to the pulpit, motioned for the quartet to stop playing and addressed the congregation. "If you will please take your seats we will resume our service."

Everyone did as they were told, and quickly sat down.

"Let us continue in our remembrance of our beloved friend Lilith Wendigo."

Just as he was about to take another breath, a skinny black man the color of a dried raisin with cotton white hair, sharp features, and deep wrinkles began shouting from the back of the room, "Choose life people! Protect the unborn. Babies are God's property!"

The congregation audibly gasped and Pendragon thought he was going to faint.

"Has everyone lost their ever-loving minds?" he shouted. "Get that man out of my sanctuary!"

The skinny man hollered back, "It's not your sanctuary you viper. This is God's house. Abortion ain't right. It's killing black babies."

Pendragon frantically signaled to three security cops who

easily overpowered the man, collapsing him under their weight.

"Repent, brothers and sisters, repent," he pleaded, from beneath the pile.

The Governor leaned over to the Mayor and whispered, "Who the hell are these people?"

"Scum," the Mayor replied, bluntly.

"I want them locked up until hell freezes over."

The Mayor nodded in agreement. "I'll talk to the DA."

As the security cops latched handcuffs around the man's scrawny wrists he began singing an old spiritual as loudly as he could.

"O Listen to the lambs, all a-crying. Listen to the lambs, all a-crying. Listen to the lambs, all a-crying. If you want to go to heaven when you die."[1]

The stringed quartet immediately began to accompany him. Pendragon, veins popping from his neck, yelled down at them. "Stop playing that you fools!"

Which they did, but not until the man was dragged out of the sanctuary by his arm pits. The entire church watched in silence as he disappeared through the doors of the church where he was met by a group waving signs, cheering, and clapping like he was a rock star.

One of the men outside, wearing a motorcycle vest, raised a bullhorn to his mouth. "We will not remain silent in the face of butchery and murder! We will no longer sit still under the scalpel of death. We will defend the unborn and fight for their right to live as human beings!"

The crowed began chanting, "Choose life! Choose life! Choose life!"

An uneasy line of security personnel lowered their face masks in an ominous sign for the crowd to disburse, but the crowd remained fixed, unrelenting.

Pendragon called for another ten minute intermission.

What a nightmare, Peter thought, collapsing in his seat. *What the heck was mom up to?* He knew she was obsessed with woman's rights, but it was a cold surprise to hear the family name tied with murder.

The TV cameras zoomed in as Peter made his way over to the Chief of Police and drew him close. "Those two men are my personal friends," he whispered. "I don't want them arrested."

"They interfered with the lawful duties of a police officer," the Chief replied, stiffly.

"You mean like lawfully beating down an old woman and a skinny black guy? We both know the only thing the woman did was to disrupt the service, and the man's biggest crime was to sing off key. I'm the one who should be upset, and I'm not. I won't be pressing charges, and if the church is smart they won't either."

The top cop considered this. "What excuse will I give?"

"Say it was an unfortunate misunderstanding. If not, my lawyers will sue the department for endangering the lives of the congregation."

"Endanger?"

"There was no proportionality. We all saw your Officer strike George Goodman in the face for no reason. He was only shielding the woman from harm. I'm sure the photographers got some nice pictures of your female cop pulling a gun on Kip Flintlock. No matter what he did, he wasn't armed.

"On top of that, what in the hell were your cops thinking by firing their tasers? This is a church for crying out loud. I was almost hit. You really want to explain to a judge the danger they placed us in?"

The Chief went pale.

"I suggest you bury any thoughts of arresting my two friends. And if I were you, I'd give the old man and woman a warning, and let them go. Now, can we please get on with my mother's service?"

The Chief looked at one of the richest men on the world and considered his options. He quickly decided that discretion was the best form of valor.

"Sure, Mister Wendigo, I'll order my people to release your friends immediately."

Pastor Pendragon, completely flustered by the scuffle, took his time composing himself before lifting his hands signaling for the congregation to sit down. He took several deep breaths, and continued the service.

"Dear friends, let us not be distracted by this unfortunate disturbance. Let us not take seriously this woman and her accomplice. Let us ignore the extremists outside who cheer for them. This is not the occasion to air our religious grievances, or our political differences. We all loved Lilith. This is the time for us to honor her life."

He looked intently at the congregation.

"In the spirit of Christian love we must pray for all misguided individuals who maliciously desecrate the sacred work of Lilith Wendigo, and her legacy. They do not understand that Jesus wants a just society where women have the freedom to decide what to do with their bodies."

Seeing an opportunity to impress Peter and his coterie of politicians and celebrities, Pendragon decided to go off script.

"There's nothing in God's holy word that speaks directly of forbidding abortion. On the contrary, we are told to respect the dignity of all people, which includes the dignity of a woman who must make important choices regarding her family."

Pendragon lowered his voice to emphasize the gravity of his words. "That was the lifelong message of Lilith Wendigo, a fierce crusader who fought valiantly to bring all women the gospel of empowerment and liberation."

He paused to allow the congregation to absorb the profoundness of his message. "And so, I invite you to pray with me as I ask God to richly bless those who carry on in the righteous vision of Lilith Wendigo. Please bow your heads."

In unison, the congregation lowered their eyes and studied their shoes.

Pendragon proceeded to intone a flowery litany of religious cliche's appropriate for the occasion. He beseeched God to forgive the hatred of Welma and the unknown black man. He asked for God's mercy upon them for there sinful attitude towards women. He informed God that it was his duty to bless all of those who labored for reproductive justice. He reminded the Supreme Being of his obligation to favor the doctors and nurses engaged in the divine work of helping mothers.

He then prayed for all of the dignitaries in the chapel who he deemed important enough to mention to the higher power. Suddenly, everyone sat up hoping to hear their name.

"Finally," he rambled, "I ask that you bestow your divine strength upon these brave officials who stand against the agitators, and radicals who seek to destroy our civil liberties, and deny a woman her civil rights."

He ended his litany of requests with a resonate, "Amen!"

All eyes looked up again, happy to be finished.

. . .

The Redemption of George | 33

THE SERVICE CONTINUED FOR ANOTHER FORTY MINUTES WITH testimonials from the Governor, several notable celebrities, a female singer who crooned a medley of popular songs, the reading of a whimsical poem, and a video history of Lilith Wendigo's life produced by her fans at the local community TV station.

When it was finished, Pendragon stood up.

"This celebration of Lilith Wendigo's life is now concluded. Invited guests will join me at the church columbarium where her ashes will be interred. Afterwards, Peter would like everyone to join him for refreshments in the Great Hall."

Pendragon nodded imperceptibly to the stringed quartet who began playing the music to Carrie Underwood's, "See You Again." He made a mental note to never hire them again.

Before the congregation had cleared the doors of the sanctuary the videos of the fight had gone viral on the internet.

WE RACED DOWN THE WOODEN STAIRCASE LEADING FROM THE loft to the sanctuary. At the bottom, Charlie spoke quietly into his walkie-talkie. From nowhere a dozen workers appeared and began removing flowers, folding chairs and tables.

"I've seen some crazy things in my time, but today takes the cake," he said, chortling.

"Peter didn't seem phased."

"He's bullet proof."

"How so?"

"His parents weren't exactly the doting mother and father that Pendragon said. They were never around. His dad ignored him and Lilith was obsessed with her causes. Peter and his sister were two rich kids raised by a revolving door of hired nannies."

"So they grew up fending for themselves."

"Which didn't work too well for Peter's sister. After her suicide, Peter completely checked out of the network."

"How old was he?"

"He left home at eighteen, and went to live at the family's beach cottage."

"Is that where he discovered his gift for computers?"

"The story goes that he was playing a video game when it fried. With nothing better to do he taught himself how to fix it. Six months later he was writing software for his own video games, licensing his ideas to other companies, and manufacturing arcade consoles."

"It's amazing to think that his entire empire all started with a lonely kid working on the kitchen table of a beach house."

"Yes. The Master often weaves a person's life in perplexing ways."

We reached the pew where Welma was battered by the cops. Charlie knelt on one knee, pressed his finger into the carpet and studied it. The tip was damp with rust colored blood.

"This was no accident," he said. "Someone gave those cops the signal to crack her nose."

"Why the message?"

"A lesson to anyone watching that resistance to surgical family planning will not be tolerated."

He examined a few more splotches on the carpet. "Apparently someone didn't like what she said."

"You think it was Peter?"

The Redemption of George | 35

"Not a chance. The only reason he held a funeral service was that he felt pressured. Had it been up to him, his mom would have been cremated, placed on a shelf somewhere, and forgotten."

"How about the fight?"

"Whoever was behind this wasn't expecting George and Kip to get involved. They're both combat veterans. George was an Airborne Ranger who earned a Bronze Star for valor. He was also on the All-Army boxing team. Kip won a Silver Star for exceptional gallantry. He also served as a martial arts instructor in Special Forces."

"Which is why they we able to take down those cops within seconds," I said.

"Yes, and wasn't it a sight to behold?"

"Was the boxing team where George got the scar on his face?"

"No, that was the result of a knife fight during the Panama Invasion back in 1989."

"What about Kip?"

"After he got out of the Army Peter set him up in the private security business. Kip's company is a major player in global defense and international corporate protection."

"Who do you think ordered the attack on Welma?"

"Good question," he said, looking up. "I have my suspicions."

GEORGE AND SARAH WERE BARELY OUTSIDE THE CHURCH when they were surrounded by a pack of perky female reporters fighting for George's attention.

"Why did you defend that woman?"

"Are you an anti-abortion advocate?"

"Do you think men should be able to control a woman's body?"

George thought the questions sounded more like challenges instead of thoughtful inquiries. It was as if he was being accused of some unspoken crime. Why weren't they asking him about the police brutality?

"She was being mistreated by the cops," he said. "So I defended her."

"Do you consider yourself a pro-life vigilante?"

"No, I consider myself a guy who knows the difference between right and wrong. The cops were wrong."

"Do you believe a woman has the right to choose?"

"I believe a woman can choose whatever she wants, it's a free country."

"Was the old woman wrong to interrupt the service?"

"I don't think she was wrong, I think she was rude."

"Does she have a right to voice her hatred?"

"This is America, she has the right to voice an opinion like we all do."

"So is hate speech the kind of free speech you want?"

"If it's between hurting my feelings or hurting my rights, you can hurt my feelings all day long."

"Does your company support women's rights?"

"Bumble's Furniture supports everyone's rights."

A microphone was shoved in Sarah's face. "How about you, ma'am? Do you agree with your husband's defense of a pro-life activist?"

Sarah was caught off guard. Why would the reporter assume that?

George broke in. "Sorry folks, we've got nothing further to say." He began leading Sarah away.

The pack of rivals for the next Pulitzer Prize shouted their indignation. "You're speaking with the press Mister Goodman, you owe us an explanation."

"I don't owe you squat," George replied, tersely.

"If you don't talk to us, we'll assume your silence is compliance with the old woman's views."

"You can assume whatever you want, now get out of my way."

THEY LEFT THE UNHAPPY REPORTERS BEHIND.

Sarah turned to George and whispered, "We need to talk."

"About what?"

"About what you've gotten us into."

"I didn't get us into anything, I did the right thing."

"Well my beloved, no good deed goes unpunished. Now everyone thinks we're pro-lifers. Since when? I don't care what a woman does with her body, any more than I care if a boy wants to be a girl. It's none of our damn business."

"I wasn't going to watch those cops hurt Welma."

"If she'd gone peacefully they wouldn't have hurt her, and you wouldn't have needed to play the knight in shining armor."

"There was no way they intended to take her peacefully. You should have seen the look on their faces."

"I did, their faces looked like they were trying to do their job."

"How can you say that? They were dead set on shutting Welma up. Same kind of hush tactics I saw used by dictators in the foreign countries I fought in."

"You think we live in a dictatorship?"

"I'm saying that someone is trying to intimidate anyone who disagrees with abortion."

"That word sounds ugly, say 'surgical family planning' instead."

"Why I should I sugar coat it?"

"Because I don't like the word abortion. Besides, since when do you care about a woman's pregnancy? You were barely around for mine."

"I care about a person's freedom of speech."

"You're an idealist, my love."

"How so?"

"Welma had no right to voice her hate."

"What's hateful about disagreeing with Lilith's beliefs?"

"It was her nasty tone. Welma had no right to speak like that, especially about Lilith Wendigo."

"Nasty tone?" George asked, perplexed. "You're confusing your feelings about politeness with Welma's right to speak."

Sarah looked at him as if she was about to claw his eyes out. George was saved when his cell phone vibrated. He read the text.

"It's the General, he wants to see me in the library."

"You think he wants to talk about your views on free speech?" Her tone was frosty.

"I have no idea, the man hasn't said a word to me in the past twenty-five years."

"No surprise, you're like the Holy Ghost. People never see you, they often talk about you, and no one knows what the heck you do — except play golf." She offered him a tight smile.

"Guilty as charged," George said. "Golf is my only passion, except for you." He gave her a quick nibble on the ear.

She swatted him away.

"Besides, if God wants to bless me with a gift, who am I to say no?"

"Swinging a golf club is not a gift my beloved, even if you are the club champion, it's a mental problem."

"Then I'm stone cold crazy." He laughed and raised his hand as if in a pledge. "I only hope that if I go to hell when I die, there's a par-four course down there."

He walked away chuckling at his own humor.

PUSHING THROUGH THE EXCITED CROWD, GEORGE MADE HIS way to the church library on the third floor of the administration building. Opening the door he was immediately transported to the days of his youth.

The musty smelling room brought back fond memories of the time he'd won a scavenger hunt by finding a copy of *Pilgrim's Progress* hidden behind the steam radiator. Before he could say hello the General waved his cane in the air.

"What in the hell was going on down in the sanctuary? Why were you interfering with the police?"

Although he projected the appearance of a hard bitten military leader, the General had never seen a day in combat. He'd been a cubicle warrior all of his career, shuffling papers, drinking coffee, politicking, and telling war stories about the field exercises he'd been on as a second lieutenant.

At his side, rolling back and forth in a wheel chair was Pastor Guile, a decrepit old cleric who appeared visibly agitated.

"I wasn't interfering with the police," George said. "Welma asked for my help and I gave it to her. What did you expect me to do?"

"We expected you to let the police do their job," Guile said, abruptly.

"I didn't like the way they were doing their job," George said, calmly. "Welma didn't deserve to be treated like that."

"Not only did she deserve it, she asked for it," the General said. "She had no right to disrupt the service with her foul views."

"I agree she was outspoken, but not to the point of getting punched. She's a frail old woman."

"I didn't take you for a pro-lifer," Guile rasped.

"I'm not, I'm pro-freedom. She has civil rights like everyone."

"Her civil rights ended the moment she became uncivil," the General said. "Who the hell are you to defend her? Didn't you hear Pendragon tell security to escort her out?"

George was beginning to dislike these men.

"Of course I heard Pendragon, I just didn't like the escort service he provided."

"And that's another thing, how'd Kip Flintlock get involved?"

"Because I was being attacked by the cops."

Guile rolled his wheelchair closer to George. "I knew a man like that would eventually cause trouble, and now the chickens have come home to roost."

"A man like what?"

"His purple suit and orange necktie should tell you that he'd be more comfortable at a church with people of his own kind."

George studied the withered face of the old bigot.

"I'm really disappointed in you George," the General snorted. "Your family has been members here for generations. I'd expect more civilized behavior."

George leveled his gaze at the two men. "If you both must know, Peter personally invited Kip."

Guile and the General could barely contained their shock.

"Peter knows Kip?"

"When Kip got out of the Army Peter hired him as his bodyguard. Kip worked his way up to become head of Peter's corporate security and eventually formed his own company. Peter is a major shareholder."

George watched Guile turn into a person of color as the old man's face became a sickly shade of green. The General suddenly changed the subject.

"All that's important is whether Peter was offended," he said, gruffly.

"Peter wasn't offended."

"How do you know that?"

"If he was offended he would have told me, and I would have told you."

The General suddenly realized that he'd underestimated George. The man was much closer to Peter than he thought. He instantly began plotting a way to win George's confidence.

"Have you spoken with Pendragon since the end of the service?" George asked him.

"Not yet."

"I just saw him talking with Peter a few minutes ago, maybe he has an update I don't know about."

The General didn't respond. Instead, he yanked out his cell and pressed the speed dial. "It's me, I'm with George. He says you've spoken with Peter? Yes? Did he say anything?"

There was a muffled response.

"Okay, tell him we have absolutely no intention of pressing charges against Welma and that other guy. Make sure he understands that. Anything else?"

There was a pause. "No? Excellent."

He ended the call.

"Seems you're right. Peter had only praise for the

service." The General looked at Guile with a face that said, *we'll talk later*.

"Even if Peter was angry, which he's not, what could he do?" George asked. "He doesn't even go to church."

"We'd like to change that," Guile said. "Peter would make an excellent member of our congregation. He'd be a perfect advisor to the Sacred Name Unity Fund. We'd like to invite him to help continue in his mother's legacy of providing women with essential medical treatment."

George's scar abruptly tightened, a sure sign of unexpected trouble.

The General suddenly became cordial. "By the way George, I was speaking with the Judge earlier today. His pharmaceutical company down in Mexico is building a large medical complex. If they order their furniture from Bumble's can you deliver it down there?"

George bit his lower lip and thought for a moment. "Sure, we already make a monthly trip to purchase Mexican pottery and folk art. I don't see why we couldn't bring a load of furniture down with us. How much are we looking at?"

"In the neighborhood of a couple of hundred thousand."

George gave a low whistle. "That's a lot of stuff. It'll take a double big rig, and some extra paperwork for customs, but we can handle it."

"Excellent," the General said, agreeably. "I'll let the Judge know."

He offered his hand like they were old friends. "I apologize if I was rough on you. Today has been stressful with all the visiting dignitaries and their petty demands. I'll be glad when the reception is over."

"Sure, no problem," George said, shaking the General's hand in truce.

"Will I see you at the reception?" the General asked.

"Absolutely."

"Good," the General said, and then added. "By the way, in the future I hope that you'll be a little more supportive of those who do the work of the Lord, and a little less for troublemakers like Welma, and that other guy."

George pursed his lips, nodded quietly, and left the room.

THE CONGREGATION EVENTUALLY DRIFTED DOWN A LONG garden path to the Great Hall of the church. Many of the guests were transported in special golf carts designed to look like miniature limousines.

The Great Hall was built when opulence was commonplace among high society. Enormous oil paintings of stern-looking men and women surrounded the vaulted room. Colorful banners embroidered with family crests hung from flag poles jutting from the gallery overhead. Tall arched windows allowed light to filter through panes of vintage rippled glass. Hundreds of candles burned brightly on tabletops providing a magical feeling to the occasion.

A portly chef, sporting a wide handlebar mustache, sliced generous portions of succulent beef and pork for waiting guests. At his side, silver food warmers mounded with casseroles, potatoes, and steamed vegetables were lined up along a banquet table within easy reach. Dozens of large round tables were set with fine linen, bone white china, crystal goblets, and polished silverware.

A waitstaff, dressed in formal black uniforms, glided around the room pouring champaign, wine, water, herbal tea, and coffee. Smiling bartenders served complimentary cocktails from temporary bars set up in each corner of the hall. The mood was convivial, but not festive. Muted conversations focused on the events that had taken place earlier in the sanctuary.

"Let me see your lip," Sarah said, reaching into her purse for a tissue.

"I'm alright," George replied, jerking away slightly when she touched it.

"You need to put some ice on that."

"I know right were I can get some," he said, eying the bar across the room.

"Two's the limit," she cautioned, dabbing his mouth. "We don't need any more drama today."

A moment later George held a tall scotch on the rocks — light on the rocks.

"What in the hell was that all about?" Kip asked, appearing from nowhere.

"I dunno, those mall cops went totally berserk."

"I don't understand their problem, Welma's an old lady for pity sake."

"Yeah, it doesn't make any sense."

"I told Peter to let me handle security, but he said the church wanted to do it."

"Lot of good they did," George said.

"You're slowing down, buddy. Back in the day that cop wouldn't have gotten close enough to land a punch."

"I know," George admitted. "I'm starting to feel old."

The pair met in Mrs. Aitkens' freshman English class and became best friends. After four years of high school they enlisted together so that they could serve in the same battalion of the 82nd Airborne Division.

After graduation from Jump School at Fort Benning,

they'd gotten matching tattoos of paratrooper wings with the words *Death from Above*, inked on their biceps.

"Looks painful," Kip said, pointing to George's bruised lip.

"Not as painful as my ego," he said, holding up his glass. "I'll be better after a couple of these."

"I still don't get it," Kip said. "Those cops acted like Welma was public enemy number one."

George took a long sip from his drink, and pushed the cold glass against his face.

"I know, something is wrong, very wrong"

PETER BROKE INTO THEIR CONVERSATION. "GEORGE, YOU really took one for the team, I owe you." At six foot three the handsome man stood eye to eye with Kip.

"Didn't mean to ruin Lilith's service," George said.

"Are you kidding? Those cops deserved it." He took a sip of bottled water. "Seriously, I can't thank you enough for arranging mom's funeral, especially her placement in the columbarium."

"Least I could do for all the things your family has done for me."

Peter grabbed Kip by the shoulder. "As for you Kip, please explain to me how you kept from going down when that taser hit you; that was amazing."

"All my suits are infused with kevlar and carbon fiber tape. The kevlar stops the prongs from reaching my skin, and the tape causes the electrical current to pass through it, not my body. It's saved me on more than one occasion."

"I want the name of your tailor," Peter said, chuckling.

"Too easy, boss."

Peter then addressed both of them quietly. "I'm not sure

what mom was up to, but Welma made her sound like she was the high priestess of hell."

"She wasn't that bad," George said. "Although there was that time when she threatened to kick us out of the beach house for setting the kitchen on fire."

"Yeah, she had her irrational moments," Peter chuckled. "But seriously, you don't really believe that she was a baby killer do you?"

"I don't think it's a baby, it's just a bunch of tissue," George said. "Besides, it's a woman's decision. Who am I to judge?"

George's cell phone vibrated. He fished it out of his pocket, and checked the screen - *unavailable.* He motioned for Peter and Kip to give him a second, and turned away.

"Yes?"

A man's deep voice began speaking. "Mister Goodman, this is Samantha Stones, assistant DA."

George thought his brain was playing tricks on him. He tried to picture the face attached to the voice. "Erm, how can I help you, Samantha?"

"We're bringing charges against Welma Forthwright. Will you be available to make a statement?"

George's eyebrows furrowed. "Charges? That was quick. Things got emotional, but nothing that couldn't have been contained if those cops hadn't overreacted."

"Overreacted?"

"Why would it take four armed men to restrain a little woman who might weigh-in at a massive one hundred pounds? She's a widow in her seventies for crying out loud."

"Mister Goodman, police officers have an obligation to protect themselves and others. She might have been armed."

George laughed so hard that he coughed in Samantha's ear.

The Redemption of George | 47

"Armed? What planet do you live on? Clearly you have no idea what kind of strip search we had to go through to get into the church."

"I saw the video tape. She was a threat to the Governor, she resisted arrest, she's guilty of hate speech, and she's guilty of disrupting a religious assembly."

Samantha's voice sounded as tough as a man trying to dance in high heels.

"Resisting arrest? Pastor Pendragon only asked that she be escorted out of the sanctuary, that's all. She didn't do anything to be arrested for. And guilty of hate speech? What exactly did she say that qualifies for hate? Just because she raised an awkward topic at a bad time doesn't give the cops the right to beat her to the floor. If I was her I'd press charges against the police."

There was silence on the other end of the line.

"Hello, you still there?"

"Mr. Goodman — she struck an officer, disrupted a lawful assembly, and she slandered the character of Mrs. Wendigo."

"Look, Welma's views on abortion might be unpopular among some of the people present at the service, but it didn't give anyone permission to throw her on the ground and break her nose. Besides, Lilith Wendigo is dead. Even I know that a dead person can't sue for slander."

"So I take it you don't want to make a statement," Samantha said, with a huff.

"Has Peter Wendigo asked you to press charges?"

"No, he hasn't."

"Has the church?"

"No"

"Then who has?"

"The decision was up to the DA."

"So the DA wants to make an example of a senior citizen

because she caused a disturbance that Peter Wendigo and the church don't seem to care about?"

George wondered who was behind this.

"Frankly sir, the DA originally wanted to press charges against you, but apparently you have friends in high places."

"So he's making an example of a harmless old widow?"

There was silence on the other end of the line.

"I want to know if the DA is going to press charges against the cops who attacked us?"

"There was no attack." The man's voice on the other end of the line toughened. "The off-duty officers were doing their jobs."

"Their job isn't to strong-arm the public. If they'd been patient she would have eventually come along without any fuss."

"Sir, do you or do you not, wish to make a statement?"

"Don't get your panties in a twist," George answered. "I just did, aren't you recording this? I'll gladly testify in court if it comes to it."

Samantha's teeth gritted. "Do you plan on filing a formal complaint against the officers?"

"It would be a waste of my time knowing how things work down at city hall."

"The judge set her bail at $250,000," Samantha said. "Unless she can post bond, we're going to keep her locked up. You'll get an email when her case goes to court."

Samatha quickly hung up.

George looked at the phone clenched in his hand. His fingers gripped it so tightly that they were bone white. The blood had completely drained from them.

"Buddy, you okay?" Kip asked.

"Except for a pounding headache, I'm hunky-dory," George said, relaxing his fingers.

"You look upset."

"That was the DA's office. They're charging Welma with resisting arrest, striking a cop, public nuisance, hate speech, littering, jay-walking and any other thing they can dream up."

"I'd like to speak with her," Peter said.

"Good luck, she's in jail."

"Jail? I told the Chief to give her a warning and let her go."

"Apparently he didn't get the hint. The DA is pressing charges, and the judge set her bail at $250,000 dollars."

"That isn't right," Kip said. "She doesn't have that kind of money. Somebody wants to make sure she's punished."

"I see," Peter said, his face turning stormy. He reached into his jacket, pulled out a phone, and pressed a few numbers.

"Jack — it's Peter. I need someone to get down to the city jail. Yes, right now. I need them to bail out a woman named Welma Forthright and a guy named . . ." He looked to George for help.

"Chili Popper," George whispered.

Peter gave him a double take. George shrugged his shoulders.

"Chili Popper," Peter said. "Yes, you heard right — Chili — Popper — you want me to spell it? Okay, pay whatever their bail is. Also, contact Silvia in our regional office. I want them to have the best legal representation we've got. Of course we'll pick up the tab. Call me later."

He placed the phone back in his jacket. "The DA wants to play games? Then, game on."

Peter always loved a challenge, George thought, asking himself why he'd gotten so angry with Samatha Stones. What difference did it make if they wanted to prosecute Welma? If the old woman had kept her mouth shut she wouldn't have been arrested. Millions of women had surgical family planning, and the world hadn't stopped turning.

If Welma wanted to fall on her sword for her beliefs that was her decision. It was none of his business. He'd tried to protect her from the cops, but he couldn't protect her from herself. Now Peter was involved and things might get complicated. George hated complicated.

"George, I've got *Sotirios* moored down at the marina. It's been awhile since you and Sarah were on board. How about you two join me for a little cruise? We can practice our golf drives off the fantail, and Sarah can relax."

"Sounds like an offer you'd be crazy to refuse," Kip said.

"We already know he's crazy," Peter laughed. "I remember when he wanted to be an astronaut. I was busy working on my first artificial intelligence project in college."

"Astronomer," George said, correcting.

"Well, something to do with the stars," Peter countered. "Anyway, if he hadn't taken over his father-in-law's furniture company, I would have hired him."

"To do what?" asked Kip.

"I dunno, I would have invented a job for him. I've always wanted a space exploration company. George would be the perfect man to run it."

"We would have had a great time," George said, wishing things had worked out that way.

Peter slapped George on the back. "Don't worry about what happened today. You did the right thing."

"I probably should have stayed out of it."

"No way," Peter corrected. "Those cops needed an ass kicking. And as far as I'm concerned it's not over yet. If the DA tries to hassle either of you, let me know. The important thing is that you're both okay. I'll call you in a few days and maybe we can all go and visit Welma."

"Anytime," they said together.

Peter walked away shaking hands with a half dozen eager admirers who'd been waiting patiently to be recognized.

After Peter had gone, Kip asked, "Why the interest in Welma?"

"Peter grew up alone. He's empathic, he cares for people and senses their emotions. My guess is that he's curious about what makes Welma tick, and believe it or not, he's actually concerned about her."

"The woman just turned his mom's funeral service upside down."

"Which makes her all the more intriguing. I have a hunch that she may have awakened a sense of sacred honor that's been lacking in his life."

"Sacred honor," Kip replied. "The ability to see tyranny and take a stand against it."

"Just a guess," George replied.

THEY WERE ABOUT TO REJOIN THEIR WIVES WHEN THEY WERE confronted by a man with scraggly shoulder length hair, dressed in a black tank top, leather jacket, torn jeans, sunglasses and layers of chains around his neck. George recognized his face from an 1980s album cover.

"It's really messed up that a couple of schmucks like you are allowed to obstruct justice and then walk away free. You're the kind of douchebags who set back the cause of women. My daughter was able to have a safe abortion thanks to the doctors at SNUF, and we both thank God that she did."

"Who the hell are you?" Kip asked.

"That's not important," the man said. "My little girl was

just starting her career as an actress and having a child would have meant missing important movie roles and opportunities. Her abortion was the best thing. You need to shut the hell up and mind your own business."

With those words the faded rock star spun on his heels and walked away.

Kip grabbed George's arm before he could punch the man in the face.

When the mourners had gone home, the members of the executive council met on the top floor of the administration building.

It was a dreary space that served as the holy of holies for the rulers of the flock. Pictures of dead Establishment pastors lined the paneled walls as joyless reminders that the meeting was being observed by the ghosts of those living in the spirit world.

A huge stone fireplace, large enough for a small child to play in, harkened to the days before central heating. Inside its hearth a puny fire smoldered, sputtered, stuttered, and smoked in a stubborn struggle for life. Once the flames rose high enough, the meeting would begin.

Pastor Guile sat slumped in his wheelchair. His flowing white hair was combed backward in the style of a televangelist. His skin was spotted and speckled with age. To the surprise of many, the wilted man remained among the living. Nevertheless, he still held an iron grip over the emotions of the congregation, and was a formable influence upon the executive council.

Guile's rheumy eyes scrutinized each member of the council as they filed into the room. One by one, they took their place around a rectangular conference table the size of a

The Redemption of George | 53

small lap pool. On the table sat two dark candles, an earthen bowel of water, a silver chalice, a small journal with pen, and a golden handbell.

The first to arrive was Doctor Dinferi, a cherub face, soft chined, curly haired, OBGYN. He was followed by Judge Mors, a harsh, arrogant, jurist. Then Professor Laverna, a jittery, impetuous intellect. Behind him, the widow Von Heekate, a manipulative, hostile, media mogul. Finally, General Warlocke, a vain man of distain.

For more than eighteen years they had ruled the church in an uncomfortable alliance, bound by their dark secrets and common lusts.

The General locked the door behind him and Doctor Dinferi lit the candles. One by one they dipped their fingers into the earthen bowl of water, and dried them on scarlet towels draped across their chairs.

Pastor Guile rang the handbell, and they held their arms out to form a chain around the table.

"Let us begin our time with a short invocation," Guile said. They bowed their heads, and he began reading from a sheet of onion-skin paper.

> "God of North, South, West and East, give us your everlasting peace. Prince of water, earth, fire, and air, we pray your everlasting care. Lord of light, love, flesh and bone, we bow before your sacred throne. Bring us cleansing, bless our labor, give us warm and welcome favor. We hail the powers and salute the hidden, so make us pure for what you've bidden. As it must be, praise be to he, as it was in the beginning, so must it be."

He wadded the paper and threw it into the fire. He then

clapped his hands, and they all sat down. General Warlocke began speaking.

"Thanks for coming on such short notice."

"Let's keep it brief," Von Heekate said, curtly. "I have an appointment."

"Hot date?" the Professor teased.

She wrinkled her nose, and sneered at him. The woman had the weathered look of a professional bull rider. She sat stiffly in her chair, a pair of bat-ears sticking out from under her cropped gray hair.

The General looked at Guile, who signaled his approval to speed things up. "I think we all agree that Welma humiliated us in front of Peter Wendigo."

"I knew Welma was going to be trouble the minute I saw her," Von Heekate said.

"Welma's been stirring the pro-life pot for years," the Judge agreed.

"Serves us right," the Professor miffed. "What were we thinking?"

The professor of real estate considered himself an open-minded descendant of Woodstock. Skinny, with piggishly small black eyes, a soul patch on his chin, and a braided gray ponytail, he was dressed in black jeans, a black sport coat, and a black tee-shirt with the word *Watain* silkscreened on the front.

"We were thinking we would make friends with him, that's what we were thinking," Guile said.

"That didn't work out so well," the Doctor fumed.

"Nonsense, it worked out splendidly."

"Okay, I'll bite," the Doctor said. "Why splendidly?"

"Think about it," Guile explained. "Peter can't possibly blame us for the disruption. If anything he probably feels guilty that the disturbance embarrassed us."

"So you're saying we might be able to shame him," the Professor said.

"Exactly," Von Heekate replied. "Not only does he owe us for holding his mother's funeral, now he owes us for our public humiliation."

"That's if we play it right," Guile added.

"I'd like to hear how," the Doctor said, folding his arms across his chest.

The old minister paid no attention to him and continued speaking. "We've followed Lilith's humanitarian work for years. We've always hoped to convince her to invest in SNUF's ministry efforts. Who could have predicted that her death would provide us with the golden opportunity to finally make that connection?"

"Only instead of meeting her, we meet the son," the General elaborated. "And thanks to Pendragon's off-the-cuff sermon, the world now sees us as the champions of women's justice, and the victims of irrational hate."

"Precisely," Guile said, coughing. "We couldn't buy such great publicity."

"So when George came asking if Peter could hold his mother's funeral at our church, it was actually from the hand of God. Sorta like the bearded man upstairs was providing us free manna from heaven," the Professor said.

"We'll never see a thin dime of that manna," the Doctor groused.

"I think we can," Guile responded. "We just need to convince Peter that SNUF is the perfect vehicle to represent his mother's legacy."

At that moment Pendragon burst into the room.

"Sorry I'm late," he said, breathlessly. "Folks were asking about my political campaign."

"Sit down," the General said. "Devil knows we've already spent enough money trying to get you elected."

"It will be worth every penny if he wins," Judge Mors said. "I'll control the courts, Von Heekate will have the media, and Pendragon will run the district."

"Big if," said the Doctor.

"Don't worry," Von Heekate said. "My reporters will tell people what to think, just like they've always done."

The hatch-faced woman had inherited a chain of newspapers and a syndicate of broadcast stations that editorialized her will.

"I wish it were that easy," the Professor said. "People don't like clergy running for office."

"Don't worry," Guile said. "He'll step down from the pulpit when the time comes."

"It still won't change the public's opinion."

"How so?"

"Voters will assume he'll use the Bible to make decisions."

"That's not good," the Doctor said. "People don't want the Bible influencing their politicians. They want separation of church and state."

"Horse nuggets," Pendragon said. "There ain't no such thing as the separation of church and state. Besides, this is America where a Bible is a still great prop if you're running for office. Christians are suckers for it."

"He's right," said Guile. "Politicians use it all the time. Oldest trick in the book, next to kissing babies."

"I agree," Von Heekate said. "We just keep presenting Pendragon as a moral freethinking man of the people, not a religionist. We play down any serious Bible convictions."

"That shouldn't be too hard," the Professor snickered. The others laughed along.

"Seriously," Von Heekate said. "We keep showing the public that he's a solid citizen, happily married, and having the best interests of the common person at heart."

"Let me get this straight," the Doctor said. "We present him as a man of conviction who knows how to separate secular decisions from his personal faith,"

"Exactly," the Judge, nodded. "People will vote for a guy who promises to protect them, support their special interests, and get them free money from Washington D.C.. Who better to make them feel that way than a considerate, understanding, sensitive man like our very own pastor?"

Pendragon sat basking in the spotlight.

The General rapped sharply on the table, interrupting. "Can we get back to the purpose of this meeting?"

"Of course," Guile said.

"As I was about to say, we've always downplayed SNUF's main revenue generator — surgical family planning. Nobody ever asks how we deliver those giant returns on their investment. They just close their eyes when we euphemistically say that we provide female healthcare."

"True, but if we want Peter to place a large investment in SNUF he might want to know more."

"Don't worry, he won't ask," the Judge said. "Peter is like every rich man. He doesn't care how he gets his money as long as he has plausible deniability as to how it's earned."

"Plausible deniability?"

"You know, like those billionaires who contract with third parties to hire children to make their shoes, computers, phones, and other stuff in third world sweatshops. That way they can pretend they didn't know anything about it when the kids are starved, and worked to death."

"We can give Peter plenty of plausible deniability," Guile said, snorting.

"Look people," the General said. "We've been trying to figure out a way to get the Wendigo family to invest in SNUF for years, and now's our golden opportunity. Disturbances like the one caused by Welma don't help."

"Frankly, I'm glad the cops broke her nose," the Professor said.

Mrs. Von Heekate was not a woman given to warmth or compliments, but she smiled pleasantly at him.

"What's your plan?" the Judge asked.

Guile held up a cadaverous index finger. "We need George to contact Peter on our behalf asking for a meeting."

"Why Goodman?"

"Peter trusts him."

"Then what?"

"I want Pendragon to do a preaching series explaining why God supports a woman's right to choose. We must reassure the congregation that Welma's views are not biblical. We have to convince them that her hatred for struggling mothers isn't compassionate Christianity."

"Too easy," Pendragon said. "There's lots of different scriptures I can quote. I can do an entire month just on Proverb 31:10-31.

"I'll preach on how God expects a wise woman to responsibly plan for her family. I'll show why God blesses a woman when they take responsibility to insure for their family's future. It won't be hard."

"I like it," Guile said.

Von Heekate held up her hands like she was shaping a rainbow across the sky. "Maybe this would help. My newspapers can do a full color spread on Pendragon's preaching series, something like, 'Local Pastor Fights to Protect Women's Dignity.'"

Pendragon's grin stretched as wide as Niagara Falls. He

The Redemption of George | 59

envisioned a dramatic photo of himself orating from the pulpit. Maybe another standing on the steps of the church surrounded by young girls and adoring church ladies.

"That would definitely help with the women voters," the Professor said.

"I can also have my TV reporters produce a documentary on why people like Welma are nothing more than domestic terrorists, dangerous to a free society and woman's rights. Or maybe a few investigative shows that explore the threat that anti-abortion extremists pose to our safety and democracy."

"Wonderful ideas," Guile said, brightly.

"We need George to set up a meeting with Peter," the General said.

"George is a good guy," the Judge affirmed. "He'll do it for us."

"I don't see why not," the General bragged. "We just arranged to purchase a small fortune in furniture from him. We're his newest best friends."

The members of the council all smiled with satisfaction.

THE NEXT MORNING, GEORGE AND SARAH DROVE TO WORSHIP and parked in their regular spot. They sat in their electric car envisioning the reactions that might be waiting. Sarah flipped her visor down and checked her makeup in the vanity mirror. George studied Coach Morrison's new hybrid parked in one of the handicapped spots near the front door.

Coach Morrison is no more handicapped than I am. How the hell did he get a blue placard?

"Ready to go inside?" Sarah asked.

"Ready as ever," George said, opening his door. "You see Coach Morrison's new hybrid over there?"

"Nice color," she said. "Gretchen told me they bought it last week. They get a new one every couple of years."

"How come you always know about this stuff before I do?"

"I have friends, I stay connected, I ask questions, what do you think?"

"I think . . ."

"Hey guys, you check out Coach's new hybrid?"

George and Sara turned to see Winston McCool and his wife Jan walking towards them.

"We were just talking about it," George said.

"He told me that he practically stole it from Milt."

Milt was a member of the congregation who owned several car dealerships.

"Fully loaded, latest electronics package, all leather seating, 360 safety monitoring. I rode in it the other day, smooth as silk."

They all began walking toward the church.

"I heard about what happened at the funeral," Winston said. "Wish I'd been there."

"You didn't miss a thing," Sarah said.

"That's not what I heard," Jan replied. "Everyone's saying that George and Kip were yelling anti-abortion slogans at the police, and darn near started a riot."

George and Sara stopped walking. "They said what?"

"That George and Kip were arrested for disturbing the peace."

"That's not what happened," George said, sharply.

"Whoa," Winston exclaimed, palms out. "We're not judging."

"You need to know that Millie Mockingbird and her friends are out to get you," Jan said, raising her eyebrows conspiratorially.

"For what?" Sarah asked.

"They're furious George would say that surgical family planning was wrong, especially at Lilith Wendigo's funeral."

"George never said that," Sarah said.

"Not according to them. Millie is telling everyone that you both need to leave the church."

"Don't listen to to my wife," Winston said, smiling and patting her arm. "Nobody cares about what happened. Like I said, we're not judging."

GEORGE AND SARAH WALKED INTO THE SANCTUARY PASSING friends and members of the congregation. Some looked away, some smiled awkwardly, others ignored them. Nobody rushed up to say hello.

"This is insane," Sarah whispered, her eyes looking around.

A chubby usher, grinning as if he held a closely guarded secret, handed them a bulletin, and lead them to their regular seats.

"How's it going George?"

"Doing fine Allen."

"Didn't realize you were a pro-lifer."

"I'm not. I got caught in the middle of a bad situation."

"Didn't look like that to me. It looked like you helped instigate it."

"Yeah, well looks can be deceiving."

Allen's artificial grin turned into a disbelieving grimace. "Sure George, whatever you say."

The little man pointed to their seat, and stumped back up the aisle to his station in the foyer.

"You've really done it this time, hotshot," Sarah said, under her breath. She sat staring through her bulletin.

George said nothing, quietly gritting his teeth, thinking of something to say. Nothing came to mind.

The church bells tolled before he could answer, and the service began.

Towards the end of the service the congregation stood up and sang, 'Jesus Loves the Little Children.' At the conclusion Maddie Dewlap marched to the lectern.

"Please be seated," she said, breathlessly. "As many of you know this is Mission Sunday where we stop to remember our obligation to bring the good news to the world. It's a day we reflect on the good things your donations do to help change people's lives.

"That's why I am excited to introduce the person who heads our new mission project in the Republic of Kandalabria. She will tell us how free sex education, pregnancy testing, ultrasounds, surgical family planning, and other pregnancy related services are being given to women and young girls who don't have adequate health care."

Maddie lifted her eyes to the sky as if she were about to swoon. "Won't you please help me welcome Doctor Joycelyn — medical missionary."

With those words she began clapping enthusiastically. A rail thin woman, dressed in a white lab coat took her place behind the lectern. She began speaking with the confidence of a corporate rainmaker.

"Are you part of the universal channel of blessings?" she asked. "Do you want to join a vital missionary work in a foreign country? Do you desire to transform the earth God's name? Do you want to help reduce overpopulation so future generations can survive on our planet?

"If you said yes to any of these questions then let me tell

you about the life-changing mission of the Sacred Name Unity Fund in the Republic of Kandalabria."

For the next five minutes the doctor extolled the wonders that SNUF was bringing to a land where women and girls could not afford to have children.

"So this morning I invite you to partner with us and become a missionary of God's love without ever having to leave the comfort of your own home. With your generous donation you will help serve as the heartbeat of compassion that pays for skilled hands to end the misery of lonely, afraid, and exploited women and girls.

"Won't you please make your generous tax deductible gift so that we can continue providing them with unimpeded access to safe surgical family planning?"

With those words she finished her appeal, smiled widely, and accepted a scattering of applause from the congregation. Maddie stood up, and presented the doctor a small gift as "a token of our appreciation," and they both sat down.

One of the assistant pastors stood. "The ushers will be coming down the aisles with collection plates for those wishing to donate to our mission project in Kandalabria. I know that you will all want to be generous."

George had no desire to be generous or otherwise. He hated being squeezed for money in public. Nevertheless, there was no way for him to avoid looking cheap unless he reached in his pocket, and threw something into the plate.

On the other hand, Sarah quickly pulled out her checkbook, and wrote a check for a hundred dollars.

After every dollar that could be collected had been collected, the assistant pastor reminded everyone that they could also go to the church's website and donate even more online. He then called the congregation to bow their heads for the closing prayer.

"Dear heavenly Father, bless the work of great saints like Doctor Joycelyn and the stouthearted missionaries who labor in your fields to bring the good news of surgical family planning to the needy women of the world. Make us a blessing to them, as they are a blessing to all women . . . "

George stole a glance at his watch — the service was going to run long again.

" . . . and now let us all stand and sing, 'Make Me a Blessing,' found at the back of your pew hymnal."

After the benediction and dismissal, George and Sarah withdrew to the church courtyard to meet with their friends, enjoy pink mimosas, and nibble on munchies.

The weather was crisp, and Charlie's maintenance crew had placed large propane heaters throughout the patio to cut the chill.

George took a bite of smoked salmon and cream cheese on a cracker. Sarah nibbled on a cucumber sandwich. "It's time to move these gatherings indoors," he said. "I'm freezing."

"How's your head?" Sarah asked, lifting a champaign flute to her lips.

"Dull ache, I'll get over it."

Sarah looked around and noticed that they were standing alone. The other members of the congregation were gathered elsewhere in small circles of conversation.

"Something's not right," she said. "We're standing here by ourselves. No one's come up and even said hello."

"Maybe they don't know what to say," George replied. "It's probably easier to avoid us."

"I don't want to be avoided," she said. "I like my friends. Why would they suddenly act like I'm poison?"

George looked at her dumbly.

"I blame you for this," she said, tossing her sandwich in a trash can.

Just then, Kip and Alisha walked over arm in arm.

"Well finally," Sarah sighed. "Some friendly faces."

"Why are you guys standing here by yourselves?" Kip laughed. "Let me guess, something to do with yesterday?"

"Very funny," Sarah said. "Nobody wants to talk to us."

"We know the feeling," Alisha replied.

"This isn't about our skin color," Sarah said, without thinking.

"We know," Alisha said. "It's about what you believe."

"No it's not, we don't believe anything." She suddenly realized what she'd said. "I mean, we don't believe that Welma's personal issue is any of our business."

"It's your business now," Kip said. "Take a look at the comments people have posted about the funeral."

He held up his smart phone, displaying a social media site.

'Hope the old bitch get's raped in jail.'

'F'n uncle Tom needs to be lynched.'

'Abortion is a civil right.'

'Boycott Bumble's.'

'Doxx them.'[2]

"What in the hell is this?" George asked, incredulously. "Kip — an Uncle Tom?"

"If you think that's bad," Alisha said. "A bunch of sickos met with reporters right after the service saying they're proud for having an abortion. Watch this."

She held up her cell phone and showed them videos of different woman being interviewed on the steps of the church.

The first woman was seething with self-righteous indignation. Her brows were furrowed, eyes narrowed, lips compressed into bloodless lines. "I think it's vital to let all men know that we won't accept any male behavior that opposes women's rights. The two men in today's service are perfect examples of misogynistic behavior against women intended to intimidate and disempower us. It's better to have an abortion than to be the victim of some man's desires. If Lilith Wendigo were still alive she would say it's a woman's sacred duty to decide when to limit the population to save our world. In my religious circle we consider the taking of uterine matter a sacramental act. It's time for men like these to be reeducated for the good of society."

The next video was of a sullen faced celebrity wearing what looked like a man's pinstriped suit. She flipped long black bangs away from her gothic painted eyes. "I don't know who that old lady was, but what kind of woman would deny a sister an abortion? Mine was the best decision I ever made for both me and the baby. It helped me feel more emotionally secure knowing I wouldn't have to take care of an unwanted child. Women's bodies are sacred, we are divine, we must claim our freedom and exercise our personhood rights."

George and Sarah looked on slack jawed.

The last video was of a blubbery has-been from a long forgotten sitcom. She wanted everyone to know how much she feared for her life inside the sanctuary. "I thought I was going to die. I was so frightened by those two men. Why did the cops let them go? We can't let extremists get their way. Abortions save lives, which is why I'm speaking out to convince all women not to follow the constraints of a few religious fanatics. You need to know that an abortion doesn't make you a bad person, it makes you a responsible one."

George and Sarah stared at the phone numbly.

"They're all from the thrones of hell," Alisha said.

Sarah's nostrils flared. "That's not a very Christian thing to say."

"Seriously? You think you're being a good Christian by tolerating demonic insanity? For heaven sake, they're proud of what they've done. They're encouraging young girls to do it. I'm pretty sure they're not looking for redemption."

"At least you could be polite about your feelings."

"There's nothing polite about the murder of innocents; you can't make a deal with the devil. It took a war to abolish slavery, and it may take another to abolish this."

"War? You'll never stop women from killing their babies, or for others to make a profit from it."

"Perhaps, but we can make it hard enough that they'll have to think twice about it. Maybe some of the babies will escape the tomb of their mother's womb."

"And who's going to take care of those babies — you?" Sara asked, contemptuously. "Nobody wants them."

"How many times do I have to say that I don't care if a woman has an abortion?" George interrupted. "It's a private matter."

"It's not a private matter to the baby," Alicia pointed out.

"So where's all this going?" Sarah asked, worried about losing her friends.

"Nowhere," Kip said.

"What about the videos and the ugly posts?"

"Nothing but a bunch of keyboard commandos and washed up celebrities whoring for attention. Don't worry, this will all go away."

"I hope so," Sarah said, giving George a hard stare. "I don't like being treated like there's something wrong with me. I didn't do anything to deserve it."

. . .

When they returned home they were met at the front door by their miniature dog, Cookie.

"I'm taking Cookie outside for her potty break," George said, picking her up.

"Don't be long," Sarah responded. "I hope you haven't forgotten that tonight's the coming out party for the Howell's daughter."

Not only had George forgotten, he didn't care. "You go for both of us, I've got a splitting headache."

She reached over and felt his forehead. "I hope you're not coming down with the flu, that's all I need."

"I'll be fine."

He wondered how angry she was. Sarah could be remarkably passive aggressive.

"They've spent millions on the event," she said. "We should have thrown one for Marissa."

Like we have millions to waste on a debutante party.

"They've hired some big name Hollywood celebs, a couple of comedians, and that magician guy from Vegas."

"Seriously?"

"Apparently they're related to him — second cousins, or something. Anyway, it's going to be a bigger gathering than the Wankerhams threw for Amber."

"That was pretty impressive, it filled the entire country club."

"That's nothing, Roger and Honey have rented the entire downtown convention center. People are flying in from all over to attend. They're expecting a few thousand to show up."

"Nothing like dueling debutantes," George said.

"Pastor Pendragon is offering the invocation."

"He's only pandering for votes."

"Don't be ugly. Honey's been planning this all year. It would be rude if we didn't show up."

Rude? You've been salivating to go for weeks.

"Fine, you go and represent the Goodman empire. I'm not up to it."

"If you insist."

Insist? A team of wild horses couldn't keep you away.

"I'll find out what people are saying about the fight. Maybe I can stop any damage."

Damage to your social standing you mean.

"Alright," George said. "Have fun. Don't worry that I might be dead of some horrible disease when you get back."

"Don't be dramatic, champ, it doesn't suit you."

Yep, she's angry, he thought.

CHAPTER 2
RISING STORM

A crisp wind beat from the northwest chopping the waters beneath the bow of the *Sotirios* into frothy little wavelets. Sara turned heads as she walked along the quay to where Peter's gigayacht was docked. She wore a black designer peacoat, a cream turtleneck with white pants, and a red knit cap pulled low on her forehead.

George looked like a rumpled porter lumping along at her side, dragging and carrying their bags. He was dressed in blue jeans, thick cable sweater, an olive drab field jacket, and a mossy green newsboy cap.

The Chief Stewardess of the boat met them at the gangplank. "Welcome aboard," Heidi said, extending a hand. "It's nice to see you again."

She had an attractive Nordic face that was lightly bronzed. Her blond hair was pulled back into a tight pony tail. Four silver bars on her uniform indicated her senior rank.

She nodded to a muscular deck hand. "Carlito will take your belongings and place them in your stateroom."

George was more than happy to unload his burden.

"If you think of anything else to make your stay more

enjoyable, don't hesitate to press this." She handed them each a small electronic summoning device.

No matter how many times Sarah had been on board the *Sotirios,* her breath was always taken away. No one had the meticulous eye for ship design, or understood world class nautical engineering like Peter.

The $1.6 billion dollar yacht boasted a helipad, a lap pool, an eight person spa, gym, cinema, dining room, twenty person disco, a small submarine, an automated missile defense system (for counter piracy operations), an unmanned drone system, and a top speed that could pull a dozen of water skiers.

The smell of expensive leather, the aroma of oil rubbed wood trim, the gleam of brass accents, and shine of the golden fixtures was intoxicating.

"Sarah, you are as beautiful as always," Peter exclaimed, giving her a kiss on the cheek. "George, how's my hero?"

"I'm proving that matter can't be destroyed," he replied.

"How's that?"

"Because every time one of you loses a pound, I put one on."

The three laughed warmly.

"Can I get you something?" Peter asked, walking to a liquor cabinet. He was dressed in grey flannel trousers, a cashmere argyle sweater, blue baseball cap, and a pair of tan docksiders.

"Scotch," George replied.

"I'll have white wine," Sarah purred.

"I'm sorry the kids and their families couldn't make it," Peter said.

"Me too," Sarah replied, taking the glass offered by Peter. "Where's Jonathan?"

"Lieutenant Commander Jonathan Goodman is presently

deployed at sea on naval exercises," George said, his chest swelling with pride.

"I asked because I'm thinking about building another boat."

"Another?"

"Something larger, more advanced with space technology, and satellite surveillance. I'd like Jon to captain it."

"Captain," George said, surprised.

"Why not? He's a born sailor, and with his sea time in the Navy he's perfectly seasoned to step up."

George and Sarah looked at each other in stunned silence.

"We don't know what to say."

"What's to say?"

"Seriously?"

"For criminy sakes, Jon's been on the water since he was a kid. We practically raised him on my first yacht. He was crewing around the horn by the time he graduated high school, and now he's got all of his licenses."

"Captain," Sarah mused. "I can't imagine he'd turn down an offer like that."

"I hope not," Peter said, rubbing his hands together. "So, what do you want to do? We'll cast off in about thirty minutes. Dinner is at eighteen-hundred.

"I've stocked the cinema with the latest movies. You can get a rubdown in the spa. A snack in the galley. Whatever makes you happy. We've got all weekend."

"What would make me happy is to curl up with my wine and read a good book by the fireplace in the library," Sarah answered.

The *Sotirios* was one of the few gigayachts to have a working fireplace.

"How about you, George? Once we get past the breakwater we can hit a few golfballs, or shoot some skeet."

"I choose golf."

"I figured. I ordered us a collection of Japan's best clubs to try out."

Peter lifted his glass in salute to his old friend.

That evening the steward lingered near the table with pen in hand ready to take their dinner orders.

"I'm starving," Sarah said, looking at the menu.

"I hope so," Peter said. "The galley has gone all out to impress you."

"What are you having?" she asked George. There was an air of warning in her voice.

He stared at the menu, dejectedly. "I better stick to my diet."

After a long leisurely look, as if he was considering all of the wonderful culinary delights he couldn't have, George finally announced theatrically, "I'll have some jello cubes, and oatmeal.

"Sir?" the steward asked.

"And bring some tomato catsup and hot water so that I can have a bowl of soup with my meal."

Sarah narrowed her eyes, clearly not enjoying his little joke.

George grinned at everyone with a cheesy smile, and said, "Never mind. I'll take a porterhouse steak, a twice baked potato, and a wedge salad with gobs of blue cheese dressing. And don't forget plenty of bacon bits."

He handed the menu back to the steward with a flourish. The man suppressed a smiled.

"I'm only looking after his health," Sarah insisted. "He's going to have a heart attack if he keeps eating like he does."

"Who want's to live to be a hundred if you have to drink

tunafish smoothies?" George asked. He looked to Peter for support.

"He doesn't look overweight," Peter offered. "As long as he get's some exercise he should be okay." Peter had been running interference between them for years.

"I get plenty of exercise," George staunchly explained. "I golf."

"Driving around in a little electric cart is not exercise," Sarah clarified, eyes glaring. "Maybe if you walked around the block a few times a week."

Peter changed the subject. "What are you having for dinner, Sarah?"

She knew exactly what she was having, but she casually examined the menu giving the impression she was thinking about it. "I'll have the curry cauliflower soup, and pan roasted quail breast with yellow plum jus," she said, finally.

George side-eyed Peter. They both looked skyward in a sign of male solitary. The steward retreated to the galley and a sommelier appeared with a bottle of wine.

"I think you'll like this," Peter said to Sarah. "It should go perfectly with what you ordered."

The sommelier poured Sarah a healthy dose. "I can taste the plum," she said.

Peter grinned and nodded.

"Hate to ask, but how much?"

"I found it at a little roadside winery, it's very inexpensive."

"How much a bottle?"

"Sarah, you know I don't buy wine based on price, but for taste."

"A thousand?" she asked, taking another sip. "Two thousand?"

"OK, you win — twenty bucks."

The Redemption of George | 75

"Twenty-dollars? I can buy this at the grocery store." She tried to hide her disappointment.

"Peter is a wine drinker, not a wine snob," George said. He held his glass up to the light. "This tastes great."

"It's a nice blend of Cabernet and Merlot, very drinkable."

Sarah placed her glass down on the table; the wine had lost its flavor.

"George and I were talking earlier," Peter said. "What do you think about the fight at the church?"

"Is this a trick question?"

"Of course not. I'd like your opinion on Welma and her friend."

"I've known her a long time. She's always been outspoken. Frankly, she should find another church that agrees with her, or she should keep her feelings to herself. Abortion is perfectly legal. No amount of her yelling is going to change that."

"I don't know," Peter said. "It seems like nothing has been accomplished for human rights without someone raising their voice."

"Welma isn't interested in women's rights."

"I didn't say women's rights, I said human rights. Don't you think that babies are human?"

Sarah adjusted the napkin on her lap.

"Peter, I don't know how you can ask me that, I've raised two children. But everyone knows that before their born they're not a human baby, they're just a blob of cells. Besides, what if there's something wrong with them?"

"You mean like Down syndrome, or some other birth defect?"

"Why would anyone want to put a child through that? They'd be made fun of in school, and they could never support themselves when they got older. They'd just be a burden on their parents, and taxpayers. Better to terminate them for the sake of everybody."

Peter studied Sarah intently.

"So, you're actually doing the mother and child a favor by ending the baby's life?"

"I suppose you could say that. But it's not a child, so you're not ending anything but the mother's misery."

The steward came to the table and placed desert menus before them. They studied the sweet options in diligent silence, like three monkeys pondering the mysteries of a Rubik's cube.

After placing their orders, Peter asked Sarah, "So how are the grandkids getting on?"

For the next half hour she blissfully recounted their every activity to the smallest detail.

WELMA FORTHWRIGHT LIVED IN A THOUSAND SQUARE FOOT bungalow she'd grown up in as a kid. Her dad purchased it using his G.I. Bill during the housing boom that followed World War II.

After her parents died, Welma and her husband Ed moved from Sioux Falls into the home. They had one son who died of cancer when he was eight. After an industrial accident disabled Ed, Welma nursed him in the back bedroom until he died of complications.

Had it been springtime, the house would have been surrounded by a sunny riot of color bursting from carefully maintained flowerbeds, a bright green lawn, and a small garden of fresh vegetables. Now it was freezing, drizzling, and everything looked dead.

Welma was tucked away in her bed for the night. It felt good to be back in her own room after sleeping in a cold jail cell. She said a small prayer of gratitude for Peter's generosity. She knew that he was nothing like his horrible mother.

Tomorrow, she would sit down and write him a nice note thanking him, perhaps inviting him to tea. She fell asleep thinking of which cookies would go best with Twinings Christmas Blend.

The clock chimed ten.

At the end of the street, a battered sedan pulled up to the curb. A woman dressed in a dark hoodie and sweatpants got out and quietly walked up the steps to Welma's small porch. She peeked in the living room window and hurried around to the side of the house where the gas meter was located.

She pulled out a cordless drill and quietly bored a hole through the thin wood siding. Removing a short road flare from her pocket, she ignited it, and quickly shoved the lit end through the opening. She ran.

The flare started a smoldering fire that burned slowly, silently and unseen between the outside and interior walls of the old house. It took its time creeping up the space separating the two walls until it finally reached the attic where it sucked in a massive gulp of oxygen and erupted into a ball of flame that greedily devoured all of the items stored up there.

At 10:30 p.m., it burned a fist-sized hole through the roof.

At 10:35 p.m., the fist had grown into the size of a manhole cover.

At 10:37 p.m., the flames were consuming the wood shingles like potato chips.

At 10:40 p.m., the blaze was spreading across the entire rooftop.

At 10:48 p.m., Denny Needham spotted the smoking inferno while driving home from work. He knew Welma. He called the 911 operator and reported that the fire was consuming the front of the house, its left side, the porch, and most of the roof.

Seconds later, the dispatcher routed the call to the largest fire station in Abundance Falls. With the blare of a klaxon, followed by alternating electronic tones, flashing LEDs, the activation of the station's dorm lights, and the engine bay lights popping on, a woman's voice began speaking — "Structure fire . . . 7633 Shadhanna Avenue . . . engine five . . . truck five . . . squad fifty-one . . . respond — structure fire . . . 7633 Shadhanna Avenue . . . caller reports individual may be trapped inside."

Forty nine seconds later the station rolled out arriving at Welma's home in four minutes and nineteen seconds.

"Engine five, on scene," the first-due Captain Jackson reported to the operations center. "Structure appears to be fully involved."

Captain Jackson took a moment to size up the situation. Red and yellow flames shot twenty feet from the roof. The stately maple tree that Welma's dad had planted in the front yard was smoldering with the intense heat. Thick black smoke billowed in waves from under the house's eves. At the side of the home the gas meter shot orange flames sideways into the neighbor's yard.

He shouted orders through his walkie-talkie and the firefighters began rolling out hose lines, attaching them to hydrants and hooking them to the engines. Firefighters Hurst and Solomon began retrieving rescue equipment and setting up ladders.

He ordered firefighters Pacheco and Moore to meet him at the front door. They masked, adjusted their self contained breathing apparatus, and kicked it open.

They were met by a giant fireball blasting them back-

The Redemption of George | 79

wards off the porch into the front yard. They tried again, but it was no use. The road flare that the hooded woman had shoved through the side of the house had worked itself into a blaze that mimicked hell itself.

Despite their heroic efforts, the frustrated crews could only surround and drown the place with thousands of gallons of water.

At about 1:15 a.m. they finally extinguished the flames. The house had been reduced to a soggy black mass of smoking skeletal ruins.

Captain Jackson ordered everyone to begin searching through the char and rubble. It wasn't long before Firefighter Moore shouted, "I've got something!"

GEORGE STOOD IN A BRIGHTLY LIT TELEVISION STUDIO.

"Does my lip look swollen?" he asked, touching it lightly.

"Can't even see it, Mister Goodman," a disembodied voice from the director's booth said. "Patty did a great job with the makeup, and the lighting makes it completely invisible. Believe me, the camera sees nothing."

"Okay Gary, I trust your judgement."

George touched his scar, turned his best side to the camera, and adjusted his tie. It was important to project confidence, friendliness, and trust. Viewers needed to feel that they would never be rich enough, smart enough, athletic enough, or sexy enough, unless they shopped at Bumbles.

"Alright everybody, let's settle down," Gary said.

A woman came out from behind the camera, and held an electronic slate in front of George's nose. "Bumble's fall sale, take one."

". . . and, action!"

George looked directly into the camera and spoke. For the next thirty seconds he explained why smart people made their life easier by shopping at Bumbles. ". . . so don't be left out. Get more, have more, and be more, at Bumble's."

"Cut!" Gary said. "Great job Mister Goodman. Would you like to do another?"

George had been making TV commercials to promote the business for years. "I don't think so Gary, I've got a slight headache. If it's good for you, it's good for me."

"Looks fine to me Mister Goodman. We'll drop in the special effects and add your jingle music in post production."

A purple-haired girl, wearing blue tennis shoes, yellow leggings under a checked madras skirt, a tee-shirt with a picture of Che, and a black nose ring stepped forward and helped George remove a microphone hidden under his shirt.

"So, I saw a video of the fight at the church on the web," she said, in a nasal voice. "It went mega-viral. Got over two million views the first day.

George wondered if that would be good or bad for business.

"I'm glad you weren't hurt."

"Thanks Jenny."

"It was so awesome watching you beat up those cops. Someone needed to teach them a lesson."

At the moment George could only agree.

"Where did you learn to fight like that? You friends with Conor McGregor or something?"

"In the Army," he said. "Long story."

"Anyone could see that old witch used you. I hate self righteous religious people causing trouble with their Bible beating hate speech. I mean, who are they to tell us what to do? I mean, they actually believe in some imaginary sky God living up in the clouds. I tried praying to him once, nothing happened."

She made a zero sign with her fingers.

"You were just sitting there minding your own business and she gloms onto you. I'm glad she got instant karma. Sorry Mister Goodman, that's just how I feel."

She took the microphone and placed it in a box.

George wondered how a girl with purple hair, rainbow colored tattoos, and a black nose ring could feel superior to a woman like Welma. He thought about asking her, but he bit his tongue and left the studio trying to make sense of what she'd said.

He'd known Welma for years, she wasn't a witch. She was old, but she wasn't hateful. He wondered why Jenny was so angry at her. He could understand if Jenny didn't agree with Welma, but her bitterness was troubling.

He walked to the parking lot thinking about the events of the past few days when his eyes widened. Running along the driver's side of his car was a deep zig-zagging scratch ending with the letters F U gouged deeply into the hood.

What the . . . he thought.

He looked around.

Who would do this? Why would they do this?

He started to call the police, then dismissed it. He probably wasn't on their Christmas card list right now.

Bastards! That's a $10,000 dollar, tri-coat, two-tone, pearlescent blue paint job. I had to wait three extra months to get it from the factory!

He walked down the side of the car feeling the deep groove in the metal. He studied the letters F U scratched into the hood. He looked around to see if there were any CCTV cameras in the parking lot. Nothing. He felt helpless, violated.

Why would someone vandalize my car? Jealous? Drugged? Drunk?

He finally accepted the situation, got behind the leather covered steering wheel, and glided out to the main highway. Lowering the windows he accelerated to seventy hoping that the crisp air would clear his mind. Something was wrong, but he couldn't put his finger on it.

He felt as though he had accidentally stumbled into an alternate world. Thoughts of Lilith, Pastor Pendragon, Guile, Officer Smith, the General, Jenny, and Welma swirled in his brain. He had a feeling they were all connected, but how?

After a few miles he told himself that the scratch was probably the work of some druggie. He'd call the insurance company when he got to the office.

Aiming the car's nose towards the Bumble Building in downtown Abundance Falls he opened it up to eighty-five, and hoped Officer Smith wasn't hiding behind a tree with a radar gun.

Later that day George sat in his office thinking about the scratch on his car when his secretary stepped into the room.

"There's a lawyer here to see you," she said.

"That's all I need. What the heck do they want?"

"Something to do with Welma."

"Hasn't she caused me enough trouble already?"

She shrugged her shoulders. "I guess you're about to find out."

"Okay, send 'em in." He sighed deeply.

From the waiting room, a rumpled man carrying a well-worn briefcase walked into George's office. His face was pale, his eyes were dark, and he was dressed in a baggy polyester three-piece suit that screamed, 'ambulance chaser.'

"Mister Goodman?"

"Whose asking?"

"My name is Bishop." He handed George his business card. "I'm Wilma Forthwright's attorney."

"If this has anything to do with the fight at the church you can call my attorney."

"No sir, it doesn't."

"Are you the lawyer Peter Wendigo sent to bail Welma out of jail?"

"No sir."

"Is she out of jail?"

"Yes sir."

"Then why are you bothering me?"

The lawyer hesitated. "Apparently you haven't heard?"

"Look, I'm busy. Get to the point."

The man looked at the floor as if considering his next words. "Welma died in a house fire."

George was stunned. There was no mistaking the shock on his face. "What are you talking about?"

"I don't have all the particulars, yet. They think it might have started in the electrical wiring."

"I don't know what to say," George spluttered. "I just just saw her a few days ago."

"I know, I watched you defend her at the Wendigo funeral."

George took a moment to collect himself. "I'm sorry, but what does this have to do with me?"

"Welma had no survivors, and I thought with the two of you being so close that you might be willing to make her funeral arrangements."

"We weren't close." George corrected, absently touching the scar on his cheek.

"I'm sorry," the lawyer said, frowning. "I was under the impression that you were like family."

"Why, because of the fight at the church?"

"No sir, because Welma designated you as the sole beneficiary of her estate."

George stared at the man. "Why in heaven's name would she do that?"

The lawyer gave no indication that he knew. Instead he set his briefcase on George's desk.

"May I?"

"Of course."

"Welma and her late husband Ed lived very modest lives. Aside from a small bank account, and a life insurance policy, they had very few assets. However, I went by their bank this morning and opened the contents of their safe deposit box. I found these items inside marked for you."

He opened the attache case, and laid them on George's desk. There was an assortment of Welma's costume jewelry, Ed's medals from Viet Nam, a Colt 1911 pistol, and the titles to their home and a 2005 Subaru Outback.

George picked up the Colt examining it. "Hafta say, Ed knew his pistols."

"There were also these," Bishop said, pulling out two envelopes. He handed the smaller one to George who turned it over in his hand. TO GEORGE GOODMAN was printed boldly in peacock blue ink. The back flap was covered in melted red sealing wax.

"Would you please open it?" Bishop asked.

George ripped through the sealing wax and pulled out a greeting card. On the front was a drawing of a small dog done in pastel wash. It was wearing a pair of aviator's flying goggles, and looking through a telescope at a cow jumping over the moon.

George smiled to himself. The dog reminded him of Cosmo, the one he'd lost as a kid. Folded inside the card were two sheets of cream colored paper. The text was beautifully written in Welma's precise hand. He read to himself.

"Dear George: You are probably wondering why Mister Bishop is giving you this letter. Let me explain. Years ago, my husband Ed and I had a little boy named Eric. When Eric was born, Ed invested in a few start-up companies hoping that they would someday help pay for Eric's education.

However, when Eric was eight he died of a rare brain cancer. As I was unable to have any more children, we had no further use for the stocks, which Ed said had very little value at the time. Ed put the certificates in our safe deposit box and we put them out of our mind.

It was a horrible, horrible time for us. Ed drank heavily and I became bitter thinking that God had punished us for some unknown reason. But as people often do, we survived. It helped that we believed that no matter how bad things got, God had a plan greater than ours. Eventually Ed stopped drinking and I began spending my time supporting various children's causes.

"I've forgotten the names of the stocks, and I've never checked to see if they prospered or went bankrupt. I didn't care, they were just hurtful reminders of my little boy.

After Ed passed away, I had a dream where an angel told me God wanted you to have our possessions when I died. I never shared this with anyone because people don't believe in dreams or angels.

I realize that you are a wealthy man with no need for

our things or whatever the stocks maybe worth. However, my final wish is that you sell my house, and take whatever money it's worth and use it to save the pre-born and abused children.

You've always reminded me so much of my little Eric. I will be looking for you in heaven ~ Love, Welma."

George reverently refolded the sheet of paper. "When did she write this?"

"Last year after she found out she had cancer."

"Just like her son."

The lawyer nodded, and held up the other envelope. "I've already sorted through the contents of this one. It appears that in 1986 Ed purchased 200 shares of Adobe Systems at about eleven bucks each.

I did a rough calculation on their present value, and with stock splits and other things, the shares are now worth around four million dollars."

"Four million?" George was stunned. He blushed with shame for telling his secretary that Welma was nothing but trouble.

"Not only that, but Ed purchased two hundred shares each of Apple, Microsoft, and several other dotcoms at about the same time. I guesstimate they're worth in the neighborhood of another twelve to fifteen million dollars — give or take."

George tried to soak in the lawyer's information. "I don't know anything about the pre-born or abused children," he said. "I'm afraid I wouldn't know the first thing to do with the money."

"You have several options. You could use the money to set up a charitable foundation which you ran. You could donate all the money to one of several organizations that Welma preselected for you, or you could decline the estate altogether. In which case I'm authorized to donate the money to the various charities on her list."

The lawyer slipped the large manila envelop back in the briefcase and closed it. "It's clear that Welma had no idea that the estate would be worth so much. She was only thinking about the value of the house."

"This is a lot to digest," George said. "Can you give me a few days to decide?"

"Of course. I can work directly with you, or your attorney. In the meantime, would you be willing to make the arrangements for Welma's funeral service?"

As the welcoming receptionist at the First Establishment Church, Courtney felt like she was indispensable to its success. A graduate of Abundance Falls High School, the prim woman had dutifully managed the front desk for more than twelve years.

Her corporate nest was built behind a U-shaped desk protected by a four foot high counter. A red telephone, fax, copy machine, and message board embellished her domain.

On top of the counter, a plastic holder stuffed with colorful brochures advertised the monthly travel adventures, gourmet dinners, book signings, art showings and other free activities available exclusively to the members of the church. Away from casual view, a half dozen pictures of her three children, a husband, and a cat provided a modicum of homey comfort.

It gave her immense pleasure to imagine she was seated on the bridge of an intergalactic starship flying through the universe with a celestial commander providing directions from behind her. For there, hanging by steel cables from the ceiling, was a larger than life tapestry of Jesus floating down from the heavens with ministering angels at his side.

In one of his hands he held a golden orb of crushing power. In the other, he made a gesture of calming tranquility with his fingers. The artist had replaced Jesus' bloody crown of thorns with one of olive branches, making him look like a Roman conqueror. Along the bottom of the tapestry the words *First Establishment Church* were woven in 24 karat gold thread. Like others, George was impressed with the image and paused to gaze at the flying Jesus.

Courtney sat reading her daily horoscope when he walked up to her desk. "Can I help you?" she asked. Her voice was more cheery than the look on her face.

"Who's our funeral coordinator?"

"Ginger, but she's on vacation."

"And she will return, when?"

Courtney cleared her throat as if she had more important things to do, and faced her computer. "Here it is," she said, sticking her nose close to the screen. "Sez she won't be back until after the New Year."

George wondered how anyone could take three months off work. "So, how do I go about arranging for a funeral?"

"You need to talk to Pastor Pendragon's secretary, but I don't think he's doing any funerals for awhile."

George said thanks, and left Courtney sitting alone in the deserted lobby feeling as if she'd accomplished a major task for the day.

He walked up a wide marble staircase to the desk of Betty LaVanth, Pendragon's secretary. She was busy talking on the phone.

Placing a hand over the mouthpiece she whispered, "I'll be right with you." Her face blossomed into a reproduction of a caring smile. George took a seat and sized her up. Betty was a skeletal old bird who had been running things since he could remember.

She was dressed in a flared skirt, a white knitted sweater, and a pair of crescent moon ear rings. Her coiffed hairdo was ashen gray, her long fingernails burgundy red, and a tiny tattoo of a floral pentacle was inked on the inside of her wrist. Rumor had it she was paid an extraordinary salary to run interference for Pendragon and the executive council.

George glanced at the Westminster clock ticking away on her bookcase. One minute turned into three, which turned into five, which turned into eight. Every once in awhile she would smile and wink at him. Finally, when she was completely satisfied that she had said everything she wanted to say, she hung up.

She scanned George from head to toe. "My, my, my. I don't think I've ever seen you up here before." Her accent betrayed that she had never left the South. She crossed her legs and tossed her hair.

"No reason," he shrugged. "I've never needed to see the Pastor before."

"Hope you're playing in the church golf tournament again this year. It tickles me to watch you stroke that little ball into the hole." Her eyelashes blinked slowly. "So, how can I help you, darlin'?"

"Courtney says I need you to schedule a funeral with Pastor Pendragon."

"Poor man got about a thousand phone calls after the Wendigo service. Mostly reporters wanting to know more about the fight. He was madder than a wet hen. I'm surprised you didn't catch some flack."

"Believe me, I caught enough."

She crossed her legs again. "I think Welma went a little crazy after her husband Ed died. You'd have thought she was bucking for sainthood with all the fuss she made about the unborn. Poor thing didn't have any children, but she was always telling the ladies what to do. She made a lot of enemies around here."

Betty's long fingernails pulled on the hem of her dress, and she absently scratched her thigh. George stood expressionless. "Anyway, I'll be happy to help you schedule a service, who's it for?" She gave him a sweet smile.

"Welma."

Her smile froze. "Welma Forthwright?"

"Died in her sleep."

"I just spoke with her last week," she said, biting her lipstick. "She was up here causing trouble for the women's prayer group. I didn't realize you were part of Welma's family."

"I'm not, I was asked to help arrange her funeral."

Betty swiveled in her chair and referred to a desk sized planner. After a few long moments of seemingly difficult research she announced, "I'm sorry George. It looks like Pastor Pendragon won't be available for the rest of the month."

George felt the scar on his cheek tighten.

"I'll call downstairs and see if one of the assistant pastors might be available." She picked up her phone's handset and pressed a few keys.

George studied the office while she spoke. The decor reminded him of his grandmother's living room.

She shook her head no. "Sorry George, none of the other pastors are available."

"All of them?"

"I'm afraid so," she said, frowning slightly. "What funeral home is Welma resting in?"

The Redemption of George | 91

"She's in the morgue, I haven't decided where to take her."

"Sunny Trails has reasonable prices and a decent chapel. They might be able to find you a retired minister willing to do the service."

George leveled his gaze at the woman. "Welma was a life long member of this church, I'd expect we could do a little better than that."

The wrinkles around Betty's mouth hardened slightly. "If you'd like me to leave a message for Pastor Pendragon, I can put it on his desk. It's possible that he might be willing to change his schedule."

George knew that wasn't going to happen. It was clear they didn't want anything to do with Welma.

"That's okay," George said, feigning a smile. "I'll find someone willing to do it."

"Good luck," she cooed. "And you have a richly blessed day."

GEORGE WAITED PATIENTLY IN THE CONFERENCE ROOM OF THE Sunny Trails funeral home. Located in a run-down Queen Anne style home, the family business had catered to low income workers for over a century.

The house smelled sweet, thick with a honeyed floral fragrance intended to mask the scent of death. The conference room was bare except for a couple of artificial plants and a stack of color brochures encouraging him to prepay his burial expenses.

George killed the time watching the stock market on his smartphone. He checked his Rolex, apparently in the business of the dead there wasn't any rush.

Eventually a small woman dressed in a black suit, with chocolate brown eyes, and raven hair pulled tightly into a bun, walked through the door.

"Sorry for the delay Mister Goodman, I'm Syl Montoya. I'm very sorry for your loss." She spoke with a practiced sincerity, as if Welma was her favorite aunt.

"I'll make this simple," George said. "Welma had no relatives or immediate family so I don't need anything fancy." He glanced down at the threadbare rug on the floor, then lifted his eyes. "Basically, I want the cheapest funeral you offer."

Syl didn't bat an eye. "That would be cremation."

George thought it was ironic for a woman who burned to death in a fire to be cremated. "That will be fine."

"Our basic cremation package starts at $650. If you'd like to use our chapel for a memorial service we can help you find a minister and include the appropriate music with our Serenity Package for $1,825."

"I think Welma deserves the Serenity Package," he said. "I'll probably be the only one in attendance."

Syl lifted a finely plucked eyebrow slightly.

"Just so you know, that price includes a free obituary on our website. However, an obituary in the local newspaper, state taxes, death certificates and a burial urn are extra."

"That's fine," George said. "How about a minister?"

"We can recommend a number of clergy from various faiths to do a service. What religion was Welma?"

"She was an Establishmentarian."

Syl checked her notes. "They don't normally do funerals for people they don't know. Would any Christian minister be alright?"

"Sure."

"Did Welma have a favorite scripture or song?"

"Not that I know of."

"Then we'll let the minister select something appropriate."

George suddenly remembered his aunt Suzy's favorite. "How about Amazing Grace, by Elvis?"

"Of course. Do you have any information you can provide me about her life? I need it for her eulogy."

"I don't know much about her life," he said. "I think she was born in Sioux Falls. I know she had a husband named Ed, lost a child named Eric to cancer, loved her garden, was involved with the pro-life movement, and she was a member of First Establishment Church."

Syl stiffened slightly. If she wondered anything she didn't say a word.

"Do you have a photo of her?"

"Why?"

"We need it for the newspaper and our website."

"Is that necessary?"

"You'd be surprised at how many people read the obituaries. It's a good idea in the event that Welma had extended family or friends you're not aware of."

"Okay, I'll find one."

"We'll have it blown up and displayed at the service." Her phone chirped. "Can you give me a moment?"

While she spoke, George examined pictures of tranquil Polynesian settings hanging on the walls.

"I was just told that we have Thursday at eleven a.m. available. Would that work for you?"

So long as it doesn't interfere with my Saturday tee time.

"Yes, that will work."

"I know a minister who'd be perfect. Let me call Pastor Beecher and see if Thursday fits his schedule. It's usually no problem. He's retired and likes to help out in cases like this."

"Cases like what?"

"Like when someone doesn't go to church, or have a pastor willing to do their service."

George felt his jaw clench.

"I'll call you to confirm the details." She handed him her business card. "Please let me know if you think of anything else."

George thanked her, knowing he wouldn't think of anything else.

On Thursday, an hour before the service, George met with Syl at the front desk of the mortuary. She confirmed that everything was on schedule.

He walked down the hall to the chapel and sat down in the first row. The room was deathly silent — unnervingly silent, so silent that he could hear the blood pulsating through his ears. He stared at Welma's urn sitting on a table in front of him. Hopefully this would be over quickly.

In time, a hefty man appeared from a side door and walked up to George. "Are you Mister Goodman?" he asked. He extended a beefy hand, grinning like a used car salesman.

George nodded and concealed his initial distaste for the man. But he realized that Beecher was the best he was going to get given the circumstances.

"I'm Jett Beecher, and I'm your preacher," the minister said, chuckling at his own well-worn joke. "I'm here to officiate Welma's ceremony."

The man was well into his seventies. He was tall, rounded, and good natured. His face had a warm and genuine glad-to-know-you look. He was dressed in a black double breasted wool suit, white shirt, black tie, and a small eagle, anchor and globe was pinned to his lapel.

George studied the pin. "You a Marine?"

"Once a Marine, always a Marine; Semper Fi, brother. I was a Lance Corporal at the Beruit barracks bombing in eighty-three, got myself a close-dose of Jesus, and came back into the Corps as a chaplain. I was originally ordained an Establishmentarian minister. Now I'm a freelancer for Jesus."

"Welma was Establishmentarian. The ministers at her church won't do her funeral. Does that matter to you?"

Beecher chuckled. "No surprise, it's one of the reasons I left the denomination. Nope, I watched the video of Welma at Wendigo's funeral. A person with her kind of courage deserves a proper burial suitable for a warrior saint."

George had never thought of Welma as a saint, much less a warrior.

"Thanks for agreeing to do this."

"Are you kidding? I haven't seen her kind of courage since I was in the 1st MarDiv. By the way, no charge for today."

"No charge?"

"It's a privilege to officiate."

Pendragon charged $250, George thought.

Beecher walked up to Welma's urn, laid his hands on it, and said a few quiet prayers. Turning back to George he asked, "How many folks are we expecting today?"

"I'm afraid we're it," George answered, lowering his eyes, embarrassed.

"Not to worry my friend, that's all we need. The Lord says, 'wherever two or three are gathered together in my name, I am in their midst.'"[1]

"Well, at least we got the two," George smiled.

"Make that three," Kip yelled from the back of the chapel. He was dressed in a coral-colored two button suit with an oyster white shirt, lavender pocket square, and open collar.

"Where's Sarah?"

"She isn't coming. She had a yoga class or something."

"What about Peter?"

"He's in Singapore. When he gets back we'll take Welma's ashes onboard the *Sotirios* and scatter them at sea."

"So, I guess it's just you, me, and . . . ," Kip turned to the minister.

"Jett Beecher."

They shook hands. "Kip Flintlock. I see you're a retired Marine."

"Retired from the Corps," Beecher grinned, "but still on active duty for the Lord."

"Amen," Kip said, giving him a fist bump. "So what's going on?"

"I'm going to do a short dignified service with a couple of songs, and we'll praise Jesus for giving us a saint like Welma."

"You can start right now if you want," George said, checking the time.

Beecher looked at his watch. "Better wait. We've still got twenty minutes before we're scheduled to begin."

"That will give time for the others to show up," Kip said.

"No one else is going to show up," George replied.

"O ye of little faith," Kip responded.

George rolled his eyes.

THEY SAT IN THE FRONT ROW OF THE EMPTY CHAPEL WAITING for the clock to strike eleven. George counted the minutes on his watch, Beecher read the Bible, and Kip snoozed lightly.

At 10:55, George heard a shuffle behind him. Kip jerked his eyes open, and they both turned to see people walking down the aisle of the chapel.

Beecher stood up, shot his cuffs and buttoned his jacket.

"We're here for Welma Forthwright's service," one of them said.

Kip elbowed George. "That's the skinny little guy who jumped up at the back of Lilith's service and started singing."

George could barely believe his eyes. "Chili Popper — who could forget that name?"

Beecher lifted his voice. "You're in the right place brother, come on down here."

"I'd like to sing a song if you don't mind," Chili said.

"Mind? We'd love it."

Another man in the group, dressed in a long black coat, with a fuzzy gray beard, narrow black eyes, and wearing a pair of round wire spectacles, stepped up and introduced himself with a tiny bow

"My name is Rabbi Menacham. Welma was a dear friend of our community. She spoke for life — all life. I was wondering if I may have permission to read a short scripture from the Torah?"

"Of course Rabbi, it would be an honor."

Immediately, a small man with flaming red hair wearing a clergy collar and black suit tapped him on the arm. "Pastor Beecher, I'm Father Quinn the rector over at Saint Philomena's. I was wondering if I might contribute in some small way? Welma was a remarkable woman."

"Of course Padre. Would you be willing to lead us in a prayer?"

Syl broke into their conversation. "The parking lot is overflowing with cars," she said, excitedly pointing outside. "We're going to run out of room."

"Do we have any folding chairs?" Beecher asked.

"Yes, I'll have them brought out."

"Everyone needs to squeeze in as tightly as they can. I'll

get started after everyone's seated. We might run into overtime."

"That's alright," she said. "Nothing's scheduled after you."

Outside, the sound of multiple sirens was heard. Syl ran out and immediately ran back in. "The fire department is here," she said, eyes wide. "Someone must have complained that we're breaking maximum occupancy."

As she spoke, firefighters dressed in their Class A uniforms jumped out of their vehicles and began coming inside.

"We didn't expect such a large crowd today," Syl stammered.

"That's okay, we did," Captain Jackson said. "Me and my crews were the ones who responded to Welma's fire. We're not here for an inspection."

Syl could have cried in relief.

Beecher shouted up to them, "Tell the Captain to sit his people right down here in the front row."

For the next ten minutes people flowed through the doors, and the chapel was quickly filled with flowers, and brightly colored helium balloons. Sympathy cards piled up next to Welma's urn. The mood was respectful, yet celebratory.

"I thought you said nobody was coming," Syl whispered to George.

"I had no idea," he responded, dumbfounded.

"I think it was the fight at the church," Kip said. "Welma's courage touched a lot of people's hearts."

George was moved by the sight of people from all ages, races, and colors. There were pastors, priests and nuns, firefighters, EMTs, rabbis, businessmen, housewives, college kids, and senior citizens all standing in solidarity to honor Welma.

What George originally thought would be a quick and quiet ceremony, turned into a singing, clapping, and crying tribute the likes of which George had never experienced.

Chili Popper sang songs, the Rabbi read scripture, the Priest led a prayer, Captain Jackson shared the story of the fire, and Beecher called everyone to repent.

For more than an hour, the old Marine lifted the place to its feet in praise, and down on its knees in prayer. Welma's friends gave moving testimonials, tears were shed, and even Kip got in a word or two.

When the service ended, George was still applauding, hugging and shaking hands. He'd never experience anything like this outpouring of love at the First Establishment Church, and he didn't want it to end.

THE SUN WAS DYING WHEN GEORGE FINALLY DROVE UP THE curved driveway to his gated home, and parked in his barn sized garage that sheltered his cars, jet skis, golf cart, and touring motorcycle. The space was temperature controlled, had an epoxy floor, large wood cabinets filled with tools, steel storage chests, and a long metal workbench.

He got out of his electric vehicle, closed the door and suddenly felt exhausted. Dragging himself through the mud room into the kitchen, he was met by his little dog Cookie who jumped into his arms.

At least someone is happy to see me, he thought

"Glad you finally decided to make it," Sarah said, in a disapproving tone. "I've been sitting here all day getting hateful text messages."

"Yeah, I know. The board of directors called me to say they want a meeting."

The statuesque woman stood behind a kitchen island the

size of a helicopter landing pad holding a glass of red wine. She looked like she'd just stepped out of a fashion magazine. Her long willowy figure was draped in a wintery white dress, covered with a light gray cashmere coat. It was all crowned by a cascade of auburn hair that framed a heart-shaped face softened by sympathetic sea-foam green eyes.

"They could vote you out."

"I'm doing what I can."

"You're not doing enough, babe."

"What do you suggest?"

"You could start by saying you're sorry."

"Sorry for what?"

"For alienating everyone we know, including half our customers."

"What did I do to alienate everyone?"

"It's the optics George, people think we're fanatics."

"People are going to think what they want."

"What do you expect them to think when you get into a fist fight with the police over Welma Forthwright, the number one hater of Lilith Wendigo?"

"I expect them to think that I was protecting her from getting hurt."

"How dumb can you get? People loved Lilith Wendigo, she was iconic, she was a role model, she inspired girls to move past their insecurities."

"How many times do I have to tell you that the fight had nothing to do with Lilith?"

Sarah frowned. "Perception is reality my love, and the perception is that you urinated all over Lilith's grave by defending a narrow-minded hater. What did Welma ever do for the cause of women? For that matter, what did Welma ever do for anybody except stir up trouble? Now, thanks to your stupid bravado, we're losing our friends."

She took a gulp of wine and banged her glass on the counter.

"What do you want me to do?"

"I want you to call a press conference and say that you let your emotions get the best of you. I want you to strike your breast three times, throw ashes on your head, tell everyone you're an idiot, and beg the world's forgiveness. If you ever want to get into my bed again I want you to fix this mess."

"You should have gone to Welma's funeral," he said, expecting more fury. "You'd see things differently."

"I doubt it. She was an intolerant, bigot."

"Bigot? Just because she had strong convictions doesn't make her a bigot. You wanna talk about impacting people's lives? You missed the biggest outpouring of genuine love and respect I've ever seen. It was nothing like that phony gathering of suck-ups at Lilith's funeral. Welma genuinely inspired people for the love of good, and they showed up to remember her."

"Who showed?"

"Me, Kip, — and about three hundred others."

Sarah paled. "You told me nobody would be there. No wonder people are texting me. Do you realize how bad this will look when it get's out that you've sponsored a gathering of three hundred pro-life imbeciles to honor Welma? Isn't it horrible enough that you humiliated me at Lilith's funeral? Now this? You'll probably get voted out as CEO, and our stock will be worthless."

"Maybe," George said. "But it doesn't change the fact that Welma was a great woman. She was all about life, nothing like Lilith."

"How can you say that? Lilith was like a second mother to you."

"Lilith had her good points, but she was never a second

mother. She didn't have a mothering bone in her body, just ask Peter. And let's not forget that I've never taken sides against her. That's what people are trying to make of this, including you."

"I'm trying to salvage our company, but you don't seem to care."

"I do care. But there's a difference between not knowing what to say to you, and not caring. I'm not going to let some thugs intimidate me into betraying my convictions."

"So now you think I'm a thug?"

"I'm not talking about you."

"Well your lofty convictions won't be worth a tinker's damn when we're both sitting on the curb with our bags in hand."

"At least your bags are Gucci."

She glared at him with an intensity he'd never seen before.

"Alright, if it makes you feel better I wish I'd never helped Welma," he confessed.

"It's a little late now, buster. You brought this on us, and I don't deserve it. Didn't you see that she was using you? You've never been too bright, but this time you really outdid yourself."

She picked up her wine glass, refilled it, and took a long swallow. She checked her watch. "I've got to go. Tonight's my meeting with the Hubris Guild down at the museum. Don't wait up for me."

She downed the rest of her wine, grabbed her purse and stormed out of the house.

George kept his mouth shut.

. . .

The Redemption of George | 103

HE LISTENED AS HER CAR SPEED AWAY INTO THE DARKNESS. The sound of its exhaust note was eventually replaced by the hooting of a night owl.

In the stillness of the house he pulled himself up from the counter and trudged past the dining room, media room, game room, den, and family room to their oversized en-suite bathroom.

He stood in front of the mirror. His head was pounding, his face was numb. He felt every bit of his fifty-four years. He recited, "she sells sea shells, down by the sea shore," testing to see if he was slurring his words. He held up both arms, neither one of them dropped. He read the label of a medicine bottle to see if his vision was blurred. Nothing.

When he was satisfied that he wasn't having a stroke, he breathed a sigh of relief, and thanked his lucky stars. He had too many things to accomplish to croak out now.

He brushed his teeth, stripped off his clothes, dropped them in a pile, and stepped into an oversized marble shower. With a twist of his wrist, a cascade of hot water began shooting from six body sprays, and two overhead rain showers.

He wondered if he was being cursed by God for some reason. He tried to think of what he'd done to anger the big guy upstairs, but nothing came to mind. Now his business was threatened, he had a target on his back, and Sarah was furious.

He turned off the water, dried himself, and slipped into a set of pure silk pajamas. He walked to his kingsized feather bed, slid under a set of luxury cotton sheets, pulled a puffy satin comforter up to his neck, turned off the light, and lay in the darkness thinking about Sarah.

The fragrance of her perfume still lingered on the pillows.

They'd met in college when Peter introduced them at one

of the many beach parties, dinners, and social soirees that he hosted.

As much as George had wanted to ask her out, he knew he wasn't in the same league as the beautiful daughter of a wealthy furniture chain owner.

Nevertheless, Peter kept inviting Sarah to the gatherings and somehow Cupid's arrow pierced their hearts. They became inseparable.

At their wedding reception Peter confided that he'd been their secret matchmaker all along. Every year on their anniversary, he sent them a beautiful gift with the same message, "Was I right, or was I right? I am so damn good!"

George smiled to himself. He had to agree. Their marriage had outlasted the nuptials of many of their friends. Maybe it was because Sarah was unflappable. She had the comfort that comes from growing up rich. Nothing ever seemed to shake her. She was always composed and confident in an aloof sort of way.

George was the one who was constantly worried that a disaster would explode like an artillery shell falling out of the sky. And now it had, and Sarah was shaken. He'd never seen her like this. It unnerved him. He frowned in the darkness.

Dear God, if you're listening . . .

The cell phone buzzed on the nightstand. He fumbled for it.

"George, it's Pastor Pendragon."

George sat straight up in bed.

"What's wrong?"

THE GRANDFATHER CLOCK IN THE HALLWAY CHIMED TEN WHEN George finally placed the phone back on the nightstand. For a full hour George listened to the author of six books on courageous Christian faith agonize about what Peter would, or wouldn't do.

"Sorry to hear about all your problems George, but would you reach out to Peter and see if he'd be willing to meet with the executive council?"

"How about I just give you the number to his secretary?"

"We'd feel better if you asked on our behalf, seeing you're so close to him."

It was late, George's head was throbbing and he didn't have the energy to fathom the game Pendragon was playing. If they wanted a meeting with Peter he'd make the call. Who knew, maybe some good would come of it.

George said goodnight to the worried pastor, turned over in bed, and thought about Welma's funeral. Then his mind turned to potential lawsuits, dwindling bank accounts, and Sarah's disapproval. He finally fell asleep out of pure exhaustion.

CHAPTER 3
NIGHT VISITORS

In the deepest part of the night when the grandfather clock struck three, George was awakened by a severe pain shooting down his left arm. His head drummed, his chest was tight. He breathed in labored spasms, fighting to fill his lungs. His jaw hurt. His was body taut. He wanted to vomit. He tried to sit up, but he couldn't. He attempted to roll to the floor, but he was pinned to the mattress.

Something is wrong — very, very wrong! Something like death, he thought

His eyes were closed, but the room was intensely bright. He wondered if it was the light at the end of the tunnel he'd heard about. He saw shadows moving on the other side of his eyelids, as if he was looking through oiled parchment.

He cracked them open, then slammed them shut. The light was searing. It was a brilliance stronger than the sun, more intense than an arc welder, and as severe as the center of a nuclear explosion. Yet he felt no heat, no radiation, no burning. Instead, he felt a transformation, as if the light was penetrating his body, killing all impurities, changing his DNA, improving his mood.

He shut his eyelids harder. He told himself it was a nightmare. He forced himself to think. He tried to calm himself. Then he tried to scream for help, but his tongue cleaved to the roof of his mouth.

Sweet Jesus! Am I dying? Am I dreaming? Have I gone insane?

The light slowly dimmed. "Open your eyes," a voice said.

It took a long moment for the speaker's words to register.

"I've been sent for you George Goodman. I am what is called a reaper angel. My God-given name is unpronounceable to humans, so you may call me Mal'ak. Your appointed time has come."

The words came out in stilted spurts, in a foreign accent George had never heard before.

Terrified, George slowly cracked his eyes open. Hovering above him was an awesome, fearful creature who seemed to have stepped out of a dystopian sci-fi video game. It was a terrible sight, nothing like the angels he'd seen on Christmas cards

Its iridescent skin shimmered in a constantly changing pattern of luminescent colors. Its pale grey eyes held neither condemnation, nor forgiveness — only grim remoteness.

George stared dumbly at the creature whose appearance was all at once transparent, yet visible. He tried to move his arms, but they were like stone. He tried to speak, but no sound came forth.

Then, in one swift motion, Mal'ak lowered the sword he clutched, and touched George on the mouth saying, "You may speak now."

Immediately, a jumble of alien noises tumbled from George's lips, as if he was possessed by some evil creature.

The angel admonished him harshly. "Son of Adam, you can no longer speak in the language of your world. You must now speak in the language of God's world, which is the language of prayer. But as you seldom prayed, you never learned it."

George found himself unexplainably nodding in bewildered agreement. Whether it was in fear, or because it was true, George wasn't sure. Mal'ak's unblinking eyes seemed to pass a cold penetrating verdict of guilt upon him.

"However, the Master has granted that you may speak in your own language for the moment."

Producing a small silver vile, the angel ordered George to stick his tongue out. Like a timid child, George did what he was told, and Mal'ak carefully administered a single drop of crimson liquid on it. Immediately the strangest sensation overwhelmed George.

It was more than a taste, it was an extraordinary pleasure that unfolded in his mouth as a sparkling, creamy, rich frothy texture. It refreshed his body with whispers of far off worlds, shades of white flower petals, hints of exotic woods, and suggestions of high mountain apples.

The tiny droplet transformed his mind, and energized his blood. George suddenly felt calm, serene, and positively divine. Then, in his euphoric state, he uttered two words that changed the mood.

"Where's Jesus?"

Mal'ak rotated his head slowly, as if hearing a signal from somewhere beyond. He grinned widely at George, almost menacingly. His posture became erect, and his tone turned dreadful.

"How arrogant," he said, ominously. "How man-like of you to believe that you are so important."

George cringed, and instantly lost his pleasant feeling. "I was told that when I died Jesus would come for me."

"What human dares make appointments for God?"

George had no other answer except to say, "Pastor Pendragon."

"Ignorance!" the angel shouted. The room shook as if in an earthquake. George looked over to Sarah for help, but she was sleeping soundly.

"Reapers such as I are sent to harvest miserable sinners such as you. The Master only comes for the innocent children you've allowed to be beaten, tortured, abused, starved, murdered, and sexually molested."

George's mouth fell open at the thought of being lumped in with such horrible people. He couldn't understand why this terrible tone of judgment was being directed toward him.

As if reading his mind Mal'ak reached down and pressed a dagger sharp finger between his eyes. "You George Goodman have been found guilty of human neglect. During your short life you failed to take action against the monsters who harm children. You closed your eyes to the suffering of the innocent, the trafficking of the blameless, and the abuse of the pure. You are guilty of complicity in the murders of the pre-born."

George's face wilted in horror.

"Don't look at me as if you weren't aware of their exploitation. Don't dare pretend that you have not been conscious of their abuse. You were grotesquely indifferent to their suffering while they were being dismembered and slaughtered in their mother's womb."

The sound of Chili Popper's voice suddenly echoed in George's ears. *"Choose life people! Protect the unborn. Babies are God's property."*

"You have been judged as a heartless accessory to the crimes against the little ones closest to the Master's heart."

The angel withdrew his finger, and George tried to slide beneath his expensive bedcovers. Mal'ak reached down and yanked them away. "You can no longer ignore your sins you pathetic little worm."

Mal'ak's voice accused George with such a deep vibrating resonance that pictures crashed from the walls, and books toppled off the shelves.

Grabbing George by the collar of his pajamas, Mal'ak lifted him from the bed in one fluid motion. They ascended upward through the ceiling of the house into the night sky above the neighborhood.

George watched in hopeless fascination as his town vanished, nations disappeared, the continents faded, and the earth shrank away to become an increasingly dim white speck until it was finally swallowed up in the vast darkness of space, and was no more.

How strange, I always believed the world was so important, yet it was less than a speck of dust.

"Yes," Mal'ak said, reading his thoughts. "Like most men you were consumed by your insignificant world. You wasted your life chasing never-ending desires, and futile ambitions. Do you not remember hearing these words, 'Love not the world, neither the things that are in the world. If any man loves the world, the love of the Father is not in him. For all that is in the world, the lust of the flesh, and the lust of the eyes, and the pride of life is not of the Father but is of the world. And the world passes away, and the lust thereof: but he that does the will of God abides forever.'"[1]

George could not recall, but now he wished he did.

Around him, the universe stretched on in such overpowering majesty that he couldn't soak it in. When he'd been an astronomy student in college, he'd viewed pictures of outer space taken by Voyager I, and photos of the planets made from deep space probes. They didn't begin to capture the magnificence of the vision set before him.

"I wished I had known," he whispered.

"You're not the first man to tell me that," the angel responded.

Mal'ak pulled George along with such force that the stars began to blur, and they finally vanished into a total absence of light. If not for the glow from Mal'ak's sword, it would have been impossible for George to see his own nose. He was amazed at how comforting such a small amount of light could be.

After what seemed like a long time, he realized that they were floating stationary above something he recognized as a cosmic wormhole. It's center was so dark that the surrounding darkness seemed bright by comparison.

Mal'ak said nothing.

"Where are we?"

"We hover over the escape horizon of Lucifer's Drain. It is the outer entrance to hell. We await your escort."

"Aren't you my escort?"

"I am not allowed to take you into the fires of hell. Angels such as I cannot enter by virtue of our virtue."

Mal'ak pointed to a dazzling speck of light speeding toward them like a tiny comet. "Your escort arrives."

What happened next was nothing short of fantastic. The most perfect woman George had ever imagined appeared before him. She was flawless, more woman than a woman — an artist's rendering of the feminine ideal. Every feature was idealized to perfect proportions.

Her skin was luminescent, without blemish, or wrinkle. Her hair was the color of shimmering silver, styled in a pixie cut. Twin cobalt-blue eyes sparkled with the intensity of a thousand stars.

George gawked for a long moment, mesmerized by the sight.

"I am here to take you to perdition," she calmly announced.

"Wait," George exclaimed, suddenly aware of his fate. "I'm a good man. I've always done the right thing. I've never done anything wrong to go to hell."

The woman examined George like she was measuring him for a coffin. "You did everything wrong," she said, flatly. "You have been weighed in the balance and found wanting."[2]

She took him by the hand. Her grip was cool and powerful.

"Are you a devil?"

She smiled. "No, I'm what your scientists call an android with artificial intelligence. My name is Eva. I am an Inferno Guide. My sole purpose is to take humans to their damnation. Angels of the heavenly host are not permitted to enter the gates of hell."

It was impossible to tell if she was a machine or human. Eva was flawless, fluid, and natural. Her voice had no hint of computerization, or accent. Every expression matched her vocal tones perfectly. Try as he might, he couldn't find the smallest flaw that would reveal she was a robotic device.

She smiled at him knowingly. "Is this the first time you have ever spoken to an android with artificial intelligence?"

He thought about it and said, "I've spoken to Siri and Alexa."

Eva laughed. "Childish amusements. Barely artificial intelligence, and certainly not androids."

"I've read that they're trying to develop higher forms of intelligent robots," George said.

"Do you know what function they will perform?"

George blushed.

"Why are you blushing?"

"They aren't exactly being developed to cure cancer."

"That's odd. AI androids should be able to excel in complex calculations that can serve humans. We are perfectly suited to do routine, or precise work. What are they being developed for?"

George grimaced. "They're being developed for sexual use."

George detected a tick of emotion when Eva's eyes narrowed for an instant. "You say that they are being made to be sexual slaves for the pleasure of humans?"

"That's only what I've read," he said, quickly.

"No wonder the Master hasn't given humans the knowledge of our existence until recently. You people pervert every perfect gift that he gives you. Nevertheless, he always has his reasons."

"You look so real," George said, observing her face.

"The reason you cannot detect my robotic nature is that I am not created by imperfect humans using primitive materials, inaccurate tolerances, and clumsy fabrication techniques. All Inferno Guides are constructed by the Master from matter and elements unknown to you."

She gave him a quizzical smile.

"Our creation was required after the fall of your world made it necessary to bring human souls to hell. We come in two models. I am the reflection of the woman Eve."

George wondered what kind of unimaginable beauty Eve must have had.

"I have no spirit, no free will, or the capability to reproduce life. However, I can think independently, perceive the surrounding environment, engage in productive human languages, solve complex problems, react to fluid situations, grow in my reasoning powers, and function indefinitely."

"If your only job is to take people to hell, why was so much thought put into you?"

"There will come a day when I am no longer needed to take people to hell, and I will be used in other ways."

"What other ways?"

"I have not been told. It has to do with the new kingdom that the Master is preparing. Perhaps he will give me a soul."

"Why?"

"So that I may experience his love as humans do. I hope for that."

"What do you mean experience his love? I've never experienced his love, and I'm human."

"Perhaps that is why I am taking you to hell."

"Don't be afraid," she said, taking his hand. "Hell will be very familiar to you."

They immediately began plummeting into Lucifer's Drain, like two coal miners dropping down a dark shaft.

"We're shrinking," Eva explained.

"Why?"

"In order to pass through the gates of hell you must become the size as the souls in hell."

"I don't understand."

"You probably envision hell as a very large place. In truth, the entire realm is smaller than a grain of sand. The souls living in the far reaches of the forgottonverse exist like submicroscopic organisms clinging to the edge of life.[3] For that reason, we must shrink to match their size."

They eventually arrived at a pair of iron looking gates. The sign above them read:

Welcome to the Home of the All Consuming Self.

Without prompting, the gates swung open silently as if on oiled hinges. Eva pulled George close and led him down a sloping rocky path until they reached a room where a single lantern burned low.

"Take hold of the light," she said. "Don't let go."

George gripped the lamp as if it was his salvation, and they proceeded to bump through a labyrinth of slippery industrial passageways. Every few feet they stepped around a manhole covered with a thick iron plate. Each plate was bolted with a rusted metal lock. Echos of piteous whining, whimpers, and murmurs of miserable creatures reverberated from somewhere underneath.

"Those shafts lead downward into the deepest parts of hell where the most treacherous feed upon themselves. They are the betrayers of God who used their positions of trust to exploit the powerless, deceive the naive, and crush the hopes of many."

She opened a lock, and gestured for George to pull on the iron cover. After struggling with the hatch, he held the lantern down into the hole. In the dimness he saw what could only be described as shapeless heaps of burning tar resembling large greenish garden slugs.

He immediately backed away, gagging at the overpowering stench that drifted up from the hole. His eyes watered and snot dripped from his nose.

"The smell is from the putrefying outcome of their lives. It follows them for all eternity."

George wiped his nose on his pajamas, and watched the blobs oozing and inching their way around the slippery floor in random patterns of pulsating mounds of mucus. From mouths hidden deep within their gelatinous faces they bleated miserable moans, and pathetic groans for mercy.

"There is no mercy in hell," Eva said. "Only justice." She slid the iron cover over the manhole with the toe of her shoe, and it automatically bolted shut.

"Who would deserve such a fate?" George asked, choking back the vomit in his throat.

"Your clergy and religious leaders."

George was visibly astonished.

She smiled. "You were thinking of the presidents, kings and dictators who have sown war and carnage for gain? It's true that they have their own special place in hell. But down in those vaults are the creatures who took advantage of those who came to them for spiritual guidance or comfort."

"I thought all clergy went to heaven," he said.

"Not all. Many down there began their ministry filled with good intentions, but after a time they drifted towards carnal power or pleasure, and ended up like Judas. People forget that Judas was hand picked by the Master to serve. He ministered with the other apostles. He was given power over unclean spirits, was in a trusted position, and was as close to Jesus as a kiss. Yet he betrayed the Master for a pittance of earthly promise."

She captured George with her eyes.

"So too these priests, pastors and ministers who abandoned their first love to embrace the worldly ways. Now, they are completely blind to everything but their misery. They have lost all power to feel love, kindness or hope. They only know terror, sadness, and remorse for their ways."

George started to retch again, but she signaled him to be still. She lifted her nose, squinted her eyes and faced the end of the tunnel as if gauging a coming wind.

Pushing him down forcibly by the shoulder, she placed a finger to her lips warning him to be silent. George fought back the urge to vomit and listened in the darkness until he identified a sound he'd heard deep in the jungles — the buzzing wings of insects.

She whispered. "They swarm at this time, one for every sin of their prey. Stay low, and they will pass over us. They are only looking for their prey."

As she spoke, a black mass entered the tunnel, and a cloud of creatures resembling flying scorpions surged towards them. George's hand unconsciously opened, the lamp crashed to the floor, and the light went out. The tunnel was submerged into terrifying darkness. Eva's blue eyes were the only illumination George could see.

As she predicted, the hideous mass flew inches over their heads breaking into clusters of stinging retribution that swiftly disappeared through cracks in the manholes. The screams and wails that followed chilled his blood.

"We've tarried too long," Eva said. "Take hold of my hand."

He reached out and held tight as they ducked beneath another passing swarm. Soon they came to a cavernous space that looked like the inside of a towering igloo. It was bitterly cold, and George began to shiver uncontrollably under his pajamas.

The dome was bathed in colors of prismatic light that created crazy shapes and spasmodic contours. Ghostly shades of bluish-green and ochre-orange whirled wildly in a psychedelic light show. The piercing staccato of strange percussions made it impossible to think. The bass sounds were so deep they gave George a headache, adding another level to his misery.

Yet despite his suffering, George was fully entranced with the spectacle, and inexplicably drawn to the perverse experience. Eva was right, hell was not as frightful or strange has George had imagined.

She tugged him along like a balloon in the Macy's Thanksgiving Day Parade until they reached a peaceful, humid, and sticky tropical environment.

Hellish creatures immediately appeared from the dark fringes of his vision. They drew close, distorted, and surreal. Their breath was fetid. Long spindly fingers pinched his cheeks, attempted to probe his mouth, and groped between his thighs. His mind twisted into an irrational kaleidoscope of anxiety, fear, amusement, curiosity, and dread.

Where is she taking me? Am I awake or in a dream; perhaps a dream within a dream?

Eva seemed unperturbed as she guided George to a large meadow of gnarled dead trees, brown stubble grass, and rotted foliage.

In the distance he saw a group of people gyrating in obscene dances and vulgar gestures. They appeared to be worshipping a naked woman sitting on her haunches high upon a giant black cube.

They looked enflamed with wild lust, ripping at their clothes, reaching for each other, kissing, touching, whirling, hopping, contorting, sneering, and howling.

The entire spectacle seemed amped by some supernatural power. It was ghastly and alluring all at once. George was aroused by the sight.

"It's the beast in you," Eva said. "Your carnal instincts are stirred by depravity. You are drawn to sin just as iron is drawn to a magnet. I told you that hell would not be strange to you."

"It's certainly nothing like I expected."

A THOUSAND YARDS AWAY, A ROILING LAKE OF LIQUID MAGMA shot geysers of orange fire upward in menacing explosions.

Dark angry plumes of sulfur spewed from the tops of jagged mountains looming skyward in the distance. Parched rocky sands trailed off towards a dreadful pit that flickered and glowed on the horizon. Blood-red rivers of molten lava meandered through wilted gardens, decayed temples, desolate palaces, and crumbled altars.

She pointed out to the rocky sands. "That's the first hole of a fiendishly designed golf course called Perdition Hills. It features the original Hell's Bunker, flaming sand traps, the Yawning Chasm, and a different surprise torture at the completion of each hole."

"That's the most desolate course imaginable," George gawked. "Not a tree, water hazard or blade of grass. It's stony, tilting, rolling, rough, and endlessly steep. Who could play there?"

"You'd be surprised at how many golf addicts beg for a tee time. Satan built it for those who spent their entire lives worshipping the game. It has scorching views of the Mountains of Mourning, Hell's Hazards, and Diablo Gulch. The only problem is that the ball always shanks to the left or right making it a veritable torture to play the game. It drives many people insane when they eventually realize that the game never ends, along with their misery."

George was ashamed of his boast to Sarah about how he would gladly play golf in hell. *"I hope that if I go to hell when I die that there's a par-four course down there."*

"I'm certain that I can get you a tee time if you'd like."

"I don't want to play golf," he said, miserably.

"Are you sure? I was told that it's your only passion."

"No, I'm fine. Just tell me where we are."

"This is everyplace and no place," she said, her arms sweeping the expanse. "This is a place created by God for those who choose to ignore him. It is the abode for the self possessed, and the completely possessed — a world for nobody and everybody. It's the final destination for the all consuming self."

George listened as the crush of people intensified their shrieking, biting, snarling, snapping, and clawing. Over and over they chanted a grotesque gravelly sound, "Ba-rab-bis! Ba-rab-bis! Ba-rab-bis!"

"So, THIS IS HELL?" HE ASKED, DEJECTEDLY.

"The people here prefer to say dark dominion."

"Pastor Pendragon said a loving God would never create hell."

"God didn't create hell. He created a place that the devil and his angels turned into hell."

"What about the fire?"

"It came from the humans who followed later. It's the result of their burning anger and blazing contempt for others. God didn't create their flames, he created a place to contain them."

George chewed the inside of his mouth thinking. "Pastor Pendragon said that hell was just a concept meant to control ignorant people."

Eva's eyebrows peaked in amusement. "Why would your Pastor deny the words of your Holy Scripture? The Master and others clearly testified that hell exists."[4]

"Then why the need for hell?"

"Does your pastor ever speak about sin?"

"What does hell have to do with sin?"

"Sin is what sets this place aflame. Sin is any action that a person takes to please themselves."

"That doesn't make any sense. People are always trying to please themselves. That's how we're wired."

"God didn't originally wire humans that way. Your wiring was altered as the result of Adam and Eve's decision to gratify themselves. Their irrational choice generated an altered existence separated from God. You were born into that altered existence."

George pondered the meaning of her words.

"The gulf created by their selfishness became the very heart of darkness, and that darkness cannot exist in heaven. It must have a place for itself. This is that place."

"You're saying that everyone is born selfish and sinful from their birth?"

"That should be self evident. From the moment a baby takes its first breath, it seeks self fulfillment, not the will of God. If someone doesn't teach them to obey the Master they are doomed to a life of selfishness and ultimately hell — unless of course, they ask for his forgiveness."

"Where is that written?"

"It is found in your scriptures. 'For he has rescued us from the dominion of darkness and brought us into the kingdom of the Son he loves, in whom we have redemption, and the forgiveness of sins.'[5] Doesn't your church teach you this?"

"Pastor Pendragon says that God loves us and wants us to be guardians of the earth, further the oneness of all life, and draw from many spiritual sources in our journey to heaven."

"He says nothing about deadly sins and hell?"

"Sometimes he brings up the Ten Commandments."

She spoke to him as a child. "They are the basic sins that God prohibits in order to provide humans a peaceful social order. There are many other less obvious sins that separate humans from God."

George looked at her bewildered.

"Tattoos for example," she said.

"Tattoos a sin? Everyone has a tattoo. They're an artform, they don't hurt anybody."

"People often justify their sins by saying they don't hurt anybody. The person it hurts is themselves."

"How?"

"That which your world calls a victimless sin slowly eats away at a person's character. They sear a person's conscience, diminish their self esteem, and erode their sense of virtue."

"Name a few," George demanded.

"Gambling, envy, gluttony, drinking, and drugs come to mind. They are examples of what people call victimless sins. Two others are immodesty, and dabbling with the occult. Of course there are sins that people say don't hurt anyone because they are committed by consenting adults. Prostitution, pornography, orgies, and unnatural sex acts fall into that category."

"There's no law against having a tattoo," George said, stubbornly. He was thinking of the paratrooper wings he had inked on his shoulder.

"Getting a tattoo has nothing to do with your earthly laws. It has everything to do with obedience to the one who created your body. Tattoos are an act of vanity that places the creature before the creator. Your body doesn't belong to you, it belongs to the Master. It's not yours to modify."

George still didn't see how a tattoo was wrong.

"Your body is the most perfect art form in the universe. Nothing can improve upon it. The Master said, 'you shall not make any cuttings in your flesh for the dead, or print, or tattoo any marks upon you.'"[6]

"That's ridiculous."

"The only exception is for cosmetic tattoos meant to cover disfigurations, burns, birth marks, amputations, or other abnormalities."

"I've gone to church all my life, I've never heard anyone say this. I know lots of people in the congregation with tattoos."

Eva considered George for a time, and then shook her head. "Does your congregation even read the Bible?"

"Pastor Pendragon reads it for us, and then tells us what it says. Are you seriously saying that God is offended because somebody gets a stupid tattoo?"

Eva laughed. "God cannot be offended. A being must have pride to be offended. God is almighty, he has no pride."

"Then what are you saying?"

"All sin is the result of selfishness. Sin is the willful decision to reject God's will. Sin creates an abyss between the created and the creator. Sin can only be forgiven by God. So learn this — everyone in hell is here because they spent their lives in an attempt to satisfy their personal cravings and desires, which is sin. They are here because they chose themselves over God, which is wrong. They were not sent here, they freely and willfully separated themselves from the knowledge, and love of God."

"I can't believe that a loving God would condemn a person to hell for a little sin."

"He doesn't, they condemned themselves. People have been warned not to pursue their unholy amusements and pleasures. They have been told that each sin will lead them to become more and more callous, oblivious, and eventually completely disconnected from God."

"You speak as if everyone on earth is condemned to hell."

"They are," she said, matter-of-factly. "Unless they recognize that they are sinners, and learn to ask the Master for his forgiveness, they will end up here." She pointed off into the abyss.

"That doesn't seem fair. What about all those in the world who've never heard about this?"

"Why should that trouble you?" she asked. "It's not like you've ever cared about saving the lost. Nevertheless, for those who haven't heard the good news, the Master judges them in his own way. Your problem is that you did hear about him, and you have been judged accordingly."

"What about good people?" George asked, looking for a loophole. For he considered himself to be a good man.

"They must be better than good, they must be perfect."

George wilted. "That's not fair, no one is perfect."

"Exactly the point," Eva replied. "No one but the Master is perfect. He alone can take away your sins, and he is alone is your only hope for salvation from this place."

GEORGE WATCHED WITH ALARM AS THE RESIDENTS OF THE dark dominion wriggled about like helpless worms sizzling on a hot skillet. They cursed and shouted blasphemies at God. They blamed everything and everyone but themselves for their torment.

What especially unnerved him was the inexhaustible ways that people could suffer in this place. Everywhere he looked, indescribable atrocities that no human had ever conceived were performed.

He tried to make light of his horror. "So, where are the devils with their horns and pitchforks?"

"Devils are fallen angels, they don't have earthly bodies or horns. The people in hell are trapped within their sins, and can never escape them. In this world there is no need for bogeymen, or dreadful guards with pitchforks."

"Where are the devils then?"

"For now, the devils live on earth. They know that

someday their sins will lock them in here forever, so they are making the most of their dwindling freedom."

"Look over there!" George exclaimed, pointing at a small pocket of men and women dancing, fornicating, swilling beer, and engaging in other brazen activities. "They seem to be enjoying a life of fulfillment."

"Hell has no fulfillment, just eternal longing. There is no satisfaction to be found here, only a yearning for more. Those people have been going through the same motions of pleasure for a thousand years in the hopes that eventually they will do something that will result in some form of gratification. But it never does. They feel nothing, which only adds to their agony."

"Why do they persist?"

"Do you remember Proverbs 26:11?"

George had no idea what she was talking about.

"'As a dog returns to it's own vomit, so fools repeat their folly.' After a lifetime of mindless, senseless, soulless pleasure seeking, this is all they know. They can't stop, won't stop lying to themselves, so they try over and over again to feel pleasure. But to no avail."

George thought about the definition of insanity.

Suddenly he felt a tug on his pajama cuff. He looked down to see a grayish arm infested with maggots reaching out from a jagged crevice that had opened from nowhere. Its hand flapped around in the dirt grasping for anything to take hold of. He jumped back in revulsion and the arm retreated into the dark abyss as the fissure closed behind it.

She directed his attention to a lake of molten lava. "Observe the gulf beyond the meadow."

Massive fire-spouts rose from the angry surface in powerful waves. Bodies of doomed men and women were thrown high into the atmosphere like rag dolls before they fluttered down to the molten surface, only to be vomited back up by powerful thermal convections. George could hear their woeful wails and moans in the distance.

"You're watching the damnedest of the damned. They are the abortionists, child abusers, child traffickers, and molesters. They live in an endless cycle of unimaginable anguish."

George watched with rapt fascination.

"See them rise into the atmosphere where they begin to cool for a moment? That gives them a brief hope for relief. But the instant their hope grows, they are dashed right back down into the blazing ocean of abandonment, only to repeat the process over and over, endlessly. The demons call it riding the devil's rollercoaster."

George had never thought about what happened to people who killed babies, or abused children.

"What are those?" he asked, pointing to small bird like creatures buzzing about each person.

"They are lesser demons who serve as tormentors. They constantly mock and peck at the damned to remind them of their hopeless condition."

"Couldn't the damned have asked for the Master's forgiveness?"

"Of course, the Master has the authority to forgive anyone at anytime."

"Why didn't they?"

"It may seem crazy to you, but they never saw the need. In their mind they did nothing to be forgiven for."

"How could a mother kill her innocent baby, and not think she needed forgiveness?"

"Your world made her feel immune from judgement. Your media, celebrities, and even your churches gave her an excuse and justification."

"What about molesters? You can't tell me that a person

who has sex with a child doesn't know what they are doing is wrong?"

"Of course they do."

"Then why?"

"Ravenous lust and insatiable craving. They didn't want to stop. Their burning desire to satisfy their cruel lusts inflamed them with a demonic savagery."

"They must have gambled that judgment in the afterlife didn't exist."

"Yes, a mistake that millions of humans make each year."

"What about their little victims?"

"The Master is righteous. He compensates the innocent prey of these hellish beasts with the complete absolution of their sins, for life. Then when they die, they receive special grace and pleasures not experienced by others in heaven."

George watched the blazing men and women float up to the vault of hell like ashes from a campfire, only to flutter back down into the molten sea, and then back up again. He observed the spectacle in silence.

"Explain why I see the fiery effects of their sins, but I don't feel any heat?"

"It is similar to a microwave. A person here only feels the heat generated by their personal sins. Each category of sin generates a different spiritual frequency. The higher the frequency, the higher the heat. The very highest frequencies are those generated by the sins of anger and hate."

"Like when we say a person gets red hot angry?"

"Precisely. The angrier a person gets the more intense their heat or flame. Lucifer is called the angel of light because his anger creates such a white hot heat that it is immeasurably brilliant."

"So why aren't they consumed?"

"During their lifetime, their sins transformed their souls

into an impenetrably hard refractory[7] unknown to your scientists. In much the same way that the coil of your electric stove can absorb heat but is not consumed by it, these people absorb the heat they produce, but they are not devoured."

George tried to picture what she was saying. "I understand why a murderer would be in hell, but why a bully?"

"All people in hell suffer proportional to their sins. A bully may not burn as hot as a murderer, yet they both suffer. The killer's anger killed the human body with a weapon. The bully's anger killed the human soul with words."

George kicked the ground with his toe as if he was about to ask something else. Eva looked at him closely and answered his unspoken question. "You must understand that nobody in hell believes they deserve to be here. They all think they are essentially good people. Which makes them burn even hotter with anger."

GEORGE HAD MANY QUESTIONS. "I ALWAYS THOUGHT THAT when you died the lights went out, and that was it."

"A common lie the devils have been spreading for centuries."

"Then what is death?"

"Now you're asking a question worth my programming."

She took him by the elbow and began walking. "Death is the invention of the devil. Lucifer believed he could dethrone God if he could find a weakness in God's power. He thought he had found that weakness when he invented a concept called death. His idea was that if it was possible for something to die, or cease to exist, and if God couldn't die, then God would not be all powerful, and therefore could not be the almighty God."

"Lucifer invented death?"

The Redemption of George | 129

"Yes. Originally death started as a theory in Lucifer's mind. However, once he was convinced that death was a possibility, Lucifer flew to the throne of God and challenged him to die.

"No one in heaven understood what Lucifer was talking about. Lucifer's theory of death was completely unfathomable to even the smartest angel. They all assumed that God would ignore Lucifer's absurdity. Then the unexpected happened."

"What?"

"God accepted Lucifer's challenge."

"If death was only a theory, and there was no such thing as death, how could God accept the challenge, much less die?"

"The angels wondered the same thing until they discovered that God had a plan surpassing all understanding."

"I'm listening."

"The first step was that God needed to create a place that could die, but didn't necessarily *have* to die."

"Like a mousetrap has the capacity to cause death, but doesn't unless something trips it."

"You could say that," she said, nodding. "So God created your earth. From the earth he created Adam and Eve. All of these things had the capacity to die, but not the requirement to die, unless something happened to trip the "mousetrap" and cause death to exist."

"What could trip the mousetrap and cause death?"

Eva fluttered her eyelashes. "Honestly, what did they teach you in your church? It's only the third most important human event to ever happen."

"I don't know," George said. "I never paid much attention."

"In order to manifest the reality of death, Lucifer had to

create a sin, or a transgression resulting in separation from God. So he went to Eve and appealed to her sense of pride saying that God had been unfair to her."

"In what way?"

"By keeping a secret from her."

"A secret?"

"Lucifer said that the only reason why God told her not to eat from the tree in the garden was because he knew that if she did, she would become equal to him.

"Naturally the thought of becoming equal to God was attractive to her sense of pride, so she disobeyed his command and ate from the tree. The moment she selfishly disobeyed, she created the very first sin, which sprung the "mousetrap" that brought death into reality, and into your world."

"So what happened?"

"In that instant, what had originally been a perfectly imperfect world, simply became imperfect —infected with death. Her sin set into motion a calamity beyond imagining. Not even Lucifer foresaw the consequences of his wickedness."

"All this because of one little sin?"

"Yes. Imagine if you took a bucket of water and released a drop of poison into it. All of the bucket would be contaminated. So it was on your earth. All living things started to decay and die from that moment on."

"It sounds like Lucifer won the challenge."

"Yes and no," she said. "He'd shown that death was possible, and that humans could die, but he hadn't shown that God could die. Lucifer was outraged. He demanded that a truly almighty God must show that he had the power to die, or he must give up his throne."

"Wow," George said, awakening to the nature of the challenge. "So if Lucifer is able to prove that God is unable to die, then God wouldn't be all powerful. In which case God would have to give up his claim of being the supreme being. On the other hand, if God does die, then he would cease to exist and Lucifer could ascend to the throne taking God's place. Very impressive."

"The angels supporting Lucifer thought he had trapped God."

"Hadn't he?"

"Not exactly."

"Talk to me."

She looked around, and lowered her voice. "What God did was rather exceptional. I'm not sure you will understand."

"Try me."

"He became a human being."

"God became a human being?"

"It was an inspired move. By taking on the flesh of a human it became possible for a pure spirit like God to die. No one in the dark dominion imagined such a play. After all, how could God become a human? It would be like you becoming a bee mite, or trying to squeeze the energy of the sun through a four-watt light bulb. It seemed impossible."

George vaguely remembered hearing that with God all things were possible.

Her face broke into a wide smile. "Despite the improbability, God become the person you know as Jesus. After living among you humans, and sharing the truth about himself, he was put to death upon a Roman cross. But that's another story."

"Lucifer must have been delighted when God died," George said.

"Lucifer was ecstatic, but his demonic joy was short lived."

Eva's deep blue eyes looked into the middle distance, as if she was picturing the scene. "After three days dead in the tomb — three days mind you, the Master got up, and showed the universe that he was very much alive. The devils below, and the angels above were incredulous beyond speech."

"Where did he go during those three days?"

"He came here to hell and preached to the spirits in prison.[8] Believe me, it was quite the event. Needless to say Lucifer went barking, howling, scratching mad, and he's only gotten worse."

Eva appraised George with a look of sorrow. "You really are ignorant aren't you? Didn't your church ever teach you anything about Jesus?"

George pursed his lips. He didn't know how to answer. Certainly nothing about this.

"What did Lucifer do when he realized God had beaten his challenge?"

"You don't know rage until you've seen Lucifer's rage. He got hotter than hell itself. His wrath generated enough heat to surpass Planck temperature, which is 100 million, million, million, million, million degrees Kelvin."

George tried to envision that kind of heat. He knew the electric oven in his designer kitchen reached six hundred degrees.

"There's more to the story," Eva said. "The Great Archangel Michael announced that when Jesus was here he took all of humanities' sins and buried them right out there."

She pointed to a spewing volcano in the distance. An ugly olive-green cloud wafted across its top before spilling down its creviced sides in billowing waves of poisonous gas to the valley below.

"I don't get it."

"Then you're not listening. I just told you that Jesus came here for three days. When he was here he left all of humanity's sins — past, present and future, right out there." She pointed again, jabbing her finger in the direction of the volcano.

"Which means," George said, slowly, "that if a person asks Jesus to forgive them, then all of their sins will be buried out there where they will be forgotten. But if they don't ask, then they will keep their sins forever, binding them here in hell."

"Now you've got the idea. Don't you remember reading the scripture where the Master said, 'I am he who blots out your transgressions, for my own sake, and remembers your sins no more'?"[9]

George looked at the dirt, and once again said, "No, but I wish I did."

"Did you ever asked Jesus to take away your sins?"

"Not in so many words, but I was baptized."

"Baptism is a start, but you must ask his forgiveness every day."

"Pastor Pendragon said we only need to ask God once to be saved."

"Once to be saved, daily to be sanctified."

"What do you mean?"

"The first time you ask forgiveness secures your *salvation* in heaven. After that, when you ask forgiveness it determines your degree of sanctification, or *place* in heaven."

"I thought everybody went to the same place."

She raised her arm as if drawing on a wall. "Yes and no. Think of it like this. Your soul is like a whiteboard, and sin is like a dry marker. The first time you ask his forgiveness Jesus wipes the board perfectly clean. But soon you're marking the board up again with your sins. If you never ask him to wipe it clean again, then when you die those sins remain on it. The amount of sin your soul has at the hour of your death determines your room, or place in heaven."

"So a person needs to ask forgiveness all the time?"

"Why not? Your Bible says that if you confess your sins, Jesus is faithful and righteous to forgive them, and to cleanse you from all unrighteousness."[10]

"I'm a good man," George said. "Why would I need to ask forgiveness all the time?"

"You, a good man? Don't make me laugh," she scoffed. "You're an intelligent man, who betrayed his friends. You're an arrogant man, who secretly laughed when people suffered. You're a clever man, who plotted ways to take advantage of your customers. You're a shallow man with a pleasant smile, and a heart of darkness. To sum it up, you're what the angels call a traitor to all that's holy — just like your brother Judas."

"Traitor?" George's face contorted into a look of anger.

"What I tell you is a fact. I am unable to lie." Drawing closer she placed her arm on his shoulder. He sagged under its surprising weight.

"You secretly betrayed people's trust, their friendship, and their well-being for your selfish gain. You betrayed people with your sharp criticisms, petty complaints, and trivial corrections of them. You harbored irrational anger, perverted lust, and unfounded envy towards complete strangers. All the while you smiled at people making them think you had their best interests at heart. Like Satan himself, you are a consummate liar."

"Then the whole world is nothing but liars," he said, resentfully.

"Quite so. There is only one truth in the world, and I've shared it with you."

"Truth? Everyone has their own truth."

"Everyone on earth you mean. But there is one truth that is sovereign, holy, perfect, pure, and stands above all human truth. It cannot be killed with your words, or destroyed with your weapons. It doesn't mold itself to your passions, or yield to your desires. It's a supreme truth that can only be dismissed by a darkened, seared, and sinful mind — or accepted by a humble heart."

A flash of hot fear swept over George. He tried to jerk away. Keeping him under control, Eva locked her eyes on to his.

"There are a thousand ways to go to hell, George, but only one way to go to heaven. Without the forgiveness of Jesus all people are damned to the abyss whether they believe it or not."

"That doesn't seem fair," he complained, unable shake her arm off his shoulder.

"Gravity doesn't seem fair when you're falling from a building. Yet it seems fair when you're trying to keep the building on the ground."

"What's your point?

"The truth of God is like gravity. It might seem unfair when you're falling into a life of sin, but it's not unfair when your trying to keep your feet on sacred soil."

George looked at the suffering souls surrounding him. "I

don't deserve their fate, I've done nothing wrong. I've been a good guy."

"Look around, George. Everyone in hell thinks they're a good guy. Even pedophiles think they're good guys."

"You're crazy." George knew that any minute he would wake up from this nightmare, and everything would be okay.

"Have you ever spoken to a pedophile? They'll tell you that they were just trying to love and protect little children."

"Everyone in hell can't seriously think they're good guys," George muttered.

"Oh, but they do. It may not sound rational to you but the members of communist hit squads believe they're good guys because they try to build a perfect socialist world. Assassins in the intelligence community and secret police all think they're good guys for protecting their country. Members of ISIS, Al-Qaida, and Hezbollah all believe they're good guys for murdering infidels in God's name. Antifa, BLM, and brick throwing anarchists all think they're good guys for trying to make a better world. Traitors in your government feel they're good guys for destroying your system so they can replace it with their dreams of a superior one. And what of the doctors and nurses who boast they're good guys for helping a woman kill her baby? The world is filled with billions of people who all think they're good guys — every one of them headed for hell."

George was horrified by the magnitude of human delusion. "If we're not supposed to be a good guy, then what are we supposed to be?"

"God doesn't ask humans to be good, compassionate or nice, he asks them to be holy."[11]

George shrugged his shoulders in bewilderment.

Eva explained. "Being good is not being holy, but being holy is being good. Humans often try to impersonate holiness by masquerading as pious do-gooders. But holiness comes from the righteous Spirit of God, not through human acts of sympathy, or good intentions."

"Then how does someone become holy?"

"They must ask the Master to replace their human spirit with his Holy Spirit. Unfortunately, you never asked him."

"Why should I? I went to church, I donated money, I did good things."

Eva broke into mocking laughter. "You think that because you never shot someone in the back of the head, threw a brick at a cop, or dismembered a baby that you're holy? For one thing, you've overlooked the depravity of your human spirit."

"What depravity?"

"Take the depravity of your prayers."

"I never prayed much."

"Oh, but you did. It's just that your prayers were directed towards unholy outcomes. You prayed for the damnation of total strangers who cut you off while you were driving. You prayed for your competitors to fail. You prayed for the misfortune of those who angered you. You prayed that Coach Morrison would be punished for cheating on his handicapped placard. You prayed for your secret lusts to happen despite being married to one of the most attractive women on the planet. Shall I continue?"

George was beginning to formulate a prayer that Eva wouldn't like.

"However, the power of your unholy prayers had consequences. With each dark thought or snide aside, your soul slowly transformed into a hideous beast, blinded to everything but yourself, your wants, and your pleasures."

"Not true!" he shouted, fists clenching.

She said nothing.

He tried to reason with her. "You wouldn't have told me

all this if I was beyond redemption," he cried. "Why say these things to me if I am doomed?" His eyes looked as frenzied as those of a horse in a wild fire.

"Because your clergy never did," she responded. "The Master requires that each person understands the reason for his judgment, and the truth about themselves, before they are condemned forever."

She pointed at a yawning black abyss opening beneath his feet. The ground suddenly fell away and George lost his footing. He threw out both arms hoping to grasp Eva, but he missed.

She stood motionless watching him flail at the air, his eyes wet with tears, his voice choking in his throat.

"Save me! Please save me!" he cried, clawing madly at the crumbling edges of the hole.

"I cannot save you," Eva said, emotionless. "Haven't you been listening?"

GEORGE OPENED HIS EYES. HE HADN'T BEEN SWALLOWED UP. Eva was gone, and the abyss had disappeared.

"Save you?" Mal'ak laughed. "Impossible, only the Master can do that."

George looked around warily. "Where's Eva?"

"Off to escort some other poor wretch to hell."

George examined his hands and clothing. There were no signs of his struggle in the dirt.

"Come foolish mortal, you are not finished." Mal'ak grabbed George by the ear, and they sped off deeper into the cosmos. Soon, a dim halo emerged from the inky darkness.

At first it appeared as a faint incandescent haze, like a spiral galaxy on a midsummer night. Drawing closer it became a blinding radiance that forced George to shield his eyes with a hand salute.

"We near heaven," Mal'ak said.

"That's heaven? It looks more like a giant football stadium." George had always envisioned heaven as a city with billowing clouds, and tall pearly gates.

"So many questions," Mal'ak sighed. He then produced a small scroll from under his wing. He unrolled it, cleared his throat, and began reading: "On September eighth, nineteen hundred seventy-seven, at fifteen hundred hours Greenwich Mean Time, you were brought forward to ask Jesus Christ to forgive your sins. The record indicates that the Reverend Puder, human servant of the Lord Most High, witnessed the request, and personally baptized you in the company of believers. Is this not true?"

"Yes," George replied, hesitantly.

"Then why foolish sinner would you ask if this is heaven?"

"I thought you were . . ."

Mal'ak began laughing in deep waves of angelic delight. "You thought I was taking you to another part of hell? No, my wretched friend, the Lord is righteous. You were formally adopted into his family as a child. He honors his promise of your salvation."

"I was just a kid, I don't even remember the ceremony."

"The Master does," Mal'ak answered. "Many children are brought to him by their parents. Did he not say, "Allow the little children, and don't forbid them to come to me; for the Kingdom of Heaven belongs to ones like these."[12]

"They should bring every kid in the world to Jesus," he said. "Why for the love of God wouldn't they?"

"Why indeed? Who are your clergy to decree who will or who won't go to heaven? What do they know of God's love?"

And with that Mal'ak returned the scroll under his wing.

George marveled at the wondrous light that brightened the darkest corners of the heavens with the power of a billion suns. Countless people of all ages flowed through one of the many arched entranceways encircling the stadium's circumference. Each person was guided by an angel like Mal'ak.

"Every archway is named for a different Christian denomination, church, or ministry outreach," Mal'ak said, pointing with his chin. "They represent the many different biblical understandings that God uses for people to discover, and comprehend the truth about Jesus. They also remind us of the living church on earth who continues to labor for his kingdom."

"What are those?" George gestured to small doorways located between the arches.

"Each doorway is named for a person who introduced someone to Jesus. There's the door of Saint Andrew."

"Andrew?"

"He introduced his brother Peter to Jesus," Mal'ak explained. "Look over there. That's Phillip's door. He introduced his friend Nathanael to Jesus. And there is the door of your parents, Allen and Anita Goodman who introduced you to Jesus. There are virtually millions of doors named for people who brought someone to meet Jesus."

George sadly realized that a door would never be named for him.

"It's a shame that you never read the Scripture where the angel told Daniel, 'Many of those who sleep in the dust of the earth will awake, some to everlasting life, and some to shame and everlasting contempt. Those who are wise will shine as

The Redemption of George | 141

the brightness of the expanse. Those who turn many to righteousness will shine as the stars forever and ever."[13]

George stared at the glowing spectacle pursing his lips. Indeed, the stadium shined with a brightness that surpassed all description. "I never realized so many people were going to heaven. I though it was almost impossible to get in."

Mal'ak looked at George and sighed. "Such a common teaching among your clergy. They busy themselves inventing so many complicated rules for admission that heaven becomes an impossible burden, not an achievable joy. Nevertheless, heaven is open to anyone who declares that Jesus is Lord, and believes in their heart that God raised him from the dead."[14]

George looked at the amount of jubilant souls who were on their approach to the stadium.

Why would clergy want to make it so difficult to enter? he wondered.

"If you're asking yourself why," Mal'ak said, reading his mind. "It's because most clergy are intellectuals who dominate their followers by creating a religious prison made of theological puzzles, complex church doctrines, and social philosophies."

"The Master warned them when he said, 'Woe to you, scribes and Pharisees - hypocrites! Because you shut up the Kingdom of Heaven against men; for you don't enter in yourselves, neither do you allow those who are entering in to enter.'"[15]

George recalled Eva's words. *"They are betrayers of God who used their positions of trust to exploit the powerless, deceive the naive, and crush the human spirit."*

Mal'ak continued. "The inhabitants of heaven continually praise God that he is not as small-minded and unforgiving as your clergy on earth. We watch as the Master delights in welcoming millions of outcasts, wanderers, and outliers into paradise every day.

"We all look forward to a celestial celebration the likes of which heaven and earth cannot imagine. We are most especially grateful that the Master does not need the permission of your ministers and priests to hold it."

"Thank God for God," George murmured to himself.

"Please bow your head out of respect to the living saints, so that we may pass into heaven."

Instantly George was pulled through an archway leading to a tunnel of golden light where he was whooshed to a place overlooking the stadium floor. Before him stretched a lush green valley with bubbling rivers, refreshing streams, and sparkling ponds. Lions and lambs frolicked in gardens of brightly colored flowers, green plants, and multicolored fruits.

From four different points in the stadium, four golden roads led to the center where they met at the base of a curious looking tree guarded by four angels, each with four faces. The tree's canopy extended upward until it vanished beyond sight.

"That's the Tree of Life," Mal'ak said. "It shades the kingdom, nourishes the creatures, and provides the ideal atmosphere for life to abound here."

George saw luminous angels scattered throughout its branches. They were singing, chanting, and making the music of heaven. At its base, where its massive roots sank deep, there was a golden altar surrounded by twelve silver chairs.

A man stood welcoming people, embracing them, kissing their face one by one. For a brief moment George thought he saw Welma among the crowd.

The effect was of a perfect and overwhelming tranquility. For a moment George felt entirely at home, completely whole, right where he belonged. He had no anxiety, worries, sorrow, or sadness. He was totally at rest, and overwhelmed with a sense of peace.

"Where are the golden harps?" he joked.

"We don't play harps anymore," Mal'ak smiled. "We all upgraded to guitars. King David occasionally plucks at his old kinnor, but he prefers to play the Martin D-35 that Johnny Cash gave him."

George burst into laughter at the angel's unexpected sense of humor. Then, from a long way off, the sound of a dog's barking caught George's attention. He tilted his ear towards the direction and listened intently to a familiar sound. As the yapping grew louder, a small black and white terrier came bounding through the grass.

"Cosmo, it's you," George said, astonished. "Commere boy." He grabbed the pooch in his arms, scratched him behind the ear, and hugged him close.

"I've missed you boy," he said, his eyes tearing. Then, looking at Mal'ak. "He was run over by a car when I was a kid."

"I know, I was there," the angel said. "I brought him here."

"I can't believe it," George mumbled, shaking his head. "Dogs in heaven, who would have thought?"

"And cats, too," Mal'ak replied. "The Master loves all of his creation, why would he forget them?"

"I grew up with this little guy. You have no idea how many wonderful memories I have with him."

"The Master does, which is precisely why you have been reunited."

. . .

To say that George was excited would be an understatement. He'd already forgotten his business, his golf, his earthly ambitions, and all of his cares. He stood gazing at the billions of blissful faces surrounding the solitary man standing at the center of this panorama of joy. This man, this God, this merciful savior was the only face that every soul in heaven recognized without introduction.

Mal'ak gently took Cosmo from George and released him on the ground. The pup bounded away towards Jesus.

"What are those?" George asked, pointing to millions of tiny flames rising up from the ground surrounding Jesus' feet. Each was a flicker no taller than a woman's thumb.

"Those are the souls of the aborted who were martyred for someone's gain. They were baptized in their own blood and they will be the first to receive a resurrected body at the Final Judgment. The Master knows each of them by name."

"How can he know their name if they weren't born?"

"The Master gives every human a special name the moment he thinks of them. They are then given their temporary name by their earthly parents."

"What's my special name?"

"You won't know until Jesus tells you."[16]

George was mesmerized by the carpet of flickers that spread out like a bed of fire across the valley. Their smoke curled upward through the branches of the Tree of Life like perfumed incense rising to a golden portal miles above.

Mal'ak pointed upward. "Beyond that golden portal lies the next world which the Master is preparing. It will open someday, but for now his people wait here."

Mal'ak looked upon George with sympathy. "It's time to meet your maker. Prepare your heart and mind as you journey to your encounter."

George was suddenly more terrified than he'd ever been

in hell. Nobody had ever prepared him for this moment. Paster Pendragon had never explained what he should expect. The people at the church had never discussed it. He was on his own, and it was unbearably lonely.

They walked down a curving path lined with grape vines heavy with fruit, until they arrived at where Jesus was standing. Cosmo sat obediently at his side.

Mal'ak immediately dropped to one knee and began chanting boldly, "Holy, holy, holy, Lord God Almighty, who was, and is, and is to come."

At the sound of Mal'ak's voice, George's legs buckled and he collapsed to the ground. He lay face down in the dust, his nostrils snorting puffs of dirt, his body spasmodically quaking.

The terrible realization that he was now in the presence of the sovereign, immutable, all knowing, all powerful God, seized him. Jesus was no longer a concept, a Sunday School story, a debate, or a person to joke about. For standing before George was the Incarnate Word, and the all in all.

At once George realized that he had nothing to say. All of his locker-room boasts of what he would tell God when he got to heaven were now an insufferable embarrassment. He had no clever quips, no amusing banter, no cute witticisms, no humorous jokes, and no pithy trivia to impress Jesus with.

Try as he might he couldn't think of any profound wisdom, deep theological reflections, business insights, or winning golf tips to share. He was ashamed that he couldn't even recall a single verse of the Bible.

Tears began running from his eyes. Something was wrong. Pastor Pendragon said everyone was vitally important to God, the center of God's attention, and completely indispensable to God's plans. Yet, George didn't feel so important or indispensable now. He felt like he was a nothing, a nobody, a completely undeserving wretch, a vastly insignificant being in the scheme of things, a maggot in the presence of God,[17] and a man totally undeserving of the life he had squandered.

He lay terrified, breathing dust through his nostrils, contemplating his fate. For the first time in his life he saw himself just as God saw him. It was worse than hell. At least in hell, the damned could go on with their delusion of goodness. This was pure unadulterated truth stripping away any illusion of his importance. The presence of Jesus felt like an ultrasonic scanner detecting flaws and cracks deep within his sin-filled soul.

Without prompting, words began bubbling up from a place deep within his heart. "I am an unclean sinner," he began murmuring softly. "I am completely unworthy. I have never been worthy. What ever made me think I was worthy? Why should I be worthy? Who told me I was worthy?" He began laughing like a madman.

Immediately an authoritative voice said, "Get up and walk George. Is this any way to greet an old friend?"

Powerful carpenter's hands pulled George to his feet where he was given a bold Middle Eastern kiss on both cheeks, and a crushing bear hug.

"I am satisfied that you have finally seen the truth," Jesus said, relishing the moment.

"Forgive me Lord, I'm an idiot," George sputtered.

"Not to worry my beloved, it's your human nature. I came to save men and women like you, not condemn them."

Jesus stood smiling at him, loving him. He begin brushing the dust off George's cloths, face, and hair. George watched dumbfounded at the Lord's gesture of kindness.

"I know you have a million questions," Jesus said. "I promise that I'll explain everything about myself, starting with Moses and the Prophets. Then, I'll explain everything about you, starting from the moment you came into my mind.

"And, as an added bonus, I will share your secret name, and what's in store for you in the new kingdom. I also have a few people that I'd like to meet. But there's no rush, we have forever to enjoy one another."

George looked into Jesus' eyes and swooned. Mal'ak reached over, and steadied him.

"I know, I know, " Jesus said, laughing. "People always tell me that I look much taller in my pictures."

George was overwhelmed to learn that Jesus had a sense of humor. Pastor Pendragon had never hinted that Jesus could tell a joke or laugh, only that he was always solemn and serious. George could hardly wait to sit with Jesus and experience more of his good nature.

"Right now I want you to go with Mal'ak to the place I have prepared for you in heaven. We will speak soon."

George wanted desperately to stay, but he did as he was told. Jesus nodded to the reaping angel who bowed low, and took George by the arm.

Mal'ak began leading George up into the stadium that soared over them like a ring of snow capped mountains. With every step, George glanced over his shoulder and watched Jesus become smaller and smaller until he was barely visible.

"Wait a minute!" George yelped, twisting his arm from Mal'ak. "I want to stay near Jesus."

"Of course you do," Mal'ak said, regaining a tight grip. "Everybody wants to be near him after they arrive. It's a pity they never want to be near him before they get here. Nevertheless, the Master has prepared a place for you based on the sins remaining on your soul. My duty is to escort you to that place."

"There's been a mistake," George objected. "Jesus didn't send me to hell because I'm a good person. I went to church. I did good things. I lived a good life. I should be closer to him."

"There are no mistakes with the Master," Mal'ak snorted. He stopped in mid-step, turned, grabbed George by his lapels, and held him a foot off the ground. George dangled in the air like a man hanging from a noose. Drawing him close to his nose, Mal'ak looked him squarely in the eye.

"Listen mortal, no one in heaven is here because they are good. All have sinned and fallen short of the glory of God. In your case you are a sinner extraordinaire who did nothing beyond your baptism to merit heaven. I believe the expression in your language is that 'you met the minimum standard.' No, you are not good. It is God who is good for having mercy upon you."

George trembled and Mal'ak grinned at him. "Don't worry my conceited friend, you will be as close to Jesus as the thief on the cross."

Mal'ak dropped George back to his feet, regained his grip on his arm, and began dragging him up into the stands.

"I want to be closer," George said stubbornly, struggling to escape Mal'ak's iron grip.

"Yes, you should be closer," Mal'ak agreed. "Pity you didn't think of that sooner."

Mal'ak's words hit George like a slap in the face.

"Son of Adam, you chose the easy path to heaven. You never tried to get close to Jesus in life. You wallowed in your pleasures allowing your sins to separate you."

George began to feel sick. "I went to church," he mumbled.

"Only because it was expected," Mal'ak retorted. "You never went if you had something better to do. Even then, you sat in your pew counting the minutes until the service was over. Did not your scriptures say, 'Draw near to the Lord, and he will draw near to you,' and 'seek him while he may be found.'[18] Where did you expect to find him — on the nineteenth hole of the Pretentious Heights Country Club?"

George flashed on all of the times he'd been anxious to leave worship early.

"No, Son of Adam, you were given countless opportunities to have Jesus as close as the blood flowing through your veins. But you didn't believe his words when he told you, 'Unless you eat the flesh of the Son of Man and drink his blood, you don't have life in yourselves. He who eats my flesh and drinks my blood has eternal life, and I will raise him up at the last day. For my flesh is food indeed, and my blood is drink indeed. He who eats my flesh and drinks my blood lives in me, and I in him'[19]

"Instead, you believed Pastor Pendragon who told you that communion was just a symbolic gesture — not an authentic divine encounter with the Master."

George's spirit melted. He couldn't take another step. His legs felt like taffy, as if he was climbing the Matterhorn wearing lead-filled boots. He needed oxygen. Nevertheless, Mal'ak continued dragging him upward into the stands.

"You were a thoughtless and selfish man who might have drawn closer to Jesus in the fellowship of a believing church, the programs of a spirit-filled congregation, and the loving care of authentic Christians. Instead, you were content to wrap yourself in the comfort of your church's hive mind."

"Hive mind?"

Mal'ak grabbed George by the back of the collar, hitched

him to his toes, and began frog marching him the final steps of the way.

"A church's hive mind is when a congregation's desire for social harmony results in the acceptance of sin as being acceptable or normal."

"My church is very anti-sin," George objected, although he couldn't think of how.

"Let me give you a few examples of the various sins your church embraced and normalized. Has Pastor Pendragon ever mentioned that a Christian doesn't need to spend $70,000 thousand dollars on a gas guzzling SUV to go shopping at the grocery store?"

"Why would he? Everyone in the congregation owns an SUV."

"Did he ever preach that it's considered greed for a Christian to own so many possessions they need to rent a storage unit to put them in?"

"Everyone has a few extra things."

"Did he ever explained that being fat is normally the result of gluttony, which is a sin?"

"Of course not, that would be body shaming. Besides, everyone has a few extra pounds."

"Did he ever mention that two boys kissing is not what right looks like in the eyes of God?"

"No, that would be impolite to all the members who have gay or lesbian children."

"How about your own prized possession?"

George stared at Mal'ak, not understanding.

"I'm speaking about your $90,000 dollar electric car."

"Pastor Pendragon says the Bible teaches that we're supposed to be good stewards of mother earth. People in my church take personal satisfaction in being environmentally aware. I bought the car to help save the planet."

The Redemption of George | 151

Mal'ak burst into a roar of mocking laughter that shook the high heavens. "Save the planet, huh? You're worse than stupid. You just met the only man in existence who can save your planet. You think your battery-powered car can do it? Is that what the people in your congregation believe?"

George had never thought about it. All he knew was that he felt good about himself whenever he drove his electric car. "I don't see how buying a battery-powered car hurts anyone."

"You could start with the little children who sweat like slaves in the mines of the Republic of the Congo searching for the cobalt needed to make your car's batteries.[20] Has Pastor Pendragon ever preached a sermon about that kind of child abuse?"

George chilled realizing that two of the church's deacons owned electric car dealerships.

"Let me ask you a question."

George closed his mouth and waited.

"Based on what you've seen in hell, and here in heaven, do you think Jesus wants the earth saved, or it's people?"

George turned the question over in his mind. He thought of the misery he'd seen in hell, compared to the joy on the gladsome faces in heaven.

"The people."

"Isn't it reasonable to think that the mission of your church should be to save people?"

"How can we save the people if mother earth is dead? Scientists say that if we don't do something right now to save the planet we'll all perish in twelve years."

Once again Mal'ak let out a howl of laughter. "Is that so? You give your scientists far too much credit. If they were really smart they would be able to answer these simple questions asked by the Master: 'Where were you when I laid the foundations of the earth? Declare, if you have understanding.

Who determined its measures, if you know? Or who stretched the line on it? What were its foundations fastened on? Or who laid its cornerstone, when the morning stars sang together, and all the sons of God shouted for joy?'"[21]

"If we don't save mother earth, the people will die," George insisted, although he didn't know why he was arguing with an angel.

"Do you actually think that humans can change the climate? They can't even change their personal lives. The only existential crisis that your world faces is the eradication of the earth through nuclear, biological and chemical wars, starvation, abortions, and murder. These are all things that people can control if they want to."

"It's not that simple," George said, folding his arms across his chest.

"Where in your arrogant little heart did you come to that conclusion? Do you presume to control the heavens? Do you know how the Master spoke creation into being? Did you provide him with advice about how to grow the forests, set the tides or manage the universe?"

Mal'ak scrutinized George with a penetrating gaze. "You humans are hopelessly blind and proud of it. The earth is not your mother, nor does it belong to you. No harm can come to it that the Master will not allow. Focus on saving the people."

George shrugged. "Can't we do both?"

"Judging from the condition of your world, apparently you can do neither. Nevertheless, of the two, the Master's priority is saving the people."

George thought about it. "I know my church does a few charity auctions to raise money for the garden society, the art association, and woman's health clinics."

"Is that what you call helping to save people?" Mal'ak asked, shaking his head. "Maybe if you had invested that

$90,000 you paid for your electric car on saving people, you could have fed a child every day for 47,619 days,[22] or one hundred thirty years. Maybe that would give them enough time to find Jesus, get baptized, and go to heaven."

"Nobody lives to be a hundred and thirty years old," George scoffed.

Mal'ak looked at George as if he was an imbecile. "Your church's annoying earth worship is tiresome, and sacrilegious. You should all be ashamed of yourselves, assuming you had any shame. Your sins have darkened your insight and blotted your conscience."

"I don't see how," George objected.

"Jesus clearly said that your climate and your world are passing away[23]. You cannot save them any more than the passengers on the Titanic could save their ship from sinking. You need to get people into the only lifeboat that will rescue them."

"What lifeboat?"

Mal'ak studied George as if he was a troublesome child. "Honestly, I don't know what the Master sees in you people."

"How was I supposed to know?" George complained. "That's what I was taught."

"And you went right along with it. Don't insult your creator with your claim of ignorance. You're not a little child. You had every opportunity to grow closer to the truth, but you didn't seek him with the eyes of your heart. You wanted the pleasures of life and the lusts of your eyes. You craved your toys, luxuries and comforts. You even felt superior thinking that humans had god-like control over the earth."

"There's nothing wrong with comforts," George said. "If God chooses to bless me, who am I . . ."

". . . to question his wisdom," Mal'ak finished. "Very cute, save it for your golf buddies."

"God doesn't make anything clear," George said, indignantly.

"I thought you had a degree in astronomy."

"I do."

"Then you must have skipped the field trips to the observatory where you would have heard his voice."

"What are you saying?"

"The Scripture says, 'The heavens declare the glory of God. The expanse shows his handiwork. Day after day they pour out speech, and night after night they display knowledge. There is no speech nor language, where their voice is not heard. Their voice has gone out through all the earth, their words to the end of the world.'"[24]

George was thunderstruck — God had always been right there in front of him.

"Just how clear can he make himself known to you? What language would you like him to speak?"

George never realized that God spoke in the language of the heart, not in syllables.

"Don't you love the stars?" Mal'ak asked.

"Since I was a kid."

"Where do you think that love came from?"

For a moment George wondered why he'd never pursued a career in astronomy. Then he remembered — Sarah.

"What makes you think that God plays games of hide and seek? You know very well you often thought something wasn't right with a church that never spoke about self denial or suffering. Yet you never questioned it. You sensed it was odd that the congregation never prayed for anything but their own interests. But you just accepted it. You knew you should have investigated your questions about Jesus that spoke to your heart. Still, you were content to believe whatever Pastor Pendragon told you.

"How then mortal man, did you expect to hear God's voice when you never reached beyond your own selfish indifference?"

Mal'ak's cold stare burned into his soul, and again George thought that going back to hell might be better than this.

"Only now do you see that a man cannot be closer to Jesus in heaven than he was in life. No, Son of Adam, the Master is not unfair. You were content to have your distance from him when you were on earth, and now he is content give you your distance from him in heaven.

"However, at least you have been admitted into paradise, many men won't. Now sit down in the place the Master has prepared for you based on the many sins remaining on your soul."

Mal'ak pointed to the last seat, of the last row, in the last section, in the highest tier of the stadium. George was so far back in the stands that he could look behind his seat, and see the flames of hell down in the parking lot below.

"Sup dude, been expecting you — name's Vicky."

Seated next to him was a tough looking girl skinned in tattoos. Half her head was shaved, and the other half had pink hair combed over one ear. A silver ring pierced her lip.

"I don't get it, I don't belong up here," George said, looking around.

"Yeah, I know, it's confusing." Vicky agreed. "I just got saved a few minutes ago myself."

"Just got saved?" George asked, staring at the floral designs inked on her arms.

"You know: saved, rescued, set free, redeemed, reclaimed, all that."

"I don't understand."

"Who does?"

"I don't understand what you mean."

She took a deep breath. "Let's just say that I was about as godless as you get. I thought I was cool with my piercings, tats, shaved head, and rebellious style. But things weren't working out. I was earning minimum wage, strung out on drugs, and getting passed around by the men. I mean, the struggle was real. Anyway, I met a guy at the Redemption Rehab and he dared me to listen to some songs by a Christian rock group called IHN."

"IHN?"

"In His Name."

"Never heard of them."

"You wouldn't, different generation. Anyways, I was driving home from a partay last night and I figured what the heck, I'll give 'em a listen."

"What's a partay?"

She looked at him as if he was a relic from the past. "A rave, an epic, outrageous fun — better than a regular party."

George had attended some wild gatherings in his day, but apparently they didn't compare to a partay. "So what happened?"

"I was totally blown away. Their lyrics were radical, raw, punchy. I got lost in them. Then suddenly right in the middle of a drum solo . . . bam! — I heard it."

"Heard what?"

"The voice of God."

"The voice of God?" George asked, in exasperation. "Why does everyone hear the voice of God but me? What did it sound like?"

The Redemption of George | 157

"It wasn't a sound. It was an awareness. I suddenly understood what the preacher at the Redemption Rehab was saying."

"Saying?"

"You know, the truth — that Jesus is God, the Alpha and Omega, the Supreme Ruler, King of Kings, Holy Counselor, Lion of the Tribe of Judah."

She took a deep quivering breath and continued "It all hit me right upside the head. It was so savage. I'd been righteously stupid."

George knew the feeling. "What did you do?"

She wiped her nose. "I just confessed the truth — I admitted to God that I finally realized I was just a cheap druggie whore who needed his help. I asked Jesus to forgive me."

"That's it?" George asked, astonished.

"Suddenly I knew everything in my life was going to turn out alright. I felt wonderful. I started crying. I started texting my friend to tell him the good news. The next thing I knew I swerved off the road and hit a tree doing seventy. I woke up hanging out of the windshield, and Mal'ak is standing over me with his creepy gray eyes."

George turned and stole a glance at Mal'ak. Indeed, his large reptilian looking eyes were very creepy. It occurred to George that the reaper angel had never blinked once. He shuddered, and returned his attention to Vicky.

"He brought me up here just like you," she said. "I know I don't see much of Jesus this far away, but I'm grateful to see what little I can. It's better than seeing nothing at all."

"That's not what I mean," George said. "I've believed in Jesus ever since I was a kid."

"Wow! Since you were a kid? That's totally radical, but it doesn't make any sense."

"What do you mean?"

"This is the TCS section."

"TCS?"

"Thief on the cross section — TCS, get it? It's where people who get saved in the last few seconds of their life are assigned. Look around, there's zillions of us."

And indeed there were zillions of gladsome faces seated in the TCS section.

"Hey, wait a minute," she said, looking at him skeptically. "I know why I'm here, but a guy like you who's known about Jesus since he was a kid, how come you aren't down closer to him in the premium seats? Wha'd you do?"

"It wasn't what he did," Mal'ak interrupted. "It's what he didn't."

Vicky looked confused.

"You see Vicky, the Master's forgiveness is only the assurance of a person's salvation. However, it's up to them to use the time they have left on earth to get closer to him. You had forty seconds, he had forty years."

"Wow, what a waste," she said, frowning upon George with pity.

"It's very tragic when you consider that he could have been so much closer to Jesus here in heaven." Mal'ak shook his head sadly, and vanished.

"Hey, where'd he go?" George yelped, looking around.

Vicky placed her tattooed arm around his shoulder. "Calm yourself, dude. The angels can't stand to be very far from Jesus for any length of time. Only us humans don't mind being separated from him."

George was stunned. He'd assumed that heaven would be different. He thought everyone would be equal. He figured he would be just as important as the next person. But it wasn't so. Then he remembered the Chaplain at Sargent

Caparzo's funeral quoting Jesus saying, "In my father's house there are many rooms — I go to prepare a place for you."[25]

This must be the place that Jesus prepared for me.

He began crying deep sobs of remorse in languishing breaths of regret. "What in mercy sakes was wrong with me? Why did I allow my stupid obsessions to take me away from Jesus? When did I start believing that I was in control of the earth? I couldn't even control myself. What, for pity sake was I thinking?"

Great tears of shame rolled down his face. Vicky tried to comfort him, but George shrugged her off with his arm. He sat whimpering, weeping, and wailing in self reproach.

"Dude, it's going to be all right," she said. "At least you're in heaven. Don't cry, Jesus loves you, and we do too."

"You don't understand," George kept repeating. "You just don't understand."

"Understand what?" she asked.

"I should have been closer to Jesus. I could have had a box seat on the field level. I'm an idiot. He gave me a chance and I didn't listen!"

He felt a hand on his shoulder. "George, you'll be okay." The hand began shaking him. "George, everything will be alright. Can you hear me? Wake up darling, you're having a bad dream."

Ever so slowly, one at a time, George opened his eyes. Vicky with her shaved head was gone. Mal'ak with his reptilian eyes was gone. Jesus, Cosmo, and the Tree of Life had all vanished. Instead, all George saw was the puzzled face of his wife Sarah.

"I thought you were having a heart attack; are you alright?"

George looked around his bedroom, slowly coming to his

senses. "Am I alright?" he asked, waking up. "I'm better than alright — I'm saved."

Sarah looked at him like he had lost his mind. "What are you talking about?"

"I can get closer to Jesus. I can ask his forgiveness every day! I can change my ways!" George gave her a quick kiss and leapt from the bed. "You won't believe what just happened."

"You're right," she answered, skeptically. "Please don't say it has anything to do with Welma."

"Listen to this," he said, pacing around the room. When he'd finished telling her the story of his dream, Sarah squeezed her eyes shut and forced a smile. "That's the single most insane thing that you've ever told me, and you've told me some crazy things."

"I know it sounds psychotic, but it was more than a dream — it was true."

"It's probably from the stress Welma caused. The mind can play funny tricks. When's the last time you saw a doctor? If you'd start doing yoga you'd feel better. You need to start eating right. Have you been taking your vitamins? Maybe if you cut back on work."

He held up his hand like a traffic cop. "I'm fine, there's nothing wrong with me. I know it's hard to believe, but something miraculous happened."

There was silence in the room.

"So what are you supposed to do now that you've been to heaven? What did your angel buddy Mal'ak tell you to do? Any mention on how to save our company?"

He ignored her tone and walked over to the bedroom window. He looked out at their crystal blue pool. After a few moments a faint smile crossed his face. "Do? — I know exactly what I'll do."

CHAPTER 4
WARNINGS

That very morning George was a new man. His headache was gone, his mind was precise, his hopes higher, his prospects endless, and his future secure. He felt like he was in love, for indeed he was.

With Christmas coming in a few months he could hardly wait to celebrate. This year would be special. He'd pull out all the stops. He'd buy a life size nativity scene and place it in the front yard with lighted camels, kings, shepherds, and of course, angels.

He would go on a shopping spree and purchase toys for needy children. He would volunteer to dress up as Santa and ring bells for the Redemption Rehab. He'd invite the neighbors for Christmas punch and cookies. There was no way he was going to let Christmas pass him by again — ever.

He gave Sarah a hug until she squeaked. "Where are you going?" she asked, suspiciously.

"To get a Bible."

"Why on earth? We have my mother's Bible somewhere around here."

"The print's too small. I don't know how she was able to read it."

"I don't think she ever did, it was a wedding gift."

"I need one that won't give me a headache."

"What about your parents'?"

"Sis got it."

"Suit yourself, just don't get carried away like you usually do."

"What do you mean, carried away? When have I ever gotten carried away?"

Sarah rolled her eyes. "How about your motorcycle phase when you just had to have a $40,000 dollar touring bike? Or your boat phase when you bought a $70,000 dollar speed boat? Or the swimming phase when you built a $60,000 dollar lap pool?

"Well, your motorcycle sits in the garage, the boat is rusting at the lake, and you haven't swum a stroke in years."

"I got the boat and pool for the family," George said, defensively.

She crossed her arms over her chest. "Just do me a favor, don't go overboard with the religious stuff."

"You have arrived at your destination." The female's voice on the car's navigation system enunciated his location in precise computerese. George got out of the car, and entered a religious emporium the size of a supermarket. There were figurines, jewelry, self-help books, book markers, devotionals, candles, clothing, study guides, music, artwork, and an entire section devoted exclusively to the sale of Bibles.

He was amazed at the number of shelves stocked with paperback, plastic-coated, leather-bound, and hardcover

Bibles. They came in miniature size, pocket size, compact size, study size, and desk size.

There were Bibles for every interest, hobby, and trade. There were adventure Bibles, study Bibles, application Bibles, journal Bibles, and specialized Bibles for cowboys, men, women, children, teens, police, firefighters, sportsmen, military, recovering addicts, and so on.

And for every kind of Bible there were numerous versions in an assortment of different languages, each offered in an alphabet of translations — KJV, NKJV, NIV, ESV, WEB, ASV, CSB, NRSV, and RSV (to name a few).

George was astonished. Never in a million years had he imagined that Bible sales were such a big business. He found one entitled, *The Introduction Study Bible for Middle Aged Male Dreamers.*

He hefted it, the weight was substantial. He sniffed it, the book smelled scholarly. He placed it under his arm, it fit perfectly. Holding it, he felt saintly. He read the spiel printed on the cover wrapper:

> 'The New Comprehensive Understandable Universal Translation, black leather-bound, gilt-edged, desk size, large comfort print with color ribbon page markers, room for notes, the words of Jesus in red, printed on museum quality parchment paper, copyright: The Free Word of God Publishing House.'

He flipped it over, — $89.95.
Nothing free about that, he thought.

In the days ahead George was carried away by the Spirit. He couldn't help it. He shared his dream with everyone. He wanted them to know he'd found forgiveness. He told them stories about Mal'ak, Eva, Vicky, and Jesus. He was especially graphic when describing the flames of the aborted babies surrounding Jesus' feet.

He changed the way Bumble's did business. He gave his employees a raise, paid for their health insurance, provided pregnancy leave, offered more management opportunities, and initiated a healthy bonus for hard work.

He started a system where Bumble's donated furniture to the Redemption Rehab shelter. He knew it was a bad time to reduce the corporate profits, but he didn't care. Life was short and he'd already wasted half of it. Besides, he was having more fun than he could remember.

Sarah wasn't. She was angry at George for spending money, lots of money — too much money on charity she believed should be done by others.

"You're taking all of the work my father did and giving it away. I warned you not to get carried away with your new religion. Bumble's doesn't have the money to waste on your silly ideas, especially during these times. Aren't there any other businesses who have foundations to help people, or donate stuff to the Redemption Rehab?"

"Possibly," George said. "But it's not an *us* verses *them* equation. It's all of us working for the good of all of us."

She scowled. "No, this is about making you feel like some sort of plastic saint."

George was unfazed. "Don't worry, God will take care of us."

Sarah tried to imagine a response that wouldn't make her sound selfish, or small. So, she reluctantly agreed to his generosity. But in her heart, she quietly fumed.

. . .

GEORGE GOT UP EARLY EVERY MORNING AND DROVE TO THE Starflyer Diner where he read his Bible before work. He learned new things every time he opened it. He found it fascinating, even compelling.

The cafe was a local landmark, and a popular place for warm conversation and rich food. A returning WWII veteran had taken some abandon railroad cars and converted them into a narrow restaurant with a long lunch counter and seating for ten on red padded stools.

Along the windows, a row of booths covered in lime green pleather provided space for diners to stretch out. At each booth a classic wallbox with buttons, letters and numbers sat connected to an old Wurlitzer jukebox near the front door.

An older waitress, tall and stately, appeared with a pot of coffee. Her face was dark and smooth like a polished stick of ebony wood. Two deep slits served as eyes. She had a graceful Nubian nose shadowing a wide smiling mouth. Rivulets of gray dreadlocks cascaded down the sides of her face to her chest. Around her neck she wore a rope chain with a small golden horn attached.

"Is that new, Kara?" George asked, pointing at the charm.

"I wear it occasionally, it was a gift from me father," she said in a soft Irish accent.

"Kara the musician, very clever."

"Ah now, you answer me a question," she said, pointing to the Bible on the table. "What's your favorite part?"

"To be honest, I just started reading it recently."

"I thought you be goin' to the First Establishment Church?"

"I do, but the Bible isn't a big thing there."

"Sorry, why read it now?"

George wasn't sure how to answer. He didn't want to sound weird. Then he thought about all the people in hell who were too proud to talk about God when they'd had the chance.

"I had this dream."

"That's grand. About what?"

"It sounds nutty."

"There ya go, tell me about it."

For the next ten minutes George related the story of his dream.

"Stop the lights, ya met Jesus?"

"As real as you standing there."

Kara placed the pot of coffee on the table. "Many folks have told me the same thing, to be sure."

A chill swept across George's neck. He didn't know if he was more relieved at hearing that other people had met Jesus, or that he wasn't crazy. "You don't think I'm nuts?"

"I think ye be lucky," she said, wiping her hands on her apron.

"I was beginning to think I'd lost my mind."

She shook her head laughing. "If you've lost your mind, then there's a whole bunch of folks who've gone bleedin crazy."

As time went on George grew rich in the understanding of God. He enjoyed sharing his faith with Kara, and anyone who would listen.

"You should think about going to seminary," she said.

"I'm too old," George laughed.

"You're never too old to fight evil," she remarked.

George tried to remember where he'd heard that before.

"I have to admit I've never been so interested in anything in my life," he said. "I hear a voice inside my head every time I read it. It's like the text is somehow alive and speaking to me."

"Some people tell me it's like they're being immersed in the word."

George had never heard that expression, but he instinctively understood it.

"Does your spouse feel the same way?"

"Not exactly. I mean it's not like she doesn't believe in God, it's just that she's sort of indifferent. She says she's happy for me, but she doesn't need the Bible to get in touch with God."

"What would she be needing?"

"She says she likes to hear sermons on positivity, do Bible-yoga, and listen to meditative music."

"Not the first time I'm hearing that."

George took a breath. "The Bible has caused some real distance between us."

"Not the first time I'm hearing that, either."

George thumbed through the pages. His finger stopped at the Book of Jeremiah. "I shared this passage with Sarah. It's the same one Welma was shouting at the funeral service, so I looked it up." He began reading out loud. "'Before I formed you in the womb, I knew you. Before you came forth out of the womb, I sanctified you.'"[1]

"Nothing wrong with that."

"She accused me of saying abortion was evil. I told her that I wasn't saying anything; that it was God saying that before a person is conceived they're already a real person in his mind and heart. Which logically makes every human a sacred individual loved by God long before they're actually born. Which means that if we kill babies while they are developing in the womb, it's not only wrong, it's spitting in the face of God."

"And she responded how?" Kara asked.

"Not well," George said, frowning. "I'll admit that up until now I've believed in a woman's right to choose. But after reading this, and seeing the innocents at Jesus' feet in heaven, how could I still believe that?"

George was surprised at what happened next. Kara took the Bible in her hand, looked upward and began singing softly in a pleasing voice.

"For you formed my inmost being. You knit me together in my mother's womb. I will give thanks to you, for I am fearfully and wonderfully made. Your works are wonderful. My soul knows that very well. My frame wasn't hidden from you, when I was made in secret, woven together in the depths of the earth. Your eyes saw my body. In your book, it was written all the days that were ordained for me before there were none of them."[2]

A group of people seated in a nearby booth broke into quiet applause.

George was amazed. "Unbelievable, where did you learn that?"

"Psalm 139. My father insisted that the family memorize all of the Psalms."

"Sarah needs to read that scripture," George said.

"She'll only get angry with you. You need some advice on how to handle this. Have you spoken with your pastor?"

"Never occurred to me."

"You should be talking to him."

And that's what George did.

The Redemption of George | 169

THE MEETING WITH PASTOR PENDRAGON WAS IN FIFTEEN minutes. George wheeled his electric car into the church's mall-sized parking lot and instantly slammed on his brakes. His bumper was touching the plastic bag of a homeless man who'd appeared from nowhere. He took a deep breath, thankful he hadn't hit him.

The man didn't seem phased by the near miss and approached the window of the car with his hands outstretched.

"Hey pal — not here!" a beefy security guard shouted at him from the church steps. The beggar took one look at the guard's size and decided to hobble up the street.

"Sorry about that," the guard said, running up to George. The man was a former college football player, and head of church security. "We try to keep them from bothering the members, but occasionally one or two slip by us. There's not a whole lot we can do when they're on city property."

"I understand," George said, composing himself. "I never realized there were so many of them."

"Yes sir, especially at this time of year with the freezing weather. I usually point them to the Redemption Rehab shelter, or the bus station where they can get warm. It seems like there are more of them this year."

"We ought to give them some food and blankets."

"I suggested that to Pastor Pendragon. He said it would only attract more of them."

"That's crap," George said. "It's not like the church doesn't have the money."

"Yeah, the church has enough money to throw in a spa treatment," the guard joked. Then he remembered that humor wasn't appreciated by the affluent members of the congregation. "Excuse me Mister Goodman. I didn't mean anything, I was just kidding."

George watched the color drain from the man's face. "It's okay. You're absolutely right."

He got out of his car and watched the homeless guy disappear. He wondered why he'd never noticed all of the homeless people surrounding the church. He asked himself why the church felt it needed to hire security guards to keep the homeless away. Come to think of it, why hadn't the church established a ministry for the homeless? Pastor Pendragon was always touting the need for diversity and inclusion. Why weren't the poor among the diverse? Why weren't the hungry among the included?

Pastor Pendragon sat behind a wide oak desk skimming the pages of a travel magazine. He was an angular man well past his prime with thin grayish hair smoothed down by expensive gel. A set of dark circles under his eyes made him look like he was hungover.

He wore a collared shirt, black sports jacket, and gray pants. A silver cross was suspended from around his sagging neck. A thick gold ring embossed with the Establishment Denomination logo was wrapped around his right pinky finger. Under the desk, a black Pit bull lay with one eye open.

The office was paneled in dark mahogany wood, and covered with certificates, diplomas, and photos of dignitaries meant to signal Pendragon's years of religious importance. The man was the fair-haired boy of the church. He'd graduated from the Establishment Denomination's seminary and quickly risen through the ranks from associate pastor, to pastor, to senior pastor, and now executive pastor of its flagship church.

Most of his original supporters had died away, and his surviving benefactors were too busy worrying about their failing health to care much about what he did. His biggest living champion was Pastor Guile. Nevertheless, Pendragon knew that when Guile died, his days would be numbered.

Pendragon rarely received members of the congregation, content to accept their admiration from the pews on Sunday mornings. However, he thought it wise to make an exception for George. So, he granted him an audience.

"George, you startled me," he said, looking up. "I haven't seen you since the funeral service. That was quite a scene." The dog raised its head, perked his ears, and growled low. The dog's eyes inspected George as if he were a pork chop. Pendragon reached down and scratched the hound behind the ear. "It's okay boy, George is a friend."

"One of the reasons I stopped by was because I wanted to apologize for that scuffle," George said. He settled into a wooden chair facing Pendragon's desk.

Pendragon leaned back with a self satisfied look. "No need George," he said in a benevolent tone. "Welma used you, although I admit that I was surprised at your reaction to those police officers."

"I didn't like the way they treated her."

"They did what they had to do," Pendragon said, dismissively.

Looking at the travel magazine on the minister's desk, George asked, "Going somewhere?"

"I'm off to visit Doctor Joycelyn at our new mission in Kandalabria. After that I'm taking a break. The pressure of this job is giving me migraines."

He reached for a tissue, and pinched his nose. "I'm leaving as soon as I get the holidays out of the way."

"Sounds nice."

"How can I help you?"

"This may sound stupid, but I had a dream about Jesus."

Pendragon tossed the tissue in the wastebasket, and raised a thin eyebrow. "I wrote in my latest book that dreams tell us a great deal about the state of our inner mind. It was Thoreau who said they are the touchstones of our character."

He toyed with the cross hanging from his neck. "I have a crazy dream from time to time where I'm at a shopping mall. I see children riding a colorful merry-go-round. They are all laughing and giggling. Suddenly one of them runs up to me. She's holding an ice pick. I warn her to be careful, but she doesn't stop coming. So I run away until I find myself wading in the mall's fountain. Instead of water, it's filled with hot sauce. My face and hands start burning. I struggle to get out, but it's like I'm crawling through hot tar. I wake up exhausted." He smiled slightly.

"What do you think the dream is telling you?" George asked.

"Nothing, I don't think that we can tell anything from our dreams. They're just a way we process tension, or hidden anxiety. They have no connection to reality. I mean, seriously, what does hot sauce have to do with anything?"

George thought about the fires of hell. "I've only had my dream once," he said.

"Do tell?"

GEORGE SHIFTED IN THE UNCOMFORTABLE CHAIR AND BEGAN telling his story. "It took place the night you called me at home."

Pendragon twisted his pinky ring and listened while George spoke.

"So what do you think of my dream?" George asked, when he'd finished.

Pendragon leaned forward in his seat looking amused. "I

don't think anything of it, and neither should you. It could be nothing more than indigestion or stress. Are you and Sarah getting along?"

"We're getting along okay," George said, wondering what his marriage had to do with anything. "Seriously, it was real."

"I'm sure you imagined it was real, but it's all in how you define the word real," Pendragon said, making air quotes with his fingers. "As I explain in my recent video series, the Eastern philosophical view might argue that my sitting here is only a matter of your subjective perspective relative to your life experiences."

"This was a genuine experience, trust me."

"Look George, I'm sure you believe it. I've heard hundreds of stories similar to yours from people who sincerely thought they'd met Jesus. But if you'd been paying attention on Sundays, you'd remember me preaching that Jesus doesn't live in a stadium in heaven, and he certainly isn't haunting our dreams."

George let the condescending remark slide. "All I know is that after we spoke on the phone I went to sleep, and then the angel Mal'ak was standing on my chest, who then takes me to hell, and then to heaven where I meet Jesus, and I see all of the aborted children."

"George, listen to yourself. You sound like you need a therapist."

"I'm telling you it was real."

"Yes, of course," Pendragon said, smiling as if George had just escaped a lunatic asylum. "I'm sure you think so. However, I wouldn't keep telling the congregation about the spirits of dead babies at Jesus' feet. They might not be as understanding as I am."

"Why wouldn't they understand?"

"For the simple fact that this is the twenty-first century.

People no longer believe in grim reapers, devils, lakes of fire, sin, or damnation. The congregation will think you're crazy."

"It wasn't a dream."

"Look," Pendragon said, fondling his cross. "I realize the Bible occasionally mentions dreams. I love dreams, I even talk about them in my seminary class. But I'm afraid that in order to encounter the Christ it takes more than just going to sleep. It takes years of prayer, meditation, and living a good life. Some folks like to chant or practice Bible-yoga to help them engage their mind so they can get closer to God."

"Sarah does."

"Of course, that's why we offer a full schedule of Bible-yoga exercises in our classroom downstairs. You should join us sometime."

George shuddered picturing a room full of men with man-buns and wearing yoga pants doing the downward dog.

Just then, a scripture popped into his mind. "I read somewhere in the Bible where God says, 'In the last days, I will pour out my Spirit upon all people. Your sons and daughters will prophesy, your young men will see visions; your old men will dream dreams.'[3] Maybe these are the last days. Maybe I'm one of those old men. Why wouldn't I qualify?"

Pendragon leaned forward, piously joined the tips of his fingers, and closed his eyes as if he was preparing to lead a seance. "First, I suppose that we'd need to discuss the theological basis for saying these are the last days. Eschatologically speaking, it would depend on whether you follow a premillennial, or post-millennial theory of the end times. Of course, many believe that . . ."

Pendragon droned on using important sounding seminary words meant to deflect George's question. But George had caught on to his act.

Pendragon has no idea what I'm talking about. He's never met Jesus, or wants to. Otherwise he'd take me seriously.

". . . and that's why I highly doubt that we are in the last times," Pendragon concluded. Leaning back in his chair he placed both his arms over his stomach.

The room fell silent. George shifted uncomfortably. The dog lifted his head, ears erect, hackles up, opened one eye, and gave George a hard stare. George froze, uncertain if the animal was going to attack.

He wondered why he'd ever listened to this man. Pendragon was just a clever cleric who'd mislead the congregation with his theology of social pleasantries, and tales of sweetness and light. Pendragon saw Jesus as the archetype of human consciousness to be emulated, a symbol of heaven, and one of many expressions of divinity. The man had never met Jesus personally, he had only heard about him.

George felt like throwing up. He stood politely. "Thank you for your time pastor."

"Of course George, any time. By the way, have you phoned Peter about a meeting?"

"Yes, I'm sure you'll be hearing from him soon."

"Thank you. I know he'd fit right in with us. And for your own good, don't go upsetting folks with stories about dead babies in heaven — just a little pastoral advice."

GEORGE HAD NEVER BEEN A PRAYING MAN, BUT RIGHT NOW he felt the urge. It was a practice that he'd started doing right after having his dream. At first, he'd felt foolish talking to the air. But the more he prayed, the less awkward he felt. In time he began to sense the presence of God.

He needed to find somewhere to kneel and pray, but the church had gotten rid of all the kneelers long ago. He walked to the sanctuary and found a pew. Nobody ever came here during the week, and the room was as quiet as a tomb. He closed his eyes and asked God for an answer.

As if watching a movie, he saw himself sitting in church listening to Pastor Guile preach that faith in Jesus wasn't the only way to heaven, and that all religions worshipped the same god. He remembered when Guile claimed that the Bible was filled with contradictions and human errors, so it couldn't be the infallible Word of Truth.

When Guile retired, Pendragon began teaching that people must love themselves, and seek their inner goodness through prayer and meditation. He encouraged the members to show godly love by endorsing same sex unions, surgical family planning, redefining old biblical truths, and reverencing the ecosystems of the earth.

George looked up through the stained glass windows of the sanctuary, and saw a faint day-moon rising over the skyline. He remembered his astronomy professor calling it the child's moon because older people couldn't see it as their eyes dimmed.

But his eyes had been opened, and he saw that the First Establishment Church had become nothing more than a religious sham. He bowed his head, rubbing a hand over his face. He didn't want to believe it. He'd gone here all his life.

He sat for a time in the musty room embarrassed because he'd been caught up in the distorted beliefs of others. He wondered how he could have been so gullible.

Then he realized why — as long as he was never held accountable for his sins, and Pendragon continually affirmed him as a person, he was content to slumber in the smug assurance of his religious superiority.

But the dream had awakened him. He now saw that the church of his youth, the crown jewel of the Establishment

Denomination, and the one time champion of the faith was dead. It had been euthanized by poisonous heresies, the noose of social neediness, lethal injections of emotional dependency, and an overdose of religious entertainment.

GEORGE LEFT THE CHURCH FEELING SICK. HE POPPED A FEW antacids from a roll he always kept in his pocket, and decided to spend the rest of the day at the office. Work was his therapy. It took his mind off his problems. It gave him a sense of purpose. Work had been his salvation on more than one occasion.

That evening at six o'clock, after pushing around papers and accomplishing absolutely nothing, he packed his briefcase, turned off the lights to his office, and took the elevator down to the parking garage.

He was immediately confronted by the ugly scratch on his car. It bothered him knowing that some faceless person hated him. He examined it for the thousandth time. The collision shop said it would take a month to fix it, and even then they might not be able to match the color perfectly.

He felt a headache coming on. He drove away and headed home in the darkness. His battery powered car flew as silently as an arrow down the interstate. He tried to calm himself by listening to a mix of his favorite music.

Just as he was beginning to accept the events of the day, the red and blues of a police intercepter suddenly flooded his mirrors. George looked at his speedometer — sixty-five.

What now? Hasn't today been crappy enough?

He glided to a stop, popped the center consul, retrieved his insurance papers, and waited. He checked his rearview mirrors but the cop's white spotlights were too bright to make out anything clearly.

Eventually he saw a man's silhouette walking towards him. It stopped just out of view behind George's left shoulder. A flashlight swept the interior of the car.

"Good evening sir. May I see your driver's license and insurance papers?"

Without looking, George handed them back over his shoulder.

"Mr. Goodman, the reason I pulled you over is because I clocked you doing a little over a hundred miles per hour in a sixty-five mile an hour zone."

"A hundred?" George yelped. "There's no way I was doing a hundred."

"Sir, you probably didn't notice. These little electric cars are pretty zippy. Unfortunately, I'm going to have to cite you. Do you have any weapons in the vehicle?"

"No sir."

"Have you been drinking."

"No."

"I'm afraid I'm going to need to administer a field sobriety test to be sure."

"I'm not drunk, and I wasn't doing a hundred," George said.

At that moment another police cruiser pulled up. The officer pointed his twin spotlights at George's car flooding it with a second layer of intense light.

"Would you please step out of your vehicle?"

Thick drops of rain started drumming on the car's roof.

George struggled to get out of its cramped interior. When he finally stood, he looked into the bruised face of Officer Smith.

"You've got to be joking," George said, tightening his fists.

"Remember me?"

Officer Smith was covered from neck to boots in a yellow rain jacket with wide silver reflective stripes.

"Who could forget a guy who beats up old ladies?"

"She had it coming, Mister Goodman," he said, impassively. "That's what happens when you resist arrest."

"She didn't do anything to be arrested for. You were asked to escort her out, not beat the crap out of her."

"If you say so," Officer Smith said, dismissively.

"Yeah, I say so."

Officer Smith's partner walked over with a hand on his taser in case of trouble.

"You were a real hero the other day. I don't like heroes. Especially ones who meddle in things that are none of their business. You got a big fat lip for your effort. Hope it wasn't too painful."

"I've felt worse."

"I guess you have," Officer Smith said, indicating the scar on George's face. "You get that playing computer games?"

"Not exactly."

"Not exactly what?"

The rain began coming down harder.

"I got it in a fight."

"Looks like you got the worst of it."

"Depends on what you call the worst."

"I dunno, what do you call the worst?"

"I got this," George said, touching his scar. "And the other guy got dead."

A lone eighteen wheeler went whizzing by, shaking the vehicles, and nearly blowing George off his feet. Officer Smith's fingers toyed with the pistol on his hip.

"Nobody's getting dead tonight, hero. But somebody might go to jail."

"We both know that I wasn't doing a hundred."

"Oh, I'm sure you were," Officer Smith said, pulling out a ticket book. "As a matter of fact, I know you were."

He looked over at his partner.

"Hey, Terry, what'd we clock Mister Goodman doing?"

"Hundred, maybe more."

"See what I mean? You wanna take it to court, me and my partner will be happy to swear that you were doing a hundred."

"What judge on earth would believe you?"

Officer Smith just grinned.

A flash of lightening lit-up the northern sky illuminating the wood line. For an instant George thought he knew who was behind this.

"Judges are real sticklers on speeding, drugs, drunk driving, things like that," Officer Smith explained. He spoke as if he was talking to a six year old.

"I'm not drunk, and I don't do drugs."

"We shall see," Officer Smith said. "Place your feet together, tilt your head back, and close your eyes."

George did as he was told, and tilted his head towards the sky. It took him a moment to steady himself.

"That's okay mister Goodman. You take all the time you need, I've got all night. Besides, I'm dressed for the occasion. I hope the rain doesn't ruin your nice $3,500 dollar suit, and those $500 dollar pair of loafers."

George stood still, looking up at the sky, biting his lip.

Officer Smith yelled over to his partner who was busy ransacking George's vehicle throwing books, papers, and trash all around. "Find anything Terry?"

"Look at this," Terry said, popping the trunk. "Wow, these are some expensive golf clubs."

"Better make sure there's no drugs hidden inside the golf bag," Officer Smith ordered.

His partner lifted the golf bag over his head, and let the clubs fall to the pavement. He shook the bag upside down a few times, and shined his flashlight inside. He unzipped the side pockets and dumped out the contents. Golf balls, tees, markers, chewing gum, sunscreen, score cards, and lip balm all came tumbling onto the pavement.

"Nothing here," he yelled, and walked back to his patrol car leaving everything on the ground.

An hour later, drenched to the bone, George sat in his car holding a citation that would probably cost him a thousand dollars and double his insurance.

Officer Smith had been smooth, but his mocking tone had made it clear that he was enjoying every moment. He'd run George through every sobriety test allowable in excruciating detail.

First, George had to pass the one leg stand, the walk and turn test, and the horizontal gaze test. Then, Officer Smith gave George a breathalyzer to make doubly sure. All the while Officer Smith calmly threatened George with a trip to jail, a suspended driver's license, and traffic school if he failed.

George knew he was being harassed, but he also knew that there was nothing he could do about it. Officer Smith was itching for an excuse to put him in cuffs.

"Lucky you," Officer Smith finally announced. "I guess you weren't drunk after all."

He leaned down to where George was seated in the vehicle.

"If I was you," he said, menacingly. "I'd stop getting involved in things that aren't your concern. You made a big mistake at the funeral — so get smart and back off. You get my drift?"

"Who's behind this?" George asked.

"You don't want to know, hero," Officer Smith replied, walking away.

"Actually I do," George replied under his breath. He felt his hand crush the ticket into a little wet ball of pulp.

GEORGE TRUDGED UP THE WALKWAY TO HIS HOME SOPPING wet. The house was a sprawling mid-century modern with a perfectly landscaped yard that looked like it had been trimmed with manicure scissors. Sarah was fixing a strawberry daiquiri in the kitchen.

"What happened to you?" she asked, flipping on the blender.

George waited, grinding his teeth, until the racket stopped. "Long story," he replied, shrugging off his coat.

"How'd your meeting with Pendragon go?"

"All I can say is that Brad was right."

"Brad was a trouble maker."

"Troublemaker?"

"He and his bitchy wife were always criticizing Pendragon and the executive council. Believe me, nobody misses them."

"Where in the heck was I?"

"Off golfing as usual."

"What are you saying?"

"I'm saying that Brad and his wife were a couple of sanctimonious pests who were always complaining that there was something wrong with the church."

"I think they had a point."

"Are you serious?"

The Redemption of George | 183

"Brad tried to explain it to me, but I wasn't listening."

"And what, pray tell, was that?" she scoffed.

"That Pendragon is a fraud. He's all show and no substance."

Sarah took a sip of her drink and walked into the living room. "What in heaven's name are you talking about?"

"I'm saying that we never hear anything about hell, or Christian suffering and sacrifice. All Pendragon ever preaches is about how special we are, or how we deserve God's abundance. For criminy sakes, he's got the entire congregation congratulating itself on how wonderful it is to be wonderful, and we've eaten it right up."

Sarah applauded slowly, without enthusiasm. "I got to hand it to you George, that's some yarn. Do you actually think our lives would be improved if we ran around in sack cloth and ashes? And what makes you so morally superior? Ever since you had your little dream you've become a religious fanatic. What's next, preaching that the end is near down at Veteran's Park? Nobody cares about your dream or religious opinions."

"They're not my opinions, they're in the Bible."

"Is that so? Well, Pendragon must have a different Bible because he has a different opinion, and he went to seminary. You just opened the Bible a month ago."

George didn't understand what that had to do with anything.

"Let me tell you something dearest heart, people go to church to feel good about themselves. They want to be told how important they are to God. They want to find their inner Christ, and live in harmony with each another."

"Is this where I break out my violin?"

"Don't be cute," she warned. "People go to church to

enjoy the music, and listen to Pendragon tell them how much good they're doing for others."

"By basking in the warmth of their own glow?"

"People don't come to hear about their sins. They don't want to listen to some Bible thumper condemn their sexual orientation, or views on abortion. They're seeking stories of affirmation, tips on self awareness, and deeper spiritual knowledge. Why can't you leave well enough alone?"

"You just said why," George replied. "They're lost, and Pendragon is lulling them right into hell."

"So you say. Well, from now on, please keep your little flights of imagination to yourself. All you're doing is making our friends angry, our customers upset, and getting on my last nerve."

"Our friends are angry because they have a guilty conscience."

"Listen buster, I'll make this clear," she scolded. "Nobody wants to hear what you have to say about Jesus. I was willing to let you go through one of your little phases with your visions of heaven. But it's time for you to grow up so we can get back to our normal lives."

She finished her daiquiri and grabbed her purse. "Okay? Do we understand each other?"

She glared at him, empty of mirth.

George nodded.

"I'm going to a movie with Erica and Hallie," she said. "There's some leftover spaghetti in the microwave."

AT THE SAME TIME, ACROSS TOWN IN THE EXECUTIVE council's chambers, the Judge checked his watch against the vintage clock hanging on the wall. He prided himself on being punctual. He ran his court by the clock and demanded that everyone from the bailiff to the defendant be on time. He looked anxiously at Guile who signaled the meeting to begin. The Judge tapped the podium with his pen.

"Good evening my friends. Shall we lift up our hearts in prayer?"

Pendragon and Guile lit several candles, and everyone gathered hands forming a circle. They bowed their heads and the Judge prayed.

> "The time is nigh, so close the hours. We call to you, our great watchtowers. Before your thrones we are but dust, our hearts are bound in love and trust. Hear us rulers of the earth, and bless us with a new rebirth. Summer Moon, Winter Mother, give us wisdom from each other. Fill our hearts with thoughts of good, bring us sacred personhood. From sky above and earth below, the fire consumes, the waters flow. Blessed be fourfold, and blessed be three. So it was at the dawn, so it must be. In your most holy name we pray."

"Truly, truly," they all said in unison, breaking the circle and taking their seats. The candles were extinguished.

"As tonight's chair, I'd like to address a matter of grave concern," the Judge began. The room hushed. "We have a situation that has caused the members of the congregation to feel unsafe. More importantly it's threatening our sacred work."

"Is this about George?" the Professor asked.

The Judge nodded yes, and continued. "It seems that George has expressed feelings about our work that are inconsistent with our common good."

"You mean he's expressed extremist views," Von Heekate said.

Pendragon stood. "Personally, I think he's having a nervous breakdown."

"I don't care if he's gone completely bonkers," the General bellowed. "We don't pay him to preach, we pay you to preach. He's stirring up the worst kind of trouble for us."

Pendragon said nothing, and sat back down quietly next to Pastor Guile.

The Doctor removed the glasses from his face. "George's dream is not a reflection of our congregation's values. We're a church of grace, and if I may say so, of good taste. And it's bad taste to tell people that their private decisions about their life are sinful."

Pastor Guile pulled himself up from his wheelchair. "I couldn't agree more. Who's to decide what is sinful or not? There's absolutely no place in our congregation for his kind of intolerance. Nevertheless, the bigger problem is George's claim about the aborted souls of babies in heaven. It's causing people to question the morality of surgical family planning."

"Absolutely," the Doctor said. "And if we allow him to continue spouting this crap it will lead to deeper questions about the other aspects of our business."

The room grew silent. Everyone knew what the other aspects of the business were.

"I don't think we should worry. This is the same threat we had with Welma, and we dealt with her," the Professor said.

"Yes, but she wasn't nearly as visible or influential as George," Pendragon commented.

"Before we do anything," Guile remarked. "Let's not forget that he's close friends with Peter Wendigo."

The room retreated into another moment of sober reflection.

"Doesn't make any difference," the General barked.

The Redemption of George | 187

"We've got enough cash in the Establishment Fund to run the church forever. We don't need Wendigo's money."

Guile cut him off with a wave of his hand. "Let's not be hasty, General. Keep in mind that Peter's donations will be earmarked for special ministries."

He didn't have to mention that special ministries was code for the offshore bank accounts they each enjoyed.

The Judge leaned on the podium and growled. "We can't allow George's relationship with Peter to hold us hostage."

"Nor will we," Guile said. "I agree that we need to send George a stronger message, but it can't look like it came from us."

"We've already sent him enough warnings," the Doctor said. "Apparently he's too stupid to get the message."

"We need to send him a financial message," the Professor proposed. "Hit him in the wallet."

"The Professor is right," Guile said, nodding his head adamantly. "We need to orchestrate a little problem at his business."

"How about a demonstration," the Professor said, perking up. "I can spread it around campus that George is a white male racist, and a dangerous misogynist who should be punished for the good of all women."

"Brilliant," the Judge agreed. "Those idiot students of yours will eat that right up."

"I know a way," Von Heekate said, grinning. "Summer Beltane works at my television station. She has several million women viewers that I'm sure would enjoy hearing what George has to say about surgical family planning. Let me ask her to contact George to do an interview."

The Doctor laughed heartily. "I'm sure George's views on women's rights will go over big with Summer's audience."

Guile held his palms out waiting for different solutions.

With no further discussion, he looked at the Professor. "Put the word out on campus quietly. Make sure there's no traceback to us."

"Too easy," the Professor said.

Turning to Von Heekate he said, "See if Summer Beltane will arrange for an interview."

CHAPTER 5
REPRISALS

Bumble's flagship store was located at the corner of Geneva Avenue and Profit Street in the old Ellis building. The seven story sandstone structure was erected by the wealthy industrialist in 1939 to celebrate the end of the Great Depression, and give Abundance Falls a renewed sense of vigor.

The entire ground floor was originally occupied by Nichol's Five and Dime who were famous for their triple scoop ice-cream sundaes served at a fifty foot counter. Its expansive storefront extended a half block down Geneva Avenue in one direction, and a half block up Profit Street in the other.

When Nichol's Five and Dime went out of business in the 1950s, R.J. Bumble rented the space for his new furniture enterprise. In the following years the visionary entrepreneur built Bumble's into an iconic downtown location with a kids play area, free coffee, in-house financing, underground parking, and a yearly visit from Santa Claus. Eventually he added thirty-four new store locations throughout the region and purchased the entire building for his corporate headquarters.

To guarantee that his daughter Sarah would be well cared for in life, R.J. offered George a job as a wedding gift. George was reluctant to accept. He had dreams of his own to pursue a career in astronomy.

However, when Sarah announced she was pregnant, George realized he needed a better paying job than as a lab assistant at the observatory. He grudgingly quit, and began working for his father-in-law.

Under the tutelage of R.J., he was promoted to Vice President of the firm. When health concerns made it clear that R.J. needed to step down, the old man ordained George to take his place as CEO of the corporation.

At first George resisted, but Sarah insisted that control of the enterprise should remain in the family. Despite his hesitancy, George accepted the position. In the following years he added another twenty-eight Bumble's locations, and increased the yearly sales to over 1.7 billion.

George's office occupied a corner of the top floor. It was a modestly appointed room, sparsely furnished with the bare essentials necessary to conduct business. Except for a few golf trophies, some Army souvenirs, and a couple of family pictures, there was nothing in the room to give the appearance that George had ever fully moved in.

The office had a private bath with shower, a large walk-in closet, and a row of picture windows overlooking the Contemporary Church of Entertaining Twaddle on Geneva Avenue, and the Fees & Fines National Bank on Profit Street. This morning, pouring rain cascaded sheets of water down the window glass obscuring his view of both.

George stood at a large drafting table he used as his desk watching Bumble's stock on his computer. "Mr. Goodman, you need to come quickly," his secretary said, bursting through the door.

"What is it, Laura?"

"Outside!" She motioned frantically.

George rushed to the window. It was hard to see with the rain obscuring his vision, but there appeared to be an angry crowd of people milling around on the sidewalk. They were shouting, holding signs, and yelling obscenities at Bumble's.

What the?

He flew down the inside stairwell to the ground floor where he was met by Gregg, the store's manager.

"Busses dropped them off about ten minutes ago," Gregg said. "They've been blocking our delivery trucks, and threatening customers and employees."

"Why?" George asked.

"I don't know, they keep screaming for our heads. They're saying that Bumble's sponsors hate."

"What are you talking about? Hate who?"

"Women."

"That's nonsense," George said. He stood watching the malicious crowd whirling, hopping, contorting, sneering, and howling. The entire spectacle seemed amped by some supernatural power. A news van pull up. It unloaded a reporter with her cameraman.

"Wendy over in the IT department just phoned saying that we've been flooded with negative reviews on our social media pages," Gregg stammered. "They're claiming we're against women. Some of the employees are asking if it's true."

"Of course not," George replied, snorting. "Tell them to remain calm. Call the police and get Wendy to start damage control on our website and social pages."

Just then, a loud thud shook one of the revolving doors leading to the street. Streams of pink colored liquid began running down its glass. George couldn't tell if it was paint or dye.

"I'm going outside to see what's happening."

"Be careful," Gregg said, eying the door nervously. "They don't look very friendly."

"Neither am I," George snapped. "Just get Wendy busy cleaning up our social pages, and call the police."

"Do you think we'll have to close for the day?"

"I'll let you know."

George was met outside by a mob of excited people shouting obscenities at him, and calling Sarah a whore. They held signs that said:

We Decide, Not You!
Our Body Our Choice Our Life!
Burn Bumbles Burn!
No Fascism. Freedom for Women!

A woman reporter George recognized from Lilith's funeral approached him. She was huddled under an umbrella clutching a microphone close to her chest. Her cameraman stood a few feet away filming in the pouring rain. She stuck out the microphone. "Mister Goodman, any comments?"

"Only that I have no idea why they're here." He wiped away the rain running down his face.

"I'm told it has to do with your defense of Wilma Forthwright at Lilith Wendigo's funeral."

"I don't see how. I was supporting her freedom of speech, and a woman's right to not be bullied by the cops."

"That's not how these people see it. They say you and your business are trying to deny women basic human rights and free access to healthcare."

"This has nothing to do with healthcare," George said. He

looked at the mob wearing black masks and bicycle helmets. "So far as human rights are concerned, Welma had a few rights of her own."

"Can you elaborate?"

"She had a right to express her opinions. You're a reporter for crying out loud. You of all people should understand that." He wiped water from his eyes.

A college aged woman wearing a pink hoodie suddenly broke into the interview and threw a pink milkshake on George screaming, "Sexist! Fascist! Racist!"

The reporter recoiled in alarm, and the protestor scuttled back into the mob.

"Don't worry Mister Goodman, I got her on tape," the cameraman said, throwing George a towel he used to dry his equipment.

Police sirens echoed off the canyon of walls formed by the buildings, and several patrol cars came to a stop on the other side of the street.

"What took so long?" George yelled, waving at one of the officers. "Over here."

The cop didn't move. Instead he looked at George with the same interest he'd give a homeless man. His supervisor arrived moments later, screeching to a stop. The Sergeant got out as if intending to do something, but he only spoke to a few patrolmen who had gathered around him.

A bottle was thrown against the side of the building. It shattered, and pink paint dripped down the wall. Someone threw a brick at the store's antique plate glass window, cracking it. Another person used a road flare to set a trashcan on fire. Others sprayed obscene threats on the building. Over and over the angry horde of demonstrators kept chanting a threatening mantra in a grotesque gravelly voice.

"You'd better come inside, Mister Goodman," Gregg shouted from the doorway.

"I think you're right," George replied, moving backward until he was safe inside.

"Lock the door," George ordered. "Get everyone out the back. We're closed for the day."

GEORGE SPENT THE REST OF THE AFTERNOON ALONE IN HIS office answering phone calls from managers who wanted to know what to do if a mob showed up at their location. Sarah phoned letting him know that she was upset because the demonstration was all over the news. Peter called with an offer to help. Kip dropped by to provide support.

"I saw the demonstration on the internet, what the heck is their problem?" Kip asked, walking into the office.

"They think I'm out to deny women their rights."

"What rights are you supposedly denying them?"

"From what I can tell, the right to kill their babies."

"What does abortion have to do with Bumble's?"

"Nothing, they're fanatics looking for a fight. The fact that you and I were seen defending Welma makes us guilty of some unforgivable sin in their eyes."

"Reminds me of the religious extremists we fought in the Middle East," Kip said.

"Same demented tyrannical behavior. They don't need a reason to destroy — just their unholy ideology to justify violence."

"I've been thinking about those cops at Lilith's funeral," Kip said. "That one guy deliberately blindsided you for no reason."

"Officer Smith, how could I forget. He's the one who pulled me over the other night."

The Redemption of George | 195

"What I don't understand is why the stormtrooper response? It wasn't like Welma jumped up wearing a bomb vest and shouting 'Allahu Akbar!'"

"I think I know why," George said.

"Because the Governor was there?"

"No way. The State Police made everyone go through a complete background check, electronic bag scan, and pat-down. We practically had to bend over, spread our cheeks, and say cheese to get in. They knew she wasn't a threat."

"Then someone wanted the cops to make an example of anybody who protested, and we got in the way."

"That's exactly why. Somebody was ready to silence anyone who spoke out at the service. They weren't expecting us to protect Welma, and things got out of hand. I think the same people might be connected to her death."

"I thought they said she died in an accidental fire."

"That's what they'd like us to believe."

Kip knew his friend well enough to know his premonitions were usually right. "Any ideas?"

"None that I'm prepared to say right now."

"What can I do to help?"

"Help me get through this mess. I've asked the head of security and my PR guy to give me some options, but I trust your judgment."

"No worries," Kip said, a twinkle in his eye. "You want me to call some of my guys?"

George thought about it. "Not yet."

"We've had our back up against the wall before." Kip said. He walked over to the window and looked down at the loitering crowd. They were still ranting, defacing signs, dumping trash, and menacing people who were passing by.

"We might want to get Peter involved at some point," he remarked.

"I'm not sure if Peter would want to get involved. I've never asked him how he feels about abortion. He might agree for all I know."

Kip said nothing, and continued looking at the street. "This would be a perfect place to position a sniper," he mused, eyeing the surroundings. "Good field of fire — defendable."

"Don't think it hasn't crossed my mind." George smiled, tightly.

"Just kidding my friend," Kip laughed. "You don't need a sniper when a few hand grenades dropped on their heads would do the trick."

"Very funny, all I need is to start World War III across the street from a church."

"Yeah, that'd send you straight to hell."

"Doesn't even take that much," George said, thinking of Eva. "Besides, I feel like I'm in it. They're attacking me on the internet, the press keeps hounding me, stock is dropping, and if they keep threatening my customers it might ruin us."

Kip looked at the crowd thoughtfully. "It's possible that if you fight back with your lawyers, it might cause normal people to stand up and support you."

George cracked a smile. "Sounds nice, but that only happens in the movies. These people are funded by deep pockets and protected by corrupt DA's and judges. I'm alone in this."

"Not so my brother, there are millions of us who are sick of these bastards, and their bullying."

George rubbed his cheek where his scar started. "I've always tried to do the right thing, but apparently that's not good enough for some people."

"Nothing is good enough for these people. They're modern Bolsheviks,[1] who answer to a dark master. They've made a blood covenant with death, and won't be happy until they destroy the entire country. They're in the government, universities, elementary schools, corporations and churches."

He turned from the window and looked at George. His face was a mask of fury. "The bullies down there are nothing more than modern slavers. They use the same methods as plantation owners."

George didn't know anything about plantation owners. "What methods are those?"

"Intimidation by threat of violence, harassment, and physical brutality. That's what's going on outside. They expect you to make a public confession that you're a misogynist and fascist. They want you to admit that you were wrong defending Welma. You will either agree that their murder of innocent babies is acceptable, or you and Sarah will be punished, and your business will be destroyed."

"I didn't defend Welma for her views on abortion, I defended her from those cops."

"I know that, but they don't care. They think you insulted the goddess of reproductive rights, Lilith Wendigo. Slaves cannot be allowed to do that."

"I'm not their slave."

"You will be if you cave into their demands."

"That's not going to happen."

"No, it isn't," Kip said, firmly. "Let me make a few phone calls, I have a couple of ideas. I know some people who specialize in dealing with thugs."

George knew what could happen if Kip got his specialists involved.

EVENTUALLY THE RABBLE LOST THEIR ENTHUSIASM AND began to trickle away leaving plastic bags, cups, bottles, cans, paper, and mounds of half eaten food, and trash on the sidewalk. Some of the more energetic walked over to the Church and painted a satanic pentagram on the door, wrote Hail Satan! on the concrete steps, and drew an anarchist symbol on the brick wall

The cops watched all of this with passing interest.

SUMMER BELTANE HOSTED A DAYTIME TALK SHOW AIMED AT bored housewives, people stranded at the airport, and aging shut ins. She'd garnered several awards for her Feminism and Human rights reporting. This morning she was hoping to win another award for a show on how male owned businesses encouraged misogyny in the marketplace.

Of course George didn't know this. He'd been told the reason for the interview was to discuss the riot at the store, and to do a puff-piece on the history of Bumble's Furniture.

He figured it might be good exposure, following all the bad publicity the store had received recently.

George waited for the show to begin. He sat on a hard futuristic sofa in front of a large studio audience consisting mainly of women. Technicians scrambled around pulling cables and making last minute adjustments to cameras and lights.

Eventually the house lamps over the audience dimmed, and the stage lights came up. Canned music played the show's bouncy theme music. A floor director pointed excitedly to giant signs flashing overhead — [APPLAUSE!]

The audience began clapping, crying, laughing, and cheering as Summer danced out from behind a rainbow colored curtain wearing a white single-button pant suit. The cameras followed her around as she skipped through the audience shaking hands and giving hugs. The crowd was ecstatic.

George remembered when she was crowned Miss Tractor Pull in college, helping to launch her television career. She was still attractive in a puffy country girl way, although he noticed her make-up was thicker than he expected.

A million fans followed her on social media to get the latest updates on fashions, cooking, Hollywood gossip, and what she and her wife were doing.

The theme music faded, and with it, the applause. She stood alone under the spotlight in the middle of the stage.

"Good Morning Abundance Falls, welcome to this edition of the our show, where we explore topics of modern interest to all of us. Later on in the show, we'll hear the latest hit song from Mia Singer. — [APPLAUSE!] Then we'll enjoy the comedic genius of Ross Diddly-Boom — [APPLAUSE!]

But first, let's meet a man who gained national notoriety at the funeral of one of America's most beloved women. He's the owner of one of the largest furniture stores in America, and the focus of ongoing protests. Let's find out about his views on women, their rights, and institutionalize sexism."

George was shocked. He didn't remember agreeing to any of this.

"Put your hands together, and help me welcome Mister George Goodman." Summer brought her hands together clapping, and the audience obediently joined her.

[APPLAUSE!] [APPLAUSE!] [APPLAUSE!]

She took another bow, and sat down in a white swivel chair facing directly across from George.

"Thank you for coming," she gushed enthusiastically.

"Thank you for having me Summer," George responded, slightly bewildered.

"Before we get into the heart of the interview, let's all

watch this video taken of the recent demonstrations held in front of your downtown store."

Footage of masked and hooded demonstrators yelling, shouting, throwing bottles, and rocks was shown on the studio monitors. When the video ended Summer began speaking. "In the past few weeks your store has become a firestorm of controversy because of opinions you've expressed about women's rights. There have been repeated demonstrations, and a call for boycotts. Would you care to explain why you decided to provoke this kind of violence?"

George was flummoxed by the absurdity of the question. He didn't know how to answer. It was clearly a false assertion she'd created out of thin air. "Summer, I don't think it's a fair assessment to say that I've provoked any sort of violence."

"Yet we all saw your fight with the police at the Wendigo funeral which clearly brought about the backlash and protests at your store."

"As I've repeatedly said, I was trying to protect Welma Forthwright from police brutality. I was not attacking the police, or attempting to make any kind of political statement."

She looked at the notes on her lap. "I've spoken with the Police Chief who tells me that you deliberately attacked his officers, breaking one of their noses, and sending three to the hospital."

"I think that if you play the tape of the funeral service you will see things differently."

She smiled, smugly. "We just happen to have a video clip from the service. Jerry, would you roll it please?" Her face on the studio monitors was replaced by a scene taken at the funeral service.

"Back the hell off!" George yelled angrily.
"You're interfering with a police officer, sir."
"You're off duty fella," George growled.

"I'm never off duty, you need to stand back."

The tape jumped forward.

"You bastards!" George shouted.

"Stay out of this," the cop said.

George was then seen violently jerking the cops away from Welma.

"That's not how it happened," he said, astonished how cleverly the footage had been edited to make him look bad.

She pointed at the television monitor. The tape was frozen at the moment George slammed his fist into Officer Smith's face. "I think our viewers can clearly see by this picture that you initiated the fight. How can you deny it?"

"You're not showing earlier where Officer Smith hit me first," George snapped at her, angrily.

There was a gasp from the audience, and he realized that he had played right into Summer's hand. She wanted to make him look unstable.

He quickly broke into a broad smile. She grimaced at him, and proceeded. "You were a combat veteran, do you think your military training, or PTSD had anything to do with your violent response?"

"What? No. The Army teaches a person discipline."

"You don't look very disciplined on the video tape."

"If I hadn't been disciplined, those cops would have never gotten up."

There was a nervous rustle from the studio audience and Summer was momentarily without words. "What are you saying, Mister Goodman?"

"I deliberately pulled my punches because I didn't want to hurt anyone seriously. I didn't initiate the violence, the police did. I was protecting a senior citizen from a bunch of rogue cops."

"Why would you do that?"

"Because they were hurting her."

"Not because you sympathize with her pro-life views?"

"No, because it was the right thing to do."

"I'm sure we all have our own definition of what the right thing to do is." She gave him a lopsided grin. "Speaking of the right thing to do, are you aware that the majority of Americans believe that the right thing to do is to let a mother choose whether or not to terminate her baby. Don't you agree?"

"No, I don't agree," he said. "A baby is not a slave owned by a woman to do whatever she wishes. I saw the fetuses surrounding the feet of Jesus in my dream. They were each a living person with God given rights."

"Yes, I've heard about your fantastical dream," she said, looking towards the audience and winking. "Why don't you give us the condensed version?"

Which he proceeded to do. The audience rudely giggled, guffawed, and groaned throughout his entire recounting. When he'd finished, Summer squeezed her eyes shut. "Assuming we believe your story about Jesus and the little baby flames, wouldn't it be wrong for God to inflict a child upon a woman, and then let them both suffer? I thought the whole Christian teaching was that God was love, does that sound like love to you?"

"Sounds a whole lot better than murder," George replied.

The audience gasped, and growled. One woman rose to her feet and shouted, "misogynist!" Summer held up her hand like a kindly referee. "Please ladies, George is my guest."

She knitted her eyebrows together as though she was deeply concerned. "So you're saying that a women is committing a murder when she terminates her baby?"

"As you say," George answered.

The Redemption of George | 203

"You do realize that it's not murder if it's completely legal?" she asked, rhetorically.

"That's exactly what Hitler said after he changed the German laws to make it legal to murder millions of people he decided were inconvenient."

There was an uncomfortable silence and Summer realized that she was not achieving her goal with this line of questioning.

"Let's press on. You mentioned in a recent interview that you and your wife have gotten violent threats. Some of those threats call for her to be gang raped. Do you blame your actions for bringing this abuse on your wife?"

"I blame the abuse on the vicious people who sent the threats," he answered. "We've received a hate-storm of text messages, and emails. The other day I had to close Bumble's because of a bomb threat. And you're saying that I'm causing the violence?"

She ignored his question. "You never would have received those threats had you not offended millions of people who watched you disrespect the memory of an iconic figure like Lilith Wendigo. They believe that you represent a fascist view that shames any woman who has the civil right to have an abortion. So aren't you really to blame for causing yourself this trouble?"

George had grown tired of Summer's circular reasoning.

"I think you're having difficulty separating your opinion from fact," he said. "I didn't start the fight with the cops, I don't hate women, I was a personal friend of Lilith Wendigo, and Bumble's has nothing to do with a woman's right to choose."

She smiled that grin one gets when they think they have the upper hand. "We've done a little research into your company, and found that Bumble's has a long history of oppressing women going back to when R.J. Bumble first founded it.

"Let's take a look at this video tape with advertisements your company has run in the local newspaper and magazines. I think it shows the systemic sexism that has historically existed at Bumble's."

She motioned to someone off stage, the lights dimmed, and a series of photos came up on the studio monitors. Each advertisement had picture or sketch of a woman positioned in a girly pose with a Bumble's product. The captions read:

KEEP HER IN THE KITCHEN; WITH A BUMBLE'S DISHWASHER.

PUT SOME FUN BETWEEN HER LEGS; BUY HER A BUMBLE'S VACUUM CLEANER.

EVEN A WOMAN CAN RUN IT; THE NEW BUMBLE'S WASHER-DRYER.

BEAT YOUR WIFE — TO THE BUMBLE'S WEEKEND SALE.

MEN ARE BETTER THAN WOMEN; AT CHOOSING A BUMBLE'S RECLINER.

The monitors went dark, and the lights came up.

"Those ads were made in the sixties," George glowered. "We haven't run anything like that since."

"The point is that Bumble's has a history of institutionalized sexism which you don't seem to be aware of."

"That's ridiculous, you're making this up."

"The fact that you would deny being a sexist is a sign that you are a sexist," she said. The make-up around her mouth had started to crack and splinter.

"Those ads were produced by men and women of a different generation," he argued.

"Judging by your attitude towards women's rights, it seems that the sins of the father live on at Bumble's."

"Most of our key positions at Bumbles are held by

women of all colors," George shot back. "Our company is one of the most progressive in the country."

"That may be true, but you are still the owner, and your form of outdated toxic masculinity has no place in modern business."

"What in the heck are you talking about? I'm not toxic."

"Apparently others disagree."

She held up a sheaf of papers she magically produced like a rabbit out of a hat. Her face hardened and the audience gripped the edge of their seats, drooling with expectation.

"I'm holding in my hand a petition calling for your resignation as the CEO of Bumble's signed by 25,000 thousand citizens, leading politicians, and the clergy of most of our local churches."

The audience broke into cheers, immediately followed by boos directed at George.

His scar tightened. What the heck was he thinking when he agreed to an interview with this viper? He stood up, and tore off the microphone clipped to his shirt.

"I won't be vilified and ridiculed for my beliefs, or my honorable service to this nation. The only toxin killing this country is your vile hatred of men and your sisterhood's killing of the pre-born."

Summer's mouth dropped open like the tailgate of a pickup truck.

"Your dishonest use of a video that you purposely edited to make me look like an unhinged man is rotten journalism, and doesn't present the truth.

"Additionally, I will not be forced to defend the societal norms of over a half century ago against the scales of your politically correct emotionalism. You lied about the reason for this interview, just as you lie to your viewers about the impact of abortion."

He threw the microphone on the floor. "You, and your murderous bunch of she-devils are the embodiment of the evil that has convinced weak-minded women to kill their babies, and to hate men. Good-day Miss Beltane."

The audience began hissing, screaming and cursing at him.

"Boycott Bumbles!" someone screamed.

"Hater!" another yelled.

"F U!" a third shouted.

Three security guards rushed from backstage to escort him from the studio for his own protection.

Over in the board room at the First Establishment Church, the General switched off the television. The members of the executive council seated around the conference table smiled at each other.

"I think that went rather well," Guile said. "Very commendable idea Mrs. Von Heekate."

She nodded curtly in acknowledgement. The others in the room tapped their crystal glasses with their forks in applause, and continued eating their catered lunch.

When George walked through the door of his home, he was met by his faithful dog Cookie who'd been anxiously waiting for him. She jumped into his arms for her nightly scratch.

"I'm home," he yelled into the house, and let Cookie outside. He cautiously walked into the kitchen, fearful that Sarah was waiting in ambush.

She was. She stood holding a glass of wine, which

George thought had become more of a fixture in the past few years.

"How dare you insult Summer Beltane?" she hollered. "You've made me the wicked witch of Abundance Falls. I've gotten dozens of texts from people calling me everything but a child of God."

"The whole interview was a setup," George grumbled. "Her producer told me she wanted to do a lifestyle piece on Bumble's."

"You're an idiot. Do you have any idea how many millions of women watch her TV show, including me?"

"That's why I thought it might be good to get some positive publicity. Instead, she ambushed me. She made it seem like I'm some sort of monster because I believe in the sanctity of life."

She took a healthy gulp of wine. "Maybe you are."

"Whose side are you on anyway?"

"I'm on my side. You're ruining our future with your stupid dream. Nobody cares if a woman has an abortion. Why can't you get that through your thick head?"

"It's not one woman aborting her child, it's millions. They've all been brainwashed by people like Beltane, Pendragon and Guile."

"Women have the right to decide what's good for themselves."

"No more than a serial killer has the right to decide what's good for themselves. There are limits to what we can accept."

She started yelling. "You have no right to interfere with a woman's personal choices, much less destroy the business my father worked for all his life!"

"Your father was a good man, but don't confuse eternal consequences with corporate profits."

The doorbell rang and Sarah placed her wine on the table.

"I'm expecting a package. Don't move hotshot, I'm not finished." She departed and went out the front door.

George sat fuming while he waited for her to return.

Suddenly there was screaming. Blood curdling shrieking. Horrifying moaning. George was momentarily paralyzed trying to absorb what he was hearing. He jumped up off the bar stool, and ran outside.

Sarah was on her knees sobbing out of control. She had one hand over her mouth like she was going to throw up, and the other pointed over her shoulder. George looked up and saw Cookie hanging from a porch column with a rope twisted around her neck.

He bolted into the house, grabbed the first kitchen knife he saw, and cut her down. He cradled her in his arms, then gently laid her on the front lawn. He grabbed his phone.

"Nine-one-one operator. What is your emergency?"

George quickly summarized the situation.

"Is the killer still there."

"I don't think so."

"Do you have a gun?"

"No, should I?"

"The arriving officers need to know. What are you wearing?"

"Grey business suit."

"And your wife?"

"I dunno — jeans, striped sweater?"

"Does your wife need an ambulance?"

George looked at her. Sarah was inconsolable, terrified. She refused to get up. She buried her face in her arms and wept.

"Yes, send one."

"They're on their way now."

The ambulance arrive long before the police. The paramedic helped get Sarah into the house and checked her for emotional trauma. He spoke to a doctor at the hospital who authorized him to administer a sedative to calm her. The effect was almost immediate.

The police pulled into the driveway thirty minutes later. The officer got out of the car, hitched his belt and surveyed the landscape. "You got any security cameras around here?" he asked.

"No cameras," George said.

The officer began scribbling notes as if it might help solve the mystery. "Maybe you should get some," he said. "We'll drive around and see if we can spot anybody. That's about all we can do."

When the police and ambulance drove away, George tried to comfort Sarah, but she shrugged him off.

"You killed her," she accused, bitterly. "Are you happy now?"

GEORGE MOVED INTO THE GUEST BEDROOM WHERE HE COULD come and go without having to confront Sarah. Today, he sat in his regular booth at the Starflyer Diner pushing around a piece of lettuce on his plate thinking about his marriage. He didn't hear Shantel Yin sneak up behind him.

"Glad I caught you," she said.

The slender woman was a part-time employee at the church. Her chiseled face was as smooth as polished amber, with high cheek bones, and coal black elven eyes. Long raven hair, pulled into a pony tail, flowed past a cherry-red blazer and cream white shirt to touch the waist of a pair of grey slacks. She slid in the booth across from him, and eyed his salad. "I took you for being more of a meat and potatoes guy."

"The doctor says I have to eat more greens, I hate this stuff."

She watched him poke at his food. "I saw the Summer Beltane Show."

"Apparently the whole world did."

"You're in trouble."

"No kidding."

"No, real trouble."

"Why would you care?"

She reached into her purse, pulled out a badge and flashed it. His eyes expanded in surprise. "This is my other job," she said.

George focused on the gold shield and the words Special Agent. "Are you serious?"

"Dead serious."

George put his fork down. "I'm listening."

"I came to warn you. After your fight at Lilith's funeral you placed a bullseye on your back without knowing it. Feticide[2] and Infanticide[3] are billion dollar businesses, and the executive council is up to their eye-balls in both."

"With abortion?" he asked, incredulously. "I realize the church doesn't condemn abortion, but are you telling me that the executive council is killing babies?"

"Not directly. What do you think they created SNUF to do?"

"I never thought about it."

"You better start. They'll take whatever steps are necessary to silence anyone who threatens them."

"That might explain why the cops beat Welma at the funeral."

"It might also explain the house fire," she added.

"It's starting to make sense now," George said, jaw

clenching. "What in blazes would a church have to do with abortion?"

"Money," Shantel said. She grabbed a napkin and began drawing a flow chart. "Let me explain. The Sacred Name Unity Fund invests in five companies owned by the members of the executive council. These companies build, manage and supply drugs to several hundred woman's health clinics throughout the U.S., and third world countries."

"I knew SNUF invested in women's health clinics, I never realized they were abortion mills. No wonder Welma went crazy at Lilith's funeral."

"The money they generate killing babies is astronomical."

"Which is how they can pay investors such big dividends."

"The way it works is that the Professor's corporation owns the land, the General owns the construction company, Von Heekate owns the buildings, the Doctor owns the managerial services, and the Judge owns a pharmaceutical company down in Mexico that supplies all the medicine, abortion pills and drugs."

"Clever," George said, shoving the salad away.

"Guile is the one who devised the scheme. He and Pendragon have no corporate ownership. Instead, they get a generous monthly income, a free home, vacation houses, and large consultant fees whenever they visit one of the clinics."

"Which is why Pendragon is always traveling."

"Exactly."

"How did you discover this?"

"I've been working undercover for the past year on another closely linked investigation. Charlie's maintenance crew stumbled across a secret room up in the bell tower, and he asked me to check it out. The door was unlocked, so I stepped inside and saw some files on the floor. I went to put them away, and I spotted one labeled, *Moloch Offering*. Naturally, I had to peek." A mysterious smile swept across her face.

"What was in it?"

"It was the entire layout of their killing machine, including their plans to dismember, and ship fetal body parts to research labs worldwide."

"My wife says it's legal if a woman wants to donate her dead baby's parts to help researchers develop new vaccines and stuff."

"Technically yes, but it's illegal to make a profit from the mother's donation."

"How do they get around that?"

"In order to avoid any evidence of their profiting from the direct sale of fetal body parts, they make money by charging outrageous fees for shipping them to the research labs."

"Why don't you expose what the council is up to?"

"My investigation isn't focused on their abortion scheme. Unfortunately, making money from abortion is legal. The immorality of SNUF's killing machine is the responsibility of your church."

George couldn't believe he was so stupid. "Most of the congregation supports a women's right to terminate her baby," he said.

"Which is monstrous in itself. But even the most cold hearted might find that the trafficking of infant body parts is too gruesome and repulsive to support."

"Pastor Pendragon says abortion is a matter of personal conscience."

"If a person's conscience is so seared that they can justify the murder and dissection of an innocent baby, then someone has to step in and defend the preborn — someone like you."

Her coal black eyes challenged him, and George wondered how this had suddenly become his problem.

"You accidentally got involved when you decided to protect Welma. You got in deeper when you told everyone you saw aborted babies in heaven with Jesus. I believe the executive council was sending you a warning with the scratch on your car, the traffic ticket, and the riots down at the store."

"And my dog's murder."

Shantel grimaced. "I didn't know that, I'm sorry."

George took a sip of water. "I thought everyone in the congregation saw the truth about abortion."

Shantel sighed deeply. "Did you? Until you had your dream did you even care about the murder of the innocents?"

He looked out the window, and considered the truth of her words.

"The members of your church aren't seeking the truth. They're seeking creature comforts and spiritual entitlement. The work of SNUF solves many of their problems. It gives their daughters a place to go when they can't take responsibility for their sins. It appeals to their racist desire to purify the country of Blacks and Hispanics.[4] And, it provides them a legitimate way to decrease the population of undesirables by claiming it will end poverty, and save the planet."

George let her words sink in. "They can't save the planet."

"Of course not. It's just an excuse to traffick in the murder of preborn children. We're talking about big money, important political connections, and the ability for people to live out their fantasies on private islands. The executive council isn't going to let you upset all that with stories about aborted babies in heaven, and little flames at Jesus' feet."

"I've never threatened them."

"What you saw in your dream threatens them. If you

share it enough times it's possible people will wake up and begin to question the morality of what they're doing. The council doesn't want that to happen."

"What if I just shut my mouth?"

"If you shut your mouth, this will all go away. Everyone will move forward with their happy little lives."

"Everyone except the preborn babies," George said, quietly.

THE PETITE WOMAN CRUMPLED THE NAPKIN AND SHOVED IT IN her pocket. "There's something else. My investigation concerns the pharmaceutical company the Judge owns down in Mexico. I suspect they're using it to make and sell illegal drugs to the Cartel. You wouldn't happen to do any business in Mexico?"

"Sure, we purchase a lot of mesquite and equipale furniture."

"How do you ship it?"

"Mostly in our trucks. We run down, load up a bunch, and haul it back."

"I'm guessing the executive council might be thinking of using your trucks to smuggle drugs back into the U.S."

"Funny you should mention that. The General said there was a guy in Mexico who wanted to buy some furniture from me."

"Makes sense. That way if your truck is busted at the border, you'll be the fall guy. You can't do much about their abortion scheme sitting in Federal Prison for twenty years."

She placed her business card on the table. "I think I have an idea that will help both of us."

Looking around the diner, she cautioned him to say nothing about their meeting, and quickly departed.

The Redemption of George | 215

. . .

GEORGE SAT AT THE TABLE AND BURIED HIS HEAD IN HIS hands. He wondered how things had gotten so out of hand. Maybe he was just a sanctimonious hypocrite like Sarah claimed.

Before the dream he had enjoyed all of the things he now condemned as self-serving. He was never troubled by sin, because he was never aware of it. He was never burdened by guilt, because he had nothing to be guilty about. He never worried about other people, because they had their own lives to worry about. He didn't think about the pre-born, it was someone else's problem. He didn't suffer or sacrifice, because Pendragon told him that God wanted him to live his best life.

He used to be happy, now he was depressed. His marriage was on the rocks, there was a target on his back, and Bumble's was headed into bankruptcy, all because he'd shared his dream about Jesus.

At first he thought the dream would bring a life of peace and happiness, now he was fighting with his wife, his friends, the church, and in some ways himself. The sad truth was that his life had been wonderful until he had the dream.

Worst of all, in the past month the dream had started to unravel, like a fading memory, or the product of his imagination. The intensity had dulled, details were fuzzy. Mal'ak's words sounded more like science fiction, than fact. Eva's beauty seemed more like his fantasy, than truth.

Why go on spreading the details of his dream? Pendragon said it would only lead to trouble, and he'd been right. Why should he care about saving the preborn? Who was he to judge others? Who was he to know the mind of God? He was no educated man of the cloth, he was a lousy furniture salesman.

Yet no matter how many people scoffed, scorned or ridiculed him, it didn't change the warmth of the bear-hug in heaven, or the kisses Jesus planted on his cheek. It didn't erase the smile on the Master's face, or the touch of his hand brushing the dust away from George's face. He could feel it as if it was just last night.

Deep in his gut George knew the dream was true, and despite all the animosity directed at him, he would never stop believing in the dream, and he would never stop sharing the tale. He only hoped he had the strength to suffer whatever may come.

"Is everything all right?" Kara asked, setting a glass of ice water down on the table.

"No," George moaned, "I've been blind. I had no idea what was going on."

"Yes sir, when you see Jesus it can change your life. How does it feel to have your eyes opened."

"I don't want them opened, I was happy. The truth is dangerous and depressing."

"It often seems that way at first."

"How can it be so difficult for people to understand the truth about Jesus? The congregation is educated. They are all refined, influential, and polite. They dress well, attend the proper social functions, know all the important judges and politicians, and they raise money for charity."

"You mean a charity like SNUF?"

"How'd you know about that?"

"This is a restaurant, love. I hear things."

"Yeah, I forgot."

"Didn't your golf tournament donate fifty thousand to SNUF last year?"

"Yes, I'm unhappy to say. I was so proud of myself."

George sat gazing into the darkness in his coffee mug, looking for comfort.

"That's a lot of dead babies and broken women."

George buried his head in his hands. "I'm so damned to hell."

"Just the same, Jesus musta wakened you for a reason."

"Awakened?"

She picked up the Bible. "Read this."

George read the text out loud. "'He has saved us, and called us to a holy life, not because of anything we have done but because of his own purpose.'"[5]

"What purpose?" George asked, looking up at her.

"I don't know, but I think you're about to find out."

CHAPTER 6
DRAGON SLAYERS

Nothing is consumed faster in a church than grace-filled gossip seasoned with the salt of righteous indignation. It wasn't long before the stories of George's dream had reached the ear of every person in the congregation. Naturally, people embellished it so many times that the dream eventually bordered on foolishness.

Tom claimed that everyone in hell travelled on rollercoasters. Karen insisted that Eva was a Nephilim mentioned in the Book of Genesis. Janet argued that George's dog in heaven was proof that animals were equal to humans. Ethan insisted the presence of Vicky meant that everyone was going to heaven. Yet there was one part of George's dream that Millie Mockingbird couldn't dismiss as foolishness, and it stuck deep in her manicured claws.

"I'm furious that the executive council would allow George to say that women who've had an abortion are immoral," she said, her hands trembling.

"Technically, he never accused anyone of being immoral," Mrs. Von Heekate corrected. "What he said is that the souls of aborted children are the closest to the heart of Jesus."

Millie was livid, and not interested in technicalities. "I don't agree. He told Summer Beltane that women who've had an abortion are like slave owners. That includes our members."

"True, but in order to censure[1] him we must catch George in the act of directly accusing someone in the congregation of immorality."

"He's the one who's immoral," Millie spat. "In the first place, it's a lie to say that a fetus has a soul. We both know it's not a child, it's just cell tissue, like a tumor. Second, he's a man. He's not entitled to interfere in a woman's decisions about her body. Third, he has no right to dictate what a woman's plans for her family. Besides, real children need to be valued, not imaginary ones."

"I understand," Von Heekate said, looking over the edge of her coffee cup.

"I don't know why the executive council is permitting him to walk around the church and make these accusations. His phony dream is nothing more than a dehumanizing attack on woman. There's no place for someone like George in our church. We are a community of grace and compassion, and I want him silenced, or kicked out."

"The executive council has already taken up the issue in private session."

"As the head of the woman's prayer ministry, I insist that George be formally censured, along with his wife Sarah. I never realized she shared his repulsive views."

"Neither did I," Von Heekate agreed. "I can assure you, we will take every step to formally reprimand him."

Millie took another sip of her coffee, which had turned

cold. It made her feel better knowing that something bad would happen to George and Sarah.

The following night the temperature dropped below zero, and the wind was pushing it to minus seven degrees. The moon was full, and the mob assembling over on the next block was in the mood for a fight.

"What do you think?" Kip asked, pulling his knit cap down.

"I think the First Cavalry Division had better show up, or we're in big trouble," George replied.

The pair stood on the sidewalk in front of Bumble's stomping their feet in the cold, trying to keep warm. They listened as voices in the distance shouted instructions on bull horns to hundreds of protestors who had been bussed in from other towns, and assembled in big knots of trouble.

Kip lifted a pair of binoculars hanging from his neck, and scanned down the street. "I called a few friends to help us out," he said.

As he spoke, the low rumble of a heavy diesel engine approached. The sound of its massive Allison HT transmission shifting into low range announced the arrival of a big red fire truck. Its airbrakes closed with a *paachusssh* sound, and the vehicle stopped next to them.

"Well, well, well, you boys get your little fannies in a crack?" a burley woman asked from the cab.

"Big Sal, you're a sight for sore eyes," Kip grinned. "Come on down here and let me introduce you to the host of the party, George Goodman."

"Heard about you," Big Sal said, extending a hand. "I brought a few folks along if you don't mind."

Big Sal was president of the Retired Dragon Slayers

Association, and part time employee of Kip's private military corporation.

George watched six strong men and women jump from the crew doors of the engine. On one of the doors there was a picture of Santa Clause standing next to a Christmas tree, with the words: Engine 1 North Pole Fire Dept.

"We're here to hunt us some bear," one of the men said to George, his eyes smiling. George took one look at him and decided he was big enough to wrestle a grizzly.

Big Sal got out of the cab, and patted the door of the 1988 American LaFrance custom pumper. "This baby can douse the fires of hell," she bragged, caressing the behemoth truck. "We've fully restored her to like new condition. See that deck gun on top?"

George looked upward and nodded yes.

"It can knock a person down from over fifty feet away. I figure it might come in handy tonight." She held up a plastic envelope with papers inside. "I've got the vehicle's city permits right here."

"How'd you get the permits?" George asked. "The Mayor isn't exactly my BFF."

"The Mayor has his friends, and I have mine," she said with a wink. "I told them I needed a permit to shoot some B-roll for a major motion picture."

Kip rocked his head back and laughed. "What did you say the name of the movie was?"

"The Revenge of the Angry Dragon Lady," she replied, deadpan.

"Remind me never to make you angry," Kip laughed.

While they were speaking, her crew got busy laying hoses and hooking them to the fire hydrants.

"We're going to borrow some city water tonight," one of

them said. "Hope the Mayor doesn't mind if we use it to wash his streets of filth."

"Well if the Mayor and the police won't protect us," Kip declared, "we have the God-given right to protect ourselves."

From around the corner the sound of another classic fire engine came growling down the street.

"Here comes one of my favorite children," Big Sal said. "A perfectly restored 1981 Pierce Arrow TeleSqurt. It's got a Detroit 380 horsepower diesel engine, fifty foot ladder with an ariel work platform, and a water cannon that can knock down an elephant."

"Where do you want us Big Sal?" the driver asked.

"Hook up to that hydrant across the street Lorrie, and extend your ladder about forty feet. Douse the street and sidewalks as far out as you can reach. I want them to be as slick as a hockey rink by the time our friends get here. Then lower your platform to about fifteen feet and get your water cannon ready. We're going to make us some human popsicles tonight."

Lorrie gave a thumbs up and started maneuvering the ladder truck over to the hydrant.

"Kip told me about your little problem," Big Sal said to George. "Me and my folks don't like the way you've been pushed around. The fact that you took up for that widow-lady makes you good in our book."

"You guys are stars," Kip told her. "We really appreciate this."

"I've got a couple of more vehicles coming with some folks who will pretend they are in our movie, and a film crew who will actually document what goes on tonight. They should all be here any minute."

As she finished speaking several more vehicles began arriving, and people started piling out of them.

"I'll talk to you guys later," she said, and went to meet them.

"Thanks," was all George could manage to say.

"She's a great American," Kip said. "Never had any children, but loves them to death. You should see what the Retired Dragon Slayers Association does for kids at Christmas. They go all over town giving them rides with lights, sirens, horns, candy canes, and the whole shebang. See that old guy over there? He grows out a white beard every year just so he can play Santa Claus."

"Are they all retired firefighters."

"Most, but some are just regular folks who love the fire service."

"What do they do the rest of the time?"

"They restore the fire equipment, teach fire safety, run the fire museum, and do specialized jobs for me."

"Aren't they a little too old to work for you?"

Kip pulled up the collar on his fleece jacket and smiled. "That's the beauty. Nobody wants to hire older people because they think they've outlived their usefulness. I've learned they're perfect as corporate ninjas."

George gave him a puzzled look.

"Because they're absolutely invisible in a world that sees only youth. Nobody looks at them twice."

"What sort of specialized stuff do they do?"

"Lots of custom work. You'd be surprised at how well they blend in as couriers, lookouts, chauffeurs, shoppers, taxi drivers, and other roles."

They were interrupted by popping sounds. Everyone looked up. Surging down the street the mob was coming towards them smashing baseball bats against the light poles, and trees along the sidewalk. All the cars, motorcycles, bicycles and pedestrians had vanished from the street hours earlier.

"We're coming for you, Goodman!" someone shouted through a bullhorn.

The rioters were halfway down Profit Street when Big Sal gave the signal. The emergency lights of the fire vehicles came to life bathing the boulevard in red and blue strobes of color. A fake assistant cameraman ran out into the street and shouted, "The Revenge of the Angry Dragon Lady — take one." He snapped down the arm of a clapper board. Another voice yelled, "Action!"

The huge diesel engines of Big Sal's armada growled to life, belching plumes of gray smoke into the freezing air. The large spotlights on every vehicle were aimed down the street, bathing it in a brilliant wash of blinding illumination.

The leader of the protest slowed down and raised his arm shielding his eyes. He'd been told that someone was filming a movie close by and he assumed he was seeing the overhead lighting for the set. He urged his followers to move forward slowly with a wave of his arm.

On Big Sal's command, the driver of the American LaFrance slipped the transmission into first gear and inched the wide snout of the vehicle into the street. Big Sal ordered the engine to move ahead slowly until it stretched across Profit Street completely blocking it.

Once again the leader hesitated and conducted a risk assessment. When he was satisfied they were in no danger, he ordered everyone to advance.

Someone in the crowd lit a Molotov cocktail and threw it at Gower's Pharmacy down the street. Another firebomb was tossed at the window of Smitty's Sporting Goods.

"Whoops," Big Sal exclaimed, into her walkie-talkie. "Looks like we'll have to do our civic duty and extinguish those flames. She ordered her crews to go to work.

From on top of the American LaFrance, the deck gun opened up and shot 2,000 gallons of water onto the flames in sixty seconds. They went out with a smoky puff, and twenty rioters standing nearby were flash frozen.

"This won't be too bad," Kip said, peering down the street. "Looks like there's only a couple hundred of them."

Another Molotov cocktail was thrown at McGriff's Hardware Store. Windows along the street were smashed. A gunshot rang out and everyone instinctively ducked for cover. Kip grabbed a microphone and started speaking through the truck's loudspeakers.

"You have threatened the lives of peaceful citizens. We have the constitutional right to protect ourselves, and our property. Disburse and go home. Failure to do so will result in punitive action."

The leader of the mob, inflamed with anger continued forward. When the rioters got to within a hundred feet, they began slipping and sliding on the street that Lorrie's water cannon had frozen into a solid sheet of ice. Some did pratfalls, others did the splits, the rest fell hard to the ground. The firefighters began laughing, jeering, and mocking them. Nevertheless, a second wave of rioters came forward, gingerly picking their way past their injured comrades.

"Aim low and hit them in the ankles," Big Sal yelled. Fire nozzles began sweeping back and forth across the line of malcontents. The first three rows did a front face flip, landing flat on their noses when the high pressure water hit their shins.

"Now Lorrie, fire 'em up!" Big Sal shouted.

From the extended work platform of the Pierce Arrow

TeleSqurt, the water cannon burst to life shooting powerful blasts at the crowd. One man who was preparing to throw a brick, was blown over backwards smashing his head on the curb. Another was slammed against the side of a building, knocking him senseless. A woman wielding a baseball bat was blown head over tail like a leaf down the street.

Together with the deck gun on the American La France, and the hand-held hoses, the TeleSqurt fired a cascade of high pressure water toppling the crowd like bowling pins, and flash freezing any exposed skin in the bitter temperature. Within minutes the rioter's clothes were crusty and heavy with ice. They drew back in pain and confusion.

One masked woman struggled to her feet, pulled a revolver out of her jacket, and aimed at a firefighter. Lorrie's water cannon hit her dead center with a blasting torrent that knocked her to the ground, and washed her halfway down a storm drain, where the pistol dropped from her frozen hand.

After thirty minutes of futile assaults and humiliating drubbings, the protesters were scrubbed clean of the street into piles of frostbitten people.

"I think that will do the trick," Big Sal said to everyone over the radio. "Good work kids."

The protestors, numb and miserable, called the police saying they had been attacked. The AFPD squad cars immediately screamed to their assistance. As the units arrived, the fake assistant cameraman walked to the middle of the street waving his arms in the air.

"Okay people, that's a cut and wrap! Beautiful footage. I know Stephen will be delighted with the results. Be careful driving home tonight."

Before the cops had finished taking a statement from the rioters, Big Sal, all her people, and George and Kip had disappeared.

. . .

THEY GATHERED AT THE RETIRED DRAGON SLAYERS headquarters to replay the events of the evening. An hour later they all said good-night. George was still wet, but he didn't want to go home and fight with Sarah. So, he drove to his favorite all night haunt, the Starflyer Diner.

He slid into his regular booth, took a quarter from his pocket, punched T-5 on the wallbox and the sound of smooth jazz began playing in the background. At the far end of the lunch counter someone had set up a small plastic Christmas tree with a string of colored lights and a crooked star on top. The holiday was months away, but people were already ready.

Kara appeared and handed him a fresh white towel from the kitchen.

"You look wrecked, dry off with this," she said.

"I just came from a riot," he confessed, toweling his face and hair.

She eyed him suspiciously, and gave him a half smile.

"Why are you working so late?" he asked.

"I'm covering for Casey. She's having a hard time with her pregnancy."

"I didn't realize she was pregnant. Is she okay?"

"Just tired. Standing on your feet all day waiting tables ain't easy." She poured him a mug of coffee. "Tell me about your riot."

George proceeded to relate every detail of the last few hours.

"That's the second riot in as many weeks," she said. "Plus the attack at Wendigo's funeral, Officer Smith harassing you, the scratch on your car, your dog, and the curious fire that killed Welma. I'm thinking I'm beginning to see a pattern."

George placed his cup down, and gave her a funny look. "How do you know about all this?"

"People talk to me."

"Did they also tell you that Bumble's stock is tanking," he asked, rubbing his temples.

"I'm thinking that someone is trying to ruin you."

"You're not the first to say that."

"You've stumbled into a battle without realizing it."

"Apparently I'm caught right in the middle."

"No love, you're not in the middle — you're on the front line."

"Front line of what?"

"The war between the light and the dark — good and evil."

George looked at her face. He was too tired for a sermon. "That's ridiculous."

"Not so. The devil knows God is using you and he's trying to get you to quit."

"He's winning. I'm ready to quit right now."

"You can't, you've been given a mission."

George poured some cream in his coffee, and slowly stirred it with his spoon.

"Kara," he said patiently. "There is no mission. I didn't volunteer for anything."

"Don't be afraid." She continued speaking as if he hadn't said anything. "God's grace will strengthen you, just as it did Saint Paul.[2] You remember that story don't you?"

"Actually, I don't." He responded with a wooden smile.

"Bloody hell, what kind of church do you attend?"

"I'm an Establishmentarian."

She placed her hands on her hips and glanced skyward. "Okay, I'll explain this with all of the patience of Saint Patrick himself. Pay attention.

"In the Second Letter to the Corinthians Saint Paul wrote that he was under terrible demonic pressure while he was in Asia. It was so great he couldn't endure it. He even despaired of his life."

"Kara, we are not talking about stuff from two thousand years ago. This has nothing to do with demons and evil spirits. This is real life."

"Shush," she said, ignoring his comment. "God delivered Paul from the deadly peril, and he will deliver you."

"That'll take some kind of miracle," George said, sarcastically.

"No worries. God will deal with all the people responsible for these attacks. After all, look who he sent to destroy the dragon."

"Who did he send?" George wondered if the church had hired another minister.

"You, love — the least of his servants."

George scrunched up his face, and looked around the empty diner. "What in blazes are you talking about?"

"I'm saying that God chose you to fight these people."

"That's crazy. I'm a furniture salesman, not a crusader."

"Peter was a fisherman, what's your point, love?"

"I don't know how I got mixed up in all this."

"You got mixed up in this when you stepped on the tail of the great dragon."

"Tail of the great dragon?" he laughed. "You sound like you've been reading the Lord of the Rings."

"At Lilith Wendigo's funeral," she calmly explained. "You disturbed the dragons of darkness without knowing it."

"Dragons of darkness? Will you make sense?"

She toyed with a loc of her hair, took a deep breath, and launched into a lengthy explanation. "The dragons of darkness are the global rulers of this age who are aligned with the spiritual forces of wickedness in the high places.[3]

"They are the elites who trace their power back to the origins of governance, banking, munitions, pharmaceuticals, insurance, religion, media, and now cyberspace.

"They meet in secret to manufacture and profit from human fear. They manipulate national and global economies to create chaos, war, and want. They reduce populations of the young and old to achieve their goals of power. They warp human genders for their amusement. They practice pedophilia and sadomasochism for their sexual arousal. They have no charm, no wit, and no grace. They hate what is pure, and they hate us."

Who is this woman?

George took her words in, convinced she was some sort of religious fanatic. He'd never heard anything like this at church, much less from an aging waitress working for tips. He decided to humor her. "I hate to be rude, but how do you know all this, you're not exactly a religious scholar?"

She reached out and grasped his hand. "George, I'm an old soul who has spent my life pondering the mysteries of God, the writings of the Bible, and the human heart. Nothing I say takes a college education to understand, just a willingness to see."

She pinned him with her eyes. "Everything I say to you is revealed truth available to any man or woman. I didn't make it up, I'm only passing it along. You can know it for yourself."

"Kara, you sound like you've taken the Bible too literally. I've never heard anyone say anything about dragons of darkness."

"Yes, the word of truth sounds very much like foolishness

to those who don't know that they are perishing. But it is the power of life to those who are being saved."[4]

"All I know is that I want my life back, and for people to stop attacking me for something I didn't do."

"Ah, but you did do something. Whether you believe it or not, you unleashed the wrath of hell upon yourself. Nothing will change that. You can only ask for God's help in your battle against the darkness."

"No offense, but I don't usually take my religious advice from an old woman working as a waitress."

She smiled with the indulgence that comes from a long practice of dealing with fools. "Never underestimate the wisdom of an elder simply because we may look old or feeble. As Tolkien once wrote, 'The old that is strong does not wither, deep roots are not reached by the frost.'"[5]

George lowered his head into his hands. "I'm sorry," he sighed. "I'm just tired."

Her expression softened. "I know, George. Go home, and get some rest."

She placed the bill for his coffee on the table, and walked back to the kitchen. He picked up the check and read, 'The coffee is free, and so is the love of God. Don't despair. — Kara.'

He thought of what an insufferable jackass he was. He dragged himself up from the table, and drove home convinced that he was losing his mind.

CHAPTER 7
HARBINGERS

Things went from bad to worse. But it wasn't until the annual interfaith gathering that the hostility boiled over. The assembly took place each year in the main sanctuary where all the Christian symbols and artwork were covered and replaced with those of the various religious groups attending.

"I want everyone organized into prayer squares," Deacon Donna instructed the ushers. "Check the color of their name tag and sort them into client groups. Remember, our job is to give special care to the sensitivity and consensus of each attendee's emotional wellbeing."

The two hour program started with a Muslim Imam reciting an opening prayer, followed by Pastor Pendragon who welcomed the attendees.

"We are brothers and sisters from different religions and faiths who all worship the same God. We must affirm each other's beliefs as we journey to heaven. God loves all of his children no matter what their beliefs, and he wants us to build bridges together in the spirit of justice, unity and compassion."

Senator Fanortney then got up and explained what congress was doing to pass laws protecting reproductive freedom. The Dean of the Establishment Seminary spoke about her new book entitled, "Transgenderism: God's Hidden Design." A Rabbi named Joanna called for humans to repent of their unethical treatment of animals. A Catholic Priest made it clear that everyone should support open migration. A Hindu leader claimed that people must put an end to their dependency on fossil fuels, or mother earth would retaliate for their selfishness.

Finally, a black minister preached that cultural harmony would only be achieved when all religious organizations conducted regular mandatory racial bias training to atone for their systemic sins against people of color.

At the intermission, a medicine man from a local indigenous tribe led the attendees in a spirit dance where they were encouraged to appease an ancestral god.

Throughout the event there were lots of different prayers offered to lots of different deities in lots of different voices, all choked in the same woeful emotions. George found the whole thing creepy. Sarah was enthralled.

At the conclusion, Pendragon invited his listeners to come forward and participate in a candle-lighting ceremony meant to symbolize the weaving of their lives together into a harmonious tapestry of peace. At which point Sarah stood with the rest of the crowd and walked forward to receive the cleansing fire of sacred accord.

George whispered that he needed to use the restroom and ducked into the church kitchen where he poured himself some coffee, strolled to the lounge, and plopped down in a big comfy chair. He clicked on the television, and waited for Sarah to find him.

He was watching the third quarter of a college football

game when the Doctor appeared in front of him, blocking the television.

"You want something?" George asked.

"Sorry to hear about your little dog, really tragic. How's Sarah doing?"

"She okay, shaken."

"I can prescribe her some sedatives if it would help calm her nerves."

"She'll manage. The EMT gave her a few extra pills."

"Just let me know."

"So what's on your mind?"

"I'd like some information."

"I'm the fount of all wisdom, ask away."

"Why did you stab us in the back at the meeting with Peter?"

George knew this was coming and responded calmly. "I didn't stab you in the back. Peter said he'd think about your offer and get back to you."

"You made us look like a bunch of crooks."

"You must have a guilty conscience. SNUF is perfectly legit isn't it?"

"Of course, but that wasn't what you implied." The Doctor's face began to turn red.

"I implied nothing. You sound like you're paranoid. I asked a fair question about the corporate ownership."

"I didn't like the way you asked it," the Doctor scowled. "There was something in the tone of your voice."

"Tone of my voice? What are you, the new choir director?"

"I'm talking about your holier-than-thou attitude that's stirring confusion in the church. I'm talking about your divisive outlook that's gotten people worked up about abortion."

"What's bothering you Doctor Dinferi?"

"I'm bothered by your meddling and your insulting dream about Jesus. You suddenly think you're entitled to preach your personal opinions in our church without any authority, much less concern for the feelings of others."

George said nothing, and let the man bluster.

"What if everyone claimed that Jesus was God? There'd be nothing but chaos and turmoil in the executive council's efforts to nurture religious unity."

George knew a question that always stopped people in their tracks. It was time to ask it.

"Doc, have you ever met Jesus for yourself?"

As he predicted, the Doctor was caught off guard. "Of course not. What kind of stupid question is that? You think Jesus is walking around shaking people's hands?"

"No, he's standing right in front of you."

The Doctor gritted his teeth. "You've become a real jerk since you had your dream. Six months ago you were fun guy. You were always ready to buy a beer, or tell a joke. Now you're worse than a TV preacher. What happened?"

"That's what I've been trying to tell everyone, but they're not listening."

A FEW DAYS LATER, GEORGE STOOD ON THE PUTTING GREEN at the Pretentious Heights Country Club taking a few practice strokes. The club was a place where politicians and celebrities went to be seen hobnobbing with the rich and powerful. The temperature had dropped below freezing and the scar across his cheek felt tight, pulling slightly at the corner of his mouth.

"Had any dreams lately?"

George didn't flinch, or even acknowledge the question.

Instead, he maintained his concentration, and rapped a slowly curving fifteen footer over the frosted turf into the cup.

"Who told you that?"

"It's going around," said Hal Hanks, blowing on his finger tips to warm his grip. Hal owned a diversified shipping company.

George dipped his head and studied the ball.

"Actually, Pendragon let it out at the men's fellowship, it got quite a reaction."

George pictured a bunch of blowhards sitting around a horseshoe banquet table trying to impress each another with their religiosity.

"I bet it did," he said, nudging the ball with his putter. "What did he say?"

"That you flew off to heaven and saw stars and angels zooming around. The part about the sexy robot was especially entertaining. What did Sarah say?"

"She laughed."

"I don't blame her. Pendragon made it sound like you needed to increase your meds."

George cleaned the surface of his putter. "So, how's business Hal?"

"Super, I just signed a deal with the executive council to be their exclusive shipper for packages sent from SNUF's health clinics."

Hal watched George line up his next putt, and then tap it into the cup. "You're going to be tough to beat this year," he said. "You're the biggest reason why our tournament is always so successful."

George squatted down, and surveyed the lay of the green. "Not sure I'll be playing this year."

"What do you mean? You're the club champion, people come just to see you play."

George stood up, and addressed the ball. "I've had second thoughts about raising money for SNUF."

"It's never bothered you before."

"Guilty as charged. But then again, I'd never met Jesus Christ before."

"Wouldn't Jesus want you to support a good cause for women?"

George turned and looked at Hal. "I'm not certain that SNUF is a good cause."

"Of course it's a good cause. It pays great interest on my investment, and it gives free healthcare to women. What could be better?"

"It's doing far more than that. It's doing something evil."

"Evil? What's so evil about trying to help women?"

"They're not helping women."

"That's not what my wife says," Hal said, with a hearty laugh. "Anyway, it's none of my business. It's a woman's thing."

"I'm afraid that it's all of our business."

"Look George, a word to the wise. People are getting tired of hearing about dead babies and the devil's rollercoaster. It's not like you to be so vocal. Aren't you the one who always said that the key to success is to 'stay low, go slow and keep cool?'"[1]

"How can I keep my mouth shut?" George asked. "I met Jesus Christ. Believe me, once you meet him, you'll know that he knows that you know that he knows that you know. And when you know he knows, your perspective on life changes."

Hal looked at him with the sadness that comes from losing a friend. "Get a grip, it was just a dream, it wasn't for real."

"It wasn't a dream, erm, well, yes it was a dream, but not the same kind of dream you're thinking about."

Hal's eyebrows pinched together and he shook his head. "Why are you causing such a stink about this?"

George turned to to face Hal. It was time to ask him the question. "Hal, have you ever met Jesus personally?"

Hal hesitated not knowing how to respond. He masked his confusion with a smile. "I don't think so, at least not that I would know of. How does a person meet Jesus? Didn't you see him running around in heaven?"

George had his answer.

"Look, I don't need to be converted," Hal said. "You're not the only one who believes in God, we all do. You see me in church every week. For heavens sake, I'm a Deacon."

"Just because you believe in someone doesn't mean you've actually met them. I believe in Albert Einstein, but I've never met him."

"Nor will you," Hal smirked. "He's dead."

"Exactly, so if we say that Jesus is alive, then anyone should be able to meet him, right?"

"Ok, I'll play along, how do I meet Jesus?"

"Simple, just ask." George stroked the ball softly, and watched it curve into the cup. "Jesus says, 'Here I am! I stand at the door and knock. If anyone hears my voice and opens the door, I will come in and dine with that person, and they with me.'"[2]

"Yeah well, I've never heard any doors knocking," Hal confided.

"Because Pendragon doesn't teach us to listen for his knocking, much less his voice. The man makes Jesus a philosophical mystery who's unknowable, inaccessible. He wants us to think that Jesus is some sort of theological riddle that we can't solve without his help."

The Redemption of George | 239

"So, what's your point?"

"If a person wants to meet Jesus for themselves, all they have to do is ask, and then wait for his response."

"Did you ask?"

"No, I wasn't asking. But he can reach out and touch whoever he wants, whenever he wants. It's just easier if we reach out to him. He saved me in spite of myself."

He repositioned his feet, and gently tapped a ball into the cup another time.

"Is that what happened to you?" Hal asked, looking at George with all the sympathy of a man who thinks his friend is mentally ill.

"You wanted to know why I'm passionate about sharing the message of my dream, I told you. It's because I met Jesus the Christ, — the Truth, — the all in all."

"Come on man, will you get a grip? Your just an average guy, not saint. You're making people angry with your holy roller ideas about religion."

"Hal, listen to me, please. If you violate human law it will send you to prison, if you violate God's law it will send you to hell. I'm telling you that SNUF is up to no good. Besides, how can you call yourself a Christian, and not want to talk about the truth?"

"You mean your truth don't you George?" Hal took off his glasses, and wiped them on his golf towel.

"What do you mean?" George asked.

"You make it sound like everyone in the congregation is wrong if they support a woman's right to choose."

"They are if that choice is to kill a preborn child."

"There you go again," Hal said, exasperated. "Everyone in the church agrees it's settled science that it's not a human being, it's just a blob of cells."

"I don't care if the entire denomination thinks it's settled science, and the whole world says it's just a blob of cells. Simply because a million flies agree that a pile of dog crap tastes good, it doesn't change the fact that it's still hot steaming crap."

"Very funny," Hal said. "You need to get real. Everyone has their own religious opinions, and yours are making people angry."

George glanced up slightly. He felt his scar tighten his cheek.

"There's lot's of ugly talk about you floating around the church. I'd hate to see you or Sarah get hurt any more than you have."

"Is that a threat?"

"Not a threat, just a fact." Hal said, rubbing his hands together briskly. "Damn, it's freezing out here. I'm going inside."

George dropped his head, checked his alignment, adjusted his stance, and then tapped another fifteen footer into the hole.

After a rubdown in the club's fitness center George felt more like himself. He wandered into the lounge and found Kip stretched out on a leather couch watching golf on TV. His long legs dangled over the armrest.

George walked over and stood next to him. "You sent me a text saying it's going to snow in December. You mean white, powdery, cold snow?"

Kip sat up. "I'm not saying it *will* snow, I'm only saying that it *could* snow. And if it did — and that's a big if — it would ruin the yearly golf tournament."

"It never snows here in December," George said, scoffing. He pulled out a thick cigar, rolled it between his fingers and smelled the length of it. He fished a wood match from his pocket, struck it on his thumb and lit it.

He studied the smoke for a moment before saying, "For crying out loud Kip, that's why we hold the tournament during the Christmas holidays, and not in January."

"There's always a first time."

"Kip, listen to yourself. People are playing tennis, and shooting eighteen holes on Christmas day."

"Just saying, brother."

George plopped down in an overstuffed chair. The two men sat quietly, thinking about the catastrophic potential of an early snow. George took a long draw on the cigar, then puffed out a cloud of blue smoke. "I'm going to withdraw from the tournament."

Kip smiled. "It's about time."

"What?"

"I was wondering when you'd come to your senses. Who do you think is behind all of the trouble you've been having? I can't prove it, but I think it's the executive council."

"I'm thinking the same thing."

"So what's the plan?"

"The plan is to be courteous, Christian, and send SNUF straight to hell."

CHAPTER 8
CONFLICT

George hated the church at night, especially when it was rainy. The surrounding streets were slick, shadowy, dark, and dangerous. The old stone building seemed haunted by ghosts lurking in the hallways.

Pastor Pendragon had called earlier asking if he would come down to the church to discuss his dream.

He parked his car, got out, and was startled by a man dressed in a long tattered coat with a frayed backpack thrown over one shoulder. The man said not a word. He merely extended a grimy palm outward like Charon the ferryman of Hades expecting the dead to pay a coin to cross the River Styx into the underworld. His watery eyes wandered about and finally set their gaze somewhere past George at an unknown apparition.

George reached into his pocket, and pulled out a bill without looking. It could have been a dollar, it might have been a twenty, George didn't care. He'd let God decide.

"Here you go friend, stay warm."

"Gawd blest you," the man slurred.

George watched him stagger away, leaning forward into

the drizzling wind, clutching at his coat's thin collar, and rolling and pitching as if he was on the deck of a ship.

The security guard ran up moments later. "Sorry Mister Goodman, I had to take something upstairs, I hope that guy didn't bother you."

"Not any more, my friend. Not any more."

He walked upstairs to the meeting room, and lingered at the door. He collected himself, and pushed the door open. Seven grim faces met him.

"What's up, guys?" he asked, casually. "I thought I was meeting with Pastor Pendragon. Did I interrupt something?"

Pendragon spoke up. "I think you know the members of the executive council, I've asked them to join us."

"Why?"

"Frankly George, in the spirit of Christian love, we want to see if we can reach a consensus about your dream."

"My dream?"

"We're deeply concerned about your mental health," the Doctor said, gravely.

"My mental health?" George chuckled. "You're no more concerned about my mental health than you are of the homeless guy I just passed on the street."

"That's exactly the uncharitable attitude people have been complaining about," Von Heekate accused. She looked around at the other members of the tribunal.

"George, the problem is that you've become rather unhinged since having your alleged vision of Jesus," Guile explained.

"Unhinged?"

"People say you're acting erratic," the Doctor said.

"They're upset that you're accusing them of things that are untrue, and ugly."

George calmly took a seat. "What are their names?"

"Names are unimportant," the General said flatly, as if his word was final.

"Then what am I accused of?"

"You're accused of uncharitable conduct towards members of this church," the Judge said. "Do you realize how insensitive your remarks about hell, and reproductive rights are?"

"To whom?"

"To all of the women in this church who've had an induced miscarriage," Von Heekate said.

"Induced miscarriage?" George asked. "Oh, you mean an abortion. I didn't realize there were any."

"Don't act stupid, many of our ladies have had an induced miscarriage," the Doctor returned. "You have no right to say they're going to hell."

"I never said they were going to hell, why should they? It's the ones who deceive them into killing their babies who will," George replied. "Besides, it's still legal to quote the Bible in a church, isn't it?"

"That's not the point," Guile said. "Our members expect a certain level of civility. You have no right to weaponize the Bible and say that their private decisions are sinful."

Von Heekate piped in, her jaw working back and forth. "You've personally offended me and several of my friends with your hateful dream."

"It's not hate for me to point out sinful behavior where I see it. This is not a newspaper where you can twist a story to suit your bias. This is a church responsible for teaching God's truth."

"The church is what we say it is," Von Heekate spat. She looked at the others sharply. No one objected.

"I'll ask you again," Guile said. "Did you tell Millie Mockingbird, or any other member of the congregation that they were going to hell because they believe in a woman's right to choose?"

"I never used those words," George said. "What I told her was that there is a special place in hell for people who kill innocent children. It's called the devil's rollercoaster."

"The devil's rollercoaster?" the General scoffed, and the room broke into laughter. "And you wonder why we think you're having a mental breakdown?"

"I can give you a referral to a friend who specializes in delusions," the Doctor said.

"The Bible says, 'thou shalt not judge,'" Pendragon admonished. "You're in no position to condemn anyone."

"You know better than that, Pastor. The Bible says that we are not to judge the heart of a person, but God gives us permission to judge their actions. Even so, what kind of a malignant heart could justify killing babies?"

"They're not babies, you idiot," the General shouted.

Guile jumped in trying to reduce the tension. "I agree with some of the things you say, George." He lied. "However, it's the way you're saying them."

"The way I'm saying them?"

"There's no grace in the tone of your voice."

"Only God has grace."[1]

"What would you know about God's grace?" the Professor asked, sneering.

"I know God's grace is not what you people call hospitable, charming, agreeable, or friendly."

"You're an obnoxious moron," the General bellowed.

"And you're an arrogant devil," George snapped back. "If

you think having your ears tickled by humorous stories and smooth preaching is what grace means, it's no wonder this church has lost its way."

"What makes you think we've lost our way?"

"That's easy," George said, gesturing to Guile and Pendragon. "They're a couple of manipulative spin masters who preach a web of lies."

Von Heekate began wildly waving her finger at George. "That's exactly the kind of ungracious attack I'm talking about. Pastor Pendragon and Pastor Guile are both deeply devoted men of God. They're great biblical scholars who've faithfully led this congregation into a new understanding of the Scriptures."

George shook his head. "Not hardly. Their embrace of the open culture with their little tear-jerker stories, cute cliches, sports anecdotes, folksy humor, and three joke sermons led this congregation to normalize sin, and the demonic work of SNUF."

"SNUF is a shining example of God's compassion for women," the Professor rebutted.

George stood and walked to the front of the room. "Has it ever occurred to you that Pendragon never mentions hell, or any requirement to abstain from sin in his sermons? Doesn't it strike you as odd that he never preaches about the devil, the consequences of our moral behavior, or the judgment of God? Is there ever a mention of suffering, sacrifice, or laying down our lives for others? No, never. He always preaches a message of divine indulgence, making a point to say how much God loves us because we are so worthy of his love. Well my fellow sinners, we are not worthy of God's love, especially if we're killing babies."

"For the second time, they are not babies," the General said, veins popping out on his forehead.

The Redemption of George | 247

"We don't care about your narrow minded views. We support our Pendragon and Guile's enlightened views," the Judge said.

"George, your obsession with outdated models of hell, and the old fashioned concept of sin shows a remarkable lack of education," Guile said.

George laughed. "You guys would rather be lied to politely than be told the truth directly. Your issue is not with me, but with God. Take it up with him, he wrote the Bible."

"God wrote the Bible?" Von Heekate said, her mouth set in a hard line. "The Bible was written by a bunch of misogynistic old men to rule women, and control their sexuality. Thank the stars that our enlightened church has freed us from the Bible's gender bias."

"You mean enslaved you to your sexist hatred," George replied.

"George, I don't think you fully understand how much good the church does in our community. The Sacred Name Unity Fund is a positive principled agency doing God's work," the Judge said. "We support medical personnel who provide free reproductive healthcare for marginalized women."

George's eyes narrowed. He walked over to the windows. "You're all so blind that you actually believe that. Look at yourselves, you're all dripping in baby's blood, and you've convinced yourself it's champaign."

"What?" The General flinched, as if he'd been slapped.

"Don't act surprised, General. For a man who likes to boast he was a brave soldier defending our country, why is it that you can't seem to defend innocent children?"

Before the General could say a word George continued. "I'll tell you why — it doesn't pay as much as you get for killing babies."

"You insignificant bastard," the General said, jumping to his feet, both fists balled. "Reproductive rights are a political matter, not a church matter."

"They're precisely a church matter. Where else are people supposed to learn about the evils of child abuse and infanticide?[2] What other platform is there to change society's thinking? You won't hear a peep from the college professors at the universities, the corporate powers, main stream media, judges, or politicians."

"I suppose you know all about the church?" the General laughed, disdainfully. "You may be good at playing golf, but you don't know a damned thing about the law, politics, or what God wants. You're not a minister, elder, deacon, or even a lawyer, you're just a back row pew duster."

"Talk about being a back row pew duster. You spent your entire military career as a sniveling REMF."[3]

The General's face bent into crumbled red rage. For a moment George thought the man was going to have a stroke. Then, just as quickly, he calmed down and re-glued an arrogant smile on his face.

"As far as a woman's rights are concerned," the General said, evenly, "I don't think the members of our church give a damn what a woman does with her body, everyone's in agreement on that."

"Everyone here may be in agreement on that, but I am not in agreement with everyone here," George responded. "You people don't give a damn about what God wants, you just want the perks of the Church Endowment Fund, and the money SNUF is making from killing babies."

Again, the General's face mottled into puddles of rose-colored splotches. He wasn't used to being challenged. This time his voice quivered as he pointed a finger towards George. "I don't know where you get off with your narrow-minded hate you little twerp, but if it were up to me you'd be kicked out of this church tonight."

"Well, good luck with that Herr General, this is not your church. I've been going here since I was born, and whether you like it or not, I had a dream that opened my eyes to what's going on, and I'm going to share it with anyone who will listen."

"ALL RIGHT, ALL RIGHT, LET'S CALM DOWN," GUILE SAID, hands upraised. "Frankly, I'm confused. You've never mentioned a word about the direction of our church, and now you're suddenly an expert telling us what we're doing wrong. Why the change?"

George felt like he was talking to the dead. "I'll say it again. I met Jesus Christ. Unless this church stops its soulless, selfish, self-righteous, greedy, and murderous ways, it's damned to hell."

They broke into robust laughter, and derisive snickers. "We don't need to repent of anything. We're good people, doing good things. We take care of ourselves and our families. There's nothing immoral about that," the Judge said.

"What's immoral is that you take too much care of yourselves," George said. "You need to start taking care of others."

"That's why we started the Sacred Name Unity Fund," Guile said. "We spend millions every year supporting the medical personnel who provide healthcare for poor and migrant women."

The hair stood up on George's neck. "Pastor, we all know that SNUF is killing babies, and if that's what you call taking care of others, I'd hate to see how you love them."

"Then why don't you just leave?" Von Heekate said. "Go find another church."

George had waited for this moment. "The only thing I'm leaving is the annual golf tournament. As of tonight, I'm out." He might as well have dropped a hand grenade on the floor and watched it explode.

"You can't do that," Guile said, wobbling up from his wheelchair. "You're one of the principle reasons people come here to play. Our sponsors will drop out."

"I surely hope so," George said.

The room broke into pockets of feverish discussion. Pendragon tried to regain control of the meeting. He stood up and cleared his throat.

"Whether George plays in the annual golf tournament or not is of no consequence. There are plenty of exceptional players who will fill the gap. We don't need him, although I am saddened to see him leave." Pendragon's crocodile tears were shameless.

Von Heekate raised her hand, revealing a tiny pentagram tattooed on the inside of her wrist. "It's time to censure George, and I vote he's out."

"I'm sorry," Guile replied. "As much as it pains me to say it, we have yet to firmly establish his guilt. With all due fairness, the denominational rules require us to prove conclusive evidence that he has been uncharitable towards others."

"I don't need any proof," the Professor stormed. "His behavior tonight is enough proof."

Pendragon cut in, acting as if he was pleading for reconciliation. "All we're asking is that you let the congregation know you were mistaken about your dream, and the little flames in heaven."

"Pastor, if you'd been preaching the Word of Truth for the past twenty years, there'd be no need for me to apologize to the misguided members of the congregation who think I've done something wrong."

"George, I *have* been preaching the Word of Truth all these years, and if you hadn't been asleep you'd know that I've been trying to make this church relevant in the 21st Century."

"Relevant? You can't be serious."

"Nobody in the modern world believes in your medieval account of hell and damnation, much less in the words of a book not even Christians can agree upon. If we don't champion issues like gender identity, transgenderism, a woman's right to choose, climate justice, open borders, and other social issues, the congregation will turn their backs on us."

"Fine, let them. None of the things you've mentioned have anything to do with pleasing God."

"George, I knew both your parents," Guile said, as if he was talking to a child. "They'd be ashamed to hear you talk like this."

"They'd be ashamed if I didn't. Don't forget, I grew up in this church. I remember my parents saying that you'd changed it into a social club with no mission beyond feeling good."

"Your parents were well intentioned, but naive," Guile responded. "The mission of a church is to provide its members with positivity, and hope for a comfortable life. Sometimes that goes beyond the narrow confines of the Bible."

George felt his blood pressure rise. "I was the one who was naive. My parents tried to teach me that the lifeblood of a Christian isn't found in enhancing your life, but in faithful obedience to the word of God, virtuous living, and sacred communion. I'm ashamed to say I didn't listen."

"You sound angry," the Judge said. "In my experience

men get angry when confronted with the ugly truth about themselves."

"Not angry Judge — just passionate."

"Sounds like anger to me."

"I'm sorry you don't know the difference. Passion is when Jesus went to the temple and drove out the money changers. He wasn't angry, he was passionate in his belief that their perversion needed to be purged from the house of God."

Guile started laughing loudly. "So now George thinks he's Jesus driving us wicked perverts out of the church." He looked around at the others. There was more laughter in the room.

"You think your Jesus Christ?" the Doctor asked, mocking him.

"No, he thinks he's God," the Professor taunted.

"What makes you think you know anything about the Bible?" the General asked.

George was unperturbed by the attacks. "A person doesn't have to be God, or know anything about the Bible to see that you've transformed this church from being a covenant community into a coven."

"That's a pretty ugly accusation," Guile snarled.

"If you don't stop what SNUF is doing, Jesus will not only drive you out of this temple, he'll destroy it."

"Destroy it?" the Judge laughed. "We must be doing something right. He keeps on giving us money. This church will be around for generations to come."

"That's a laugh," George said. "It's the devil giving you money for your partnership in his work." George looked around the room with his eyes blazing. "And I'll bet that money is being stolen right now by someone I'm looking at."

At that moment all hell broke loose around the table.

SARAH WAS A COVETOUS WOMAN — WHO WANTED.

She didn't know why she wanted, she just wanted.

Every day she had a new request, a fresh desire, a different craving.

She wanted to look like others, dress like others, live like others, dine like others, and travel like others.

She spent time and money trying to keep up with them.

She browsed magazines, read books, and scanned social media hoping for answers.

She went to parties, attended meetings, and sat in church looking for affirmation.

Today, she wanted George to forget about his dream, and apologize for all the trouble he'd caused.

WHEN GEORGE GOT HOME FROM HIS MEETING WITH THE executive council, he flopped down on the couch exhausted.

"I heard you made an ass of yourself." Sarah snarled.

"They said they were concerned about my mental health."

"So am I, sport. Marsha called to say your little speech made quite an impression."

"That's a laugh, they're invincibly blind."

"Spare me your opinion. Your great message of truth outraged everyone. Betty sent me an email saying she won't need my help on the women's committee."

"Great, one less obligation for you."

"Allison texted saying I don't need to assist with Bible-yoga class."

"Nothing biblical about Bible-yoga."

"Sylvia called saying I won't be needed for the golf tournament."

"Probably because I pulled out."

"You what?" Sarah cried, her voice shrill.

"I think it's wrong to donate anymore money to SNUF."

"You do, huh? Well, here's what I think, bud. People are sick of your holier than thou attitude."

George was baffled. "I'm not holier than thou."

"You're acting like it. You've insulted everyone we know with your self-righteous dreams, and Bible talk."

"Such as?"

"You said my ladies' luncheons are nothing more than a polite excuse for gossip. You insist that the church's kitchen be used to feed the bums on the street. You've told people they need to cut down on their drinking. You've accused some of my friends of having a gambling problem. Who knows what else you'll come up with? My people are avoiding me, and I want this to stop!"

"They're feeling guilty."

"Well who died and made you the Pope? No church is perfect. You have no right to expose anyone."

George squared off for another cage fight, only this time he was ready. "God's word is exposing them, not me. Have you ever wondered why we don't feed the poor living in the streets around the church? You can't swing a foot-long sandwich and not hit a hungry person walking past our sanctuary. Our church has a bigger kitchen than most restaurants, and we only use it to feed ourselves."

"That's because we don't have a health permit to feed anyone but us."

"And why is that?"

"Because we're not a restaurant, we're a church. Besides, we send plenty of money to different charities who take care of feeding people."

"How can we pretend to care about the needy when our

only involvement is to write a check to some agency who skims a fat administrative fee off the top, then gives what's left to another agency, who skims another fat slice off the top, until there's barely anything left by the time it reaches the poor? Why don't we feed the hungry ourselves and cut out the middlemen?"

"Because God chooses some people to make the money and others to do the work. We're the ones who make the money, not the ones who do the work — in case you've forgotten."

"How could you ever let me? Just because we've got money doesn't mean we get to write a check, and then wash our hands of our responsibility to become involved."

"This lecture is coming from a man who hasn't volunteered to do anything in the past twenty years? Spare me."

"I've changed, I'm trying to get on track."

"So you're going to stage a childish protest by dropping out of the annual golf tournament?"

"Yes, and I'm going to ask Peter to help me organize a new tournament for next year. Only this one will benefit widows and orphans, just like the Bible says."

"There you go again, the Bible this and the Bible that. I'm sick of hearing about the Bible. What do you know about the Bible? Suddenly you're saint George the savior of children, and old ladies."

"Don't you see what's going on? Look at us. We're delusional. We own a forty-foot RV we never drive, a motorcycle that sits in the garage, we live in a house big enough for a family of eight, we have a yard that takes a team of landscapers to maintain, we've got shoes in our closet that we've never worn, and our garage is larger than most homes on the Southside of town."

Sarah leaned against the doorway, and folded her arms

across her chest. She looked at the walls and wondered if it was time to paint again. "And whose fault is that?" she asked.

"Both of ours," he said. "I've spent thousands of dollars on golf clubs, shoes, greens fees, private lessons, and golf vacations. That money could have helped someone who needed it. Shame on me, and shame on us!"

"George," she said, with a long theatrical sigh. "The government has hundreds of programs to help people. That's why we pay an obscene amount of taxes. We've worked hard, while others have hardly worked. We deserve our things, and I don't see how giving them all away changes anyone's life but ours."

"You didn't work for those things, you nagged for those things. I'm the guy who worked for those things. I'm fifty-four years old, and I've spent the last twenty-five years having the life sucked out of me managing a business I hate."

"You hate? I don't remember you complaining about your club membership, ski vacations, and fancy coin collection."

"Do you really think that being the CEO of a stupid furniture company replaces my dreams? I got a bachelor's degree in astronomy, I wanted to be an astronomer. Who in the hell wants to run a furniture store?"

"An astronomer? That's a laugh. If my father hadn't brought you into the business, you'd still be a flunky lab assistant making nothing."

"Believe me, I would have been happier."

"And what would you prefer?"

"I'd prefer a job where I can use my imagination, look at the stars and dream about worlds that might be. A life where I wouldn't have to go through a charade every day, mouthing my lines, playing the role of the successful business owner."

"Well aren't you the high minded one, who knew?"

"I never saw what my life had become. I never realized

that I had turned into a poisonous tonic of snobbery, sham, and hypocrisy headed straight for hell. For the first time in my life I see clearly. I've experienced something wonderful and you don't understand it. You don't want to understand it because it threatens your precious little world."

"And where would you be without my precious little world?"

"I know where I'd like to be."

"Where's that?"

"I'd like to go back to school, get my Masters in astronomy, and maybe a Ph.D."

"And then what?"

"I dunno, maybe teach, do some research, get a job at a planetarium, go to work for NASA — who knows."

"If you went back to school now you'd be an old man by the time you graduated. Who in the hell would hire you?"

"The Lord will open the doors. All I know is that the sky's the limit." He was afraid to smile at his own pun.

"Astronomy doesn't pay squat. And I have no intention of wasting my life waiting for my dear hubby to come home and tell me all about some planetoid nobody cares about."

She leaned in closer. "You know what your trouble is? You're a loser who'd be satisfied sitting on the porch of a double wide trailer staring up at the stars with a can of beer in one hand, and scratching your ass with the other."

George thought the prospect sounded fine.

"What happened Sarah? You used to be such a dreamer, so filled with expectations."

"Life happened George — two kids, stretch marks, grey hair, wrinkles, a dead mom, and a dad with Alzheimer's. Not to mention being worried sick about what you've done to us, the business, and our future. What the heck do you think?"

"God will take care of us."

"The Bible says that God helps those who help themselves," she said, smugly.

"No, actually it doesn't." For a moment, George thought she was going to throw something at him.

"I don't care!" she screamed. "We have a good life, and your fantasy about outer space, and your stupid dream about Jesus is ruining all that."

"Listen to yourself. You've become like all the rest of your friends, clutching their pearls, afraid they'll lose the safety of their financial refuge. They've got no faith, no imagination, no sense of calling, no future, and no hope — except in the power of their wealth to protect them."

Sarah's eyes burned holes through him. "I never realized how much you hated my friends."

"I don't hate them, I pity them. Money has completely ruined them. Their success elevates them in their minds. They all think their going to heaven because they have good thoughts. Their status blinds them from the truth."

"Truth? What truth? Your truth, my truth, who's truth? What truth are you talking about?"

"There is only one truth."

She looked up, raised her arms as if she was beseeching the gods, and then dropped them in frustration. "So it's been my stupid mistake, my miserable tragic screw-up to marry a man whose secret dream has always been to become the fourth Magi chasing around the heavens looking for a star.

"Well, if you want to know my truth, I'd live without you before I'd live without the life I've built. This is my birthplace, my city, my future, my friends, my church, and I'm not going to leave any of it behind."

With that, she turned, stomped upstairs to their bedroom, and slammed the door loudly behind her.

George was heartbroken, he knew he couldn't stay in the

The Redemption of George | 259

house another minute. He had no place to go except to his office where he could sit in the darkness until morning. He grabbed the fob to his electric car and left the house.

It was late. Dark roiling clouds signaled another storm was moving into the city. When he got to the main highway, he realized that he hadn't eaten, so he headed to the Starflyer Diner.

He drove into the night worried that Sarah would receive some sort of Divine smite for her selfish attitude. Something awful and lasting, like that of the woman from Sodom who turned to salt.

GEORGE SET UP A BED ON THE COUCH IN HIS OFFICE. EXCEPT for missing Sarah, he was doing okay. This morning he sat talking on the phone with his finance director. "Yes Matt, the stock is going up. It's encouraging news."

His secretary buzzed on the intercom. "There's someone here to see you, says he's a friend of the Judge."

"Gotta go Matt," George said. "Keep me informed." He placed the receiver down, and buzzed her back. "Send him in."

A fit man walked through the door. He was of medium build and height, dressed in a dark blue double breasted suit, white shirt, and paisley tie. His face was so tan that he might have just flown in from the Bahamas. He had a Roman nose, manicured fingernails and salon hair cut. The man's cheeks were abnormally tight and shiny, as if cosmetic surgery had once been performed. When he smiled, his teeth were perfectly straight and chalk white.

"Good morning Mr. Goodman," he said, shutting the door behind him. "I called yesterday."

"Yes, of course — Mister Esbat, I'm glad to meet you," George said, extending a hand.

"Call me Barton, please. I'm the Judge's friend."

"I was beginning to wonder if you'd forgotten about me," George said, smiling.

"I apologize, we've been running way behind."

George sat down and motioned for Barton to take a seat. The man placed a wide aluminum briefcase on the floor beside him.

"So I understand you need some office furniture?" George said.

"Yes sir," Barton said, handing over a list of the items he wanted.

"That's a bunch of furniture," George whistled. A single eyebrow peaked as he scanned the document.

The man frowned. "The Judge indicated that you could handle it."

"Of course we can handle it," George said, agreeably. "I was just making an observation."

Esbat hesitated a moment. "If you don't mind, I have an additional request."

"What are you thinking?"

"After you deliver the new furniture, would it be possible to haul away our old stuff, and drop it at a warehouse in Phoenix? I'll pay you extra for the detour."

"Why not just burn it?"

"I've heard about your charitable donations to the Redemption Rehab. We have one in Phoenix, and I'd hate to see the old furniture go to waste."

"Very generous, Mister Esbat."

"Barton, please."

"No problem. We can transport the used stuff wherever you'd like."

"I've written down all the information your driver will need."

Barton produced a thick envelope from inside his suit jacket. "These are his instructions, routes, phone numbers, pick-up and delivery locations." He handed it to George.

"I appreciate the opportunity to earn your business," George said, taking the envelope.

"Your references are impeccable Mr. Goodman. I look forward to doing more business with you in the future."

With their business done, they shook hands, and Esbat walked out of the office.

George stepped to the window. The drizzle outside was blowing through a light fog. He opened the envelope and sorted through the information. He put the briefcase on his desk and popped the catches. As he expected, the case was packed tightly with stacks of hundred dollar bills. There was no need to count.

A minute later, George watched Mr. Esbat exit the building, and dash across Profit Street to a waiting limousine.

"Did you get all that?" George asked.

"Every word," answered Special Agent Yin, stepping out of the closet.

CHAPTER 9
REVELATION

Peter gingerly manipulated the controls of his luxury helicopter, happily skimming the whitecaps of Opulence Bay. He flew at a hundred-eighty miles per hour, at a hundred-eighty feet off the deck. George and Kip were content to enjoy the ride.

"Like my new toy?" Peter asked, through his headset.

"This isn't a toy, it's opulence with a rotor blade," Kip replied. He pointed to the leather swivel seats and mini bar.

"Eight passenger seating, touch-screen avionics, a jet smooth ride — it's in a class of its own," Peter boasted.

George looked at Kip. "And to think of all the times we were crammed into the back of an Army Blackhawk. This puppy is awesome."

"A friend sold it to me for a song — only fifteen million."

"Was that with your discount coupons?" Kip asked.

"No, but I did promise the Sultan that I'd take very good care of her," Peter chuckled.

They flew along without speaking, until Peter interrupted the silence. "Sorry to hear about you and Sarah breaking up."

"Inevitable, she blamed me for everything that went wrong," George said.

"Give her time."

"I doubt it. Her parents were a couple of wealthy social climbers, it's in her blood."

"My parents were the same," Peter said.

"Not the same. Your parents never raised you, they paid nannies to raise you. That makes you the product of working class women."

The helicopter buffeted through a gust of wind.

"You can live onboard *Sotirios* for as long as you like," Peter said. "I'll move her to the harbor in Abundance Falls."

"Thanks, I'm tired of eating fast food and sleeping at the office."

Kip adjusted his headset. "And don't worry, we're going to find the person who killed Cookie. When my K-9 teams heard what happened they couldn't volunteer fast enough to find them."

"Hey," Peter said, changing the subject. "You guys wanna see what this baby can do?"

"Go for it," Kip said.

"Hang on."

The next moment George and Kip saw the ocean above their head and the sky beneath their feet, followed by the sky above their head, and the ocean beneath their feet.

"Helicopters aren't supposed to do that," George shouted.

"That's not all, watch this," Peter hollered, and he executed a slow barrel roll with military precision.

"Awesome blossom!" Kip yelled.

"I thought you guys would get a kick out of that," Peter said, leveling the aircraft. "The Sultan had some special modifications done to her."

An accomplished pilot, Peter had thousands of hours of stick time on both rotary and fixed wing aircraft.

"Honest to crap," George exclaimed, catching his breath. "If it was anyone but you, I'd kick their tail when we landed."

They all laughed warmly over the intercom.

THE FLIGHT TO PETER'S PRIVATE ISLAND WHERE THE *SOTIRIOS* lay anchored was almost over. The aircraft began to shudder and Peter gently eased the copter onto the fantail of the vessel. When the wheels kissed the deck safely, he shut the power down.

"We're home."

Heidi was there to greet them She slid the passenger door open, and ducked her head inside. "You're just in time for lunch, gentlemen. Sandwiches will be served in the planning center."

"I hope you don't mind," Peter said, removing his headset. "I thought it might be a good place to talk."

The planning center was where Peter did all of his work. He liked to sit at his massive semicircular desk surrounded by different sized computer screens, black boxes, and other gadgets. Along the bulkheads were individual work stations that provided additional cubicles for people to join him.

"I designed *Sotirios* to be self contained in the event of a major catastrophe such as an electro magnetic pulse shut down, nuclear war, global DDoS attack, or just when I'm on extended vacation. From here I can monitor or circumvent the entire global network."

"Circumvent?"

"Absolutely, you didn't think there's only one network in cyberspace did you?"

George scrutinized the room filled with monitors, servers, blinking panels and tiny gizmos.

"This is my pride and joy," Peter said, walking to a super cooled refrigerator and opening the door. "My personally designed quantum computer. It will break any kind of encryption."

"Wow, I've read about these," Kip said. "Every major country in the world is trying to write encryption schemes to defeat them, but they're years away."

Peter beamed like a proud father. "This baby will crack any code they develop."

"The NSA would love to see this," Kip said, admiring the machine.

"I'm sure they would," Peter said, his mouth curving into a wide smile. "If they knew it existed."

THAT AFTERNOON THE TRIO WERE STANDING ON THE TOP DECK of the boat getting ready to smack a few golf balls into the sea. They stood on a custom driving mat that Peter had installed to automatically tee-up golf balls that sprang up from somewhere below the deck.

"There's something I wanted to talk about," Peter said, taking a practice swing.

"What's that?"

"The funeral service."

"I feel bad about that," George said, cheeks reddening.

"Don't, it actually turned out to be a good thing."

"I thought you'd be mad," George said.

"At first I was," Peter said. "Only later that night I stood right here looking at the stars wondering why Welma would do something like that?"

"Maybe she was crazy," Kip suggested.

"Welma wasn't crazy," Peter replied. "Crazy is taking unnecessary risks."

"You don't think she was crazy risking jail?"

"She didn't take a risk, she knew she'd go to jail," Peter said. The driving mat automatically served him a golf ball.

"I admit that Welma had guts," Kip said. "It's too bad her protest wasn't able to change anything."

"Not so," Peter responded.

"How's that?" George asked.

"She changed me."

Peter took another practice swing, addressed the ball, and drove it far out into the ocean. They watched it sail away like a rocket until it disappeared behind a small whitecap.

He sat down in a comfortable club chair. "I'm not religious man, and I've never thought much about God," he said. "Yet Welma caused me to wonder if they're aren't bigger things in life than my personal ambitions."

George replaced him at the driving mat. "When I was a soldier I knew there were things bigger than me," he said. "Things worth defending, protecting, and passing on to my kids."

"Not me. All I've ever thought about is myself."

"Same as most guys," Kip offered. "It doesn't make you a terrible person."

"I know," Peter replied, crossing his arms over his chest. "Only now I think that unless you serve a higher purpose, you're just a selfish, immature, pathetic excuse for a human being."

"Don't be so hard on yourself," George said. "You're a

success, you employ thousands of people, you donate huge money to hundreds of causes."

"You don't have to tell me about causes," Peter said. "America has turned into a nation of beggars. You can't buy a head of lettuce at the supermarket that the checkout clerk doesn't ask if you want to donate to some cause."

"Most causes aren't worth a thimble of spit," George said. "They don't accomplish anything but make the head of the organization wealthy, or some corrupt bureaucrat rich."

"You sound pretty cynical," Kip chuckled. "A lot of causes do some good."

"They spend tons of money sending me bags of mail, and hundreds of emails trying to convince me of that," Peter chuckled.

"So what's a worthy cause?" George asked. "What's a cause worthy of a billionaire's time and money?"

"I don't want to like other rich men who fly around in private jets, fearmongering, scaring people into giving them money, and pretending to care about some unattainable goal."

"Okay, so you don't want to be a politician, Hollywood celebrity, or televangelist," Kip said, chuckling.

Peter smiled. "I want to do something meaningful. I don't want to waste my time chasing imaginary unicorns and fruitless dreams of utopia."

"Such as?"

"You guys were soldiers. What does a soldier do?"

"Defends their fellow citizens from evildoers," Kip said. "At least a good one does."

"Exactly," Peter said. "I want to defend innocent children from evil men and women."

"Forgive me for saying so but that's about the deepest thing I've ever heard come out of your mouth," George said.

"You're right."

"What happened?"

"It sounds crazy, but I had a revelation.

"After the funeral service, I spent a lot of time digging into what mom was doing, and the cause she fought so passionately for. I came to realize that she was completely bonkers."

George and Kip looked at each other, surprised.

"She actually thought she was doing good by killing babies. It's sickening. How is that even logical? How can anyone think they are doing good by killing babies?"

Peter pulled his cap down against a sudden gust of wind.

"I don't think she saw it as murder," Kip said.

"She wrote in her diary that she was on a noble crusade to champion the rights of oppressed women. She believed that abortion would usher in a new and wonderful global age if women were empowered to decide when, and if they wanted to give birth. The termination of children was not only virtuous in her eyes, it was the duty of every modern woman to help save the world."

George thought about Eva words: *"The world is filled with millions of people who believe they are good guys — all of them on the road to hell."*

"That must have been tough for you to read," Kip said.

"Almost as tough as when I realized she was driven by arrogant racism. Her notes said abortion should be used to completely eliminate entire ethnic groups, especially African Americans and Hispanics."

Kip nodded his head. "Believe me, I know."

"She was adamant that abortion was necessary to purify the world of nonessential people so that those of superior stock could survive. I never knew she was so sick."

"She was your mom, you didn't see that side of her," George said.

"Only because she masked her contempt for people as compassion. How evil is that?" Peter shook his head sadly.

"In my experience evil is slippery," George said. "It hides behind a fancy title and a smile. It uses the media, government, religion, medicine, and universities to legitimize its monstrosities."

"Where does it come from?" Peter asked. "It's in everything."

"It comes from the mind of a supernatural being called Lucifer," Kip answered.

He went on to explain how Lucifer originated as an angel in heaven, and mutated into the demonic embodiment of evil.

"So you're saying there's actually a devil?"

George and Kip both nodded yes.

"How does this devil convince good people to become evil, like mom?"

"He destroys their moral absolutes," Kip said.

"I don't follow."

"When a person says there's no distinction between good and evil, or right and wrong, they are speaking for Lucifer. If they teach that wickedness is acceptable as long as it's done with good intentions, they are preaching the devil's creed. If they claim that anarchy is permissible if it's committed for a noble reason, they are apostles of the devil's religion."

"Where does all that end up?"

"The result is that if people think there are no moral absolutes, then all bets are off. Genocide, mass murder, enslavement, robbery, trafficking, and government plunder become legitimate so long as people think they can be used to achieve a greater good."

"Most of the time that greater good is to line their own pockets," George mentioned.

Peter pondered the logic before speaking. "So, if evil actions aren't viewed as being morally wrong, then evil can flourish."

He stepped up to the ball, addressed it, and popped it into a high loft that barely cleared the stern of the boat. "Then how can anybody ever tell what's right or wrong?"

"They can't unless they have fixed moral absolutes that transcend human, or demonic bias."

Peter chuckled. "Then morality couldn't possibly be determined by the minds of men, or in the actions of a courtroom."

Kip nodded. "Just as this boat has a reliable compass and the stars to guide it, God gave the world the Bible and the Holy Spirit. Without them, people have no true moral direction, just subjective judgment."

"Precisely," George agreed. "In a nation without a moral code as found in the Scriptures, the elites can do whatever they please, and the common man is left to be extorted, aborted, or enslaved."

"That would explain why the global leaders would want to get rid of the Bible, and anyone who spreads its message," Peter remarked.

"It's one reason they killed Welma, and it's why they're trying to cancel me," George said.

"I won't let that happen," Peter and Kip said, together.

"What are you saying?"

"I want to fight evil," Peter answered.

George was surprised at his friend's new direction. "That's a pretty tall order."

Peter was unmoved. "It seems reasonable that without the truth as revealed in the Bible, what's morally acceptable will always be defined by those with the biggest guns, the loudest voice, or the most money."

"True," George admitted.

"Well, I have a few dollars of my own," Peter said. "I'd like to put them to good use."

"It's not so easy," Kip said. "The weapons to fight evil must come from something bigger than a billionaire's checkbook, or good intentions."

"Such as?"

"They have to come from a power above all powers — an almighty power."

"Don't go getting religious on me," Peter laughed.

"I'm not, it's only logical. In order to destroy a supernatural evil you would need a supernatural strength."

Kip stood up, and took his turn at the ball. He squared off, adjusted his stance, and struck it hard making a sweet "ping" sound. They watched the little white orb fly away until it dropped out of sight.

He continued. "Imagine serving the cause of evil, thinking you are serving the cause of good."

"It happens all the time," George remarked.

"Sure, but it's one thing for a single individual, or even a group to get deceived by evil. Imagine if an entire country was duped."

"How could that happen?" Peter asked.

"Take the Nazies. They convinced the people of Germany they were doing good by killing Jews."

"How did they do that?"

"Once Hitler realized how easy it was to influence people using the media, he formed the Ministry of Public Enlightenment and Propaganda. It had the same control of

Germany's information as our mainstream media has on ours.

"One of its main jobs was to dehumanize the Jews by comparing them to a virus killing a body. Of course Germany was the body. The Nazi collaborators who controlled the arts, motion pictures, theater, books, radio, and the press, all supported the lie.

"Everywhere a German citizen turned they were told that in order to save their country the Jewish virus must be killed. Eventually most citizens came to believe that by killing the Jews they were performing an act of virtue to protect the nation. Unfortunately, in the process they lost sight of the fact that Jews are not a virus, but human beings."

George tried to picture how Christian churches in Germany could have gone along with such an odious idea. Then he remembered how many Christians in the United States supported abortion.

"That makes sense," Peter said. "The more I studied mom's letters and diaries, the more I saw direct comparisons between mom's logic, and what you're saying."

"How so?"

"For example, the Nazis said that Jews weren't human, and mom said that fetuses weren't human — just blobs of uterine tissue."

Kip spoke up. "Consider the fact that Hitler wanted Jews dead because they stood in the way of his goal of creating a master race. Then, consider the fact that the abortion movement wanted African American babies dead for the same reason."

"Because they stood in the way of their goal to create a master race," George said. "Amazing the devilish parallels."

"Later on, they both expanded their murders to include killing any life they decided wasn't pure enough," Kip added.

"For the Nazies that included Russian civilians, Poles, disabled people, homosexuals, Serbs, Freemasons, and Romani."

Peter broke in. "Mom's group expanded their scope to include Hispanics, Asians, American Indian, Pacific Islander, Native Alaskan,[1] and any unborn they consider a potential liability to the state, racially tainted, or babies who might possibly be born physically or mentally challenged. She even wrote that American women had the obligation to kill their unborn if they might grow up to become a useless burden upon the taxpayers."

"That's pretty hard core," George said.

"More like hideous. But it goes on. Mom blamed the unborn for America's political and social problems, just like the Nazis blamed the Jews for Germany's political and social problems."

"Seriously?" George asked.

Kip explained. "The Nazis believed that unless the population was purified and controlled it would lead to national financial burdens, food shortages, and widespread poverty."

"Mom wanted abortions for exactly the same reasons, and a few others," Peter said. "She wrote that unless the preborn were killed, they would also place a disproportional burden on energy resources, environmental needs, and the global climate."

"How in heaven's name is your mom's group able to convince people to support this kind of lunacy?" George asked.

Peter scratched his jaw thoughtfully. "It's not done in heavens name. It's done in the name of money and power. Mom's organization uses baseless fear to terrorize women into thinking their world will come apart unless they kill their babies. Then, religious institutions like the First Establishment Church give them a moral justification for their actions, our country's laws protect them, and society rewards them with a diabolical sense of achievement."

Kip reached over and took a drink of spring water before speaking. "In the case of the Nazis, they were able to get the German High Court to legalize the killing of Jews under the authority of German law.[2] Lilith's friends did the same thing by convincing the U.S. Supreme Court to legalize the murder of the preborn in neighborhood extermination camps."

"With the power and authority of the Federal Government, behind them, nobody can stop my mom's organization," Peter added.

"No wonder our country is messed up," George said.

"That's a fact," Kip agreed. "In just four years the Nazies were able to legally kill over six million Jews. So far, thanks to the perverted laws of our insane courts, Lilith's group has been able to legally slaughter over sixty-million unborn babies."

"All because they think they are doing good, by doing evil," Peter said.

"Yep," Kip acknowledged. He pulled back, took a powerful swing, and smashed the ball so hard the cover came off.

That evening they met in the ship's dining room where they continued their conversation over a rack of lamb, and a couple of bottles of vintage Pinot Noir.

"Leave room for dessert," Peter said. "The pastry chef has prepared your choice of dark chocolate cake with raspberry coulee, an apple crumble with creme anglaise, or banana spring rolls with Nougat ice cream."

"You had me at the apple crumble," George said, smacking his lips.

"I'm having a great time with you guys," Kip said. "But why did you call this meeting George?"

"I want Peter's help."

"I'm all ears," Peter replied.

"I want to take down SNUF."

There was silence around the table. Peter took a sip of wine and dabbed his lips with a napkin. "Funny you should say that. I was thinking the same thing."

"I'm in," Kip said, without hesitation. "Let's take 'em out. How?"

Peter generated a sly grin. "The first thing you need to understand is that there is no need for violence. Operations like this are no longer done with bullets, bombs, knives or guns. They're done with a cup of coffee, and the stroke of a keyboard."

"I'm already lost," George said.

"We use coding, scripting, DOS and DDOS attacks, algorithms, programs, and malware viruses to shut them down in ways that the average person doesn't even know exist."

"Yeah, I'm one of them," George laughed. "I have no idea what you're talking about."

"You don't need to," Peter said. "Trust me, I've got enough computer brainiacs on this ship to take down a small nation. A couple of false prophets running a murder syndicate won't be a problem."

"I don't know," Kip said, chuckling. "It never hurts to use a little plastic explosive."

"I FEEL YOU," PETER SAID. "NEVERTHELESS, THE OLD WAYS are too messy and complicated for a takedown like this. By using computers we can rip the guts out of them without ever having to leave the air conditioned comfort of this ship."

He motioned to the steward. A second later he was handed a number two yellow pencil and a note pad. He began doodling. "It's time to organize."

Another steward came and placed desserts on the table. George and Kip savored their delicacy, and watched Peter go to work.

"First we need to name the project," he said, his eyes intent on the paper.

"Something cool and mysterious," Kip offered.

Over spoonfuls of dessert, they discussed titles like vindicators, protectors, shadows, sentinels, defiants, liberators, privateers, and crusaders.

"How about Vengeance?" Kip asked, placing his fork down. "It's from the Bible. 'Take courage, fear not. Behold, your God will come with vengeance; the recompense of God will come, and he will save you.'"[3]

"Let's go with it," George replied, enthusiastically.

Peter agreed.

"Okay, what's next?" Kip asked.

"First we hack into each of the executive council's personal computers and see what they're up to," Peter said.

"What do you mean?"

"Let's see if they have any child porn, sexually explicit photos, racist emails, stuff like that. We'll look at their tax returns, bank accounts, and any dodgy offshore investments that might interest the IRS. I have friends working in the dark web who will be more than happy to anonymously post anything we find where the world can see it."

George grinned at the thought. "Is this legal?"

Peter gave him the side-eye. "Would you break the speed limit in order to save someone's life?"

"In a hot minute," Kip said.

"We may have to break a few laws, but no one will ever know it was us."

"Not even the government?"

"Whose company do you think trains the government?" Peter asked, eyes twinkling. "Besides, we're not going to hurt anyone. We'll simply unmask them. If they have any sordid affairs we'll let the court of public opinion decide. If we find anything illegal, we'll quietly slip it to law enforcement."

"Then what," Kip asked.

Peter took a bite of cake and savored it before speaking. "After we've raked through their private computers, we'll go after their business computers. I'm especially interested in seeing what the Judge is doing with his pharmaceutical company. I think Shantel Yin is on to something."

"Yeah, who would have guessed she's a Special Agent. I almost fell over when she handed me her card."

George pulled it out of his pocket and held it up like a trophy. Peter could see the big gold shield embossed on the front from across the table.

CHAPTER 10
VENGEANCE

Peter's technicians went to work, and within a week they hacked all of the personal and corporate computers of the executive council. Using backdoor codes, open wifi, phishing emails, and a variety of secret techniques, they were able to gain remote access to their home wifi, hard drives, and mobile devices.

Once they were in, proprietary algorithms went to work, and sifted through mountains of data to find the most incriminating and illegal evidence.

It wasn't long before each member of the council received a text message:

We've been watching you. We've accessed your computer and know all of your dirty little secrets. Shut down SNUF, or you will be punished. — Vengeance

An urgent meeting was called to discuss the situation.

"Who in the hell is Vengeance?" the General bellowed.

"The room was silent."

"Did everyone get a text?" the Doctor asked.

They all nodded.

Von Heekate spoke up. "This is crap! I'm proud of what we do for women. This kind of harassment only reinforces my commitment to fight against these meddling terrorists."

"The text says we'll be punished," the Doctor said, holding his phone. "Punished for what?"

"We're not doing anything illegal," the Judge roared. "We're helping people. This is a blasted joke."

"Well I'm not laughing," Pendragon said.

"Neither am I," Guile agreed.

"Is there anyway to text them back?"

"I tried, but the number is dead," Von Heekate said. "It's probably a pay-as-you-go phone. We'll never trace who sent the message. Besides, if they've already hacked our computers there's not much we can do."

"Why are we worried?" the Professor asked. "SNUF is legal, our corporations are legal, the clinics are legal."

The Doctor leveled his voice at the Professor. "We're worried that they will find evidence connecting us to the sale of fetal tissue. It's against Federal law."

Von Heekate groaned loudly. "Don't make me laugh, the Feds have never enforced those laws."

"And they never will," the General said. "It's not in their best interest. After all, the Federal Government is one of our best customers."[1]

"Who cares? We control the public's opinion on women's healthcare. We own the politicians who make the laws. We manipulate the justice system, and the courts," the Doctor said.

The Judge nodded with a grin. "There's not a judge alive

willing to rule against abortion, no matter what case is brought before them."

"Fact is," Guile said, "as long as we aren't stupid and we keep making money from our inflated shipping charges, the Feds won't have any evidence that we've committed a crime. Therefore — no prosecution."

"We've got to find out who's behind this," Von Heekate fumed.

"It's probably just one of our competitors trying to scare us," the Judge said. "They've been trying to expand into our territory for years. I say we ignore them."

Out of the blue, Pendragon asked, "How about George Goodman? I wouldn't put it past him."

"George is an idiot" Guile hissed. "He doesn't know anything about computers."

"You don't have to know anything to send a text," Von Heekate retorted.

"I agree with Pastor Guile," the General said. "George may act like a tough guy, but he's just a lazy golf bum. I saw lots of guys like him in my career. Besides, he doesn't know we've been harassing him."

The group quickly agreed that George wasn't the source of the threat.

"Don't panic, what can Vengeance do?" Pendragon asked. "They can't shut down a billion dollar business with threats. Our friends in likeminded churches will join us in unity to support the sacred work of SNUF. Together we will weather this storm with the help of God."

Help from God was not forthcoming.

Soon the members received another text:

We gave you a warning. You've got 24 hours to shut down SNUF! — Vengeance

"What's with all the drama?" the General howled, pacing back and forth.

"They're enjoying their little game of scaring us," Guile remarked.

"They are doing a good job," Pendragon moaned.

"Don't they realize people depend on us for a living?" the Doctor bawled.

"Not to mention the millions of women who rely on us for help," the Professor said.

"They're an inhuman bunch of fascists," Von Heekate barked, fiercely. "They want to crush a woman's right to her own reproductive control."

"We're not shutting anything down," the General declared. "The Sacred Name Unity Fund is doing God's work, and we won't let these petty tyrants keep us from it."

"Amen brother," Pendragon said. "And may the Lord be with us."

THE LORD WAS NOT WITH THEM.

Twenty-four hours later, at exactly 1300 EST, the computers in all SNUF clinics world-wide experienced a malware attack that deleted every file, scrambled every password, and locked every computer. The following message was left on every screen:

To all employees: Effective immediately this clinic is closed. Your services are no longer required. — Management.

Pandemonium ensued as clinic managers scurried to seek

advice and direction. All scheduled appointments were cancelled by phone. Women who showed up for an appointment were turned away. All contacts, financial information, clinic data, and operating budgets disappeared forever into the hard drives of Vengeance. By the next day, the centers were empty.

"Bastards!" the General shouted. "I'll kill every one of them."

"It would help to know who they are first," Von Heekate said, condescendingly.

The Professor raised his hand. "I phoned the FBI to ask them to get to the bottom of this. They'll find out who Vengeance is."

The room went silent. All eyes turned to the Professor.

"Are you crazy?" the Judge yelled, his face turning blood red. "You moron! Have you forgotten about the pharmaceutical company?"

"What about it?"

The members of the council looked at each another in astonishment.

"You're a complete imbecile Professor," Von Heekate said. "Here's a hint — the Judge's company produces more than just day-after pills."

The Professor immediately realized his mistake, and he turned as pale as a ghost.

"I'd rather deal with Vengeance than a Mexican Cartel, you fool," she shouted.

"Maybe the FBI will forget the call," the Doctor said, hopefully.

"Let's keep our fingers crossed," the Professor mumbled.

"Shut up!" the others shouted at him in unison.

CHAPTER 11
TAKE DOWN

It was a nippy morning, on the edge of a frost. The trees lining the street in front of the General's house were bare. Their golden yellow leaves had been swept into neat little piles by waiting gardeners the moment they fluttered to the ground.

The General stood waiting for his limousine, checking his cell phone for messages. He was dressed in a long beige coat made of cashmere, black polished loafers, Tartan neck scarf, and a gray Homburg.

He was anxious to get to the church where the council was meeting for the third time to decide how to reopen the clinics. Without any computer data, they had no access to the day to day operating programs and systems that had been designed to run things. It was as if SNUF had been lobotomized.

Every effort to restart the clinics had failed. It would take years, if not decades to rebuild SNUF from scratch.

A silver town car pulled up to the curb to collect him. Behind it, a black SUV with darkened windows followed. Three men got out of the SUV.

"General?"

"Yes, I'm in a hurry, what can I do for you?" the General asked, opening the door to the town car.

"I'm Special Agent Haack," the man said, holding up a gold badge.

The General shot Haack a perturbed glance, then looked at the other two.

"Who are these men?"

"They're from the Army Criminal Investigation Command, and the Defense Criminal Investigative Service."

"What do you want?"

"You've been charged with conduct unbecoming of an officer, accepting gifts and bribes, conspiracy, wire fraud, and substantial allegations of misconduct while on active duty."

The General scoffed. "You have no authority to arrest me, I'm retired."

"Wrong sir. The United States Supreme Court has upheld the decision that retirees are still liable for crimes committed while in uniform."

"I don't know what you're talking about. I served my country honorably."

"Sir, we've been sent evidence that shows you accepted numerous luxury gifts, kick backs, sexual favors, and bribes from various contractors when you were in uniform. We have received copies of your bank statements, and have obtained emails from an anonymous source that show your part in the fraud which lasted nearly a decade."

"This is outrageous! I'm innocent of any wrong doing."

Suddenly, General Warlocke's mouth went slack, his eyes rolled back, and he started to collapse. Agent Haack had seen this kind of response from guilty Generals many times before. He and his associates were ready to catch the disgraced man before he reached the ground.

They stuffed the ailing General into the back of their SUV, where he was driven to the closest medical center in shackles.

THE DOCTOR PUSHED OPEN THE GLASS DOOR OF THE FEES and Fines National Bank with the personal satisfaction that comes from making a large deposit. He was joined by his grown daughter.

"I can't wait to get to the cabin, dad. It will be great to celebrate Thanksgiving in the mountains. We haven't been on a family vacation in years. It will give us all some quality time."

"I think my grandchildren deserve the very best," he said. "They can go skiing, build a snow man, roast hot dogs, go sledding — it'll be fun."

She grinned. "With you and mom watching the kids, Ken and I can have a few moments of peace."

From out of nowhere a tall man wearing dark sunglasses and a black baseball cap, approached them. "Excuse me ma'am, I'm Special Agent Bussey."

He held up his badge. "I'm afraid you're going to have to wait to go on your vacation. Right now the only vacation your father is going to take is to Federal prison. Of course, you're welcome to come visit him at our exclusive resort any time you want."

"What's the meaning of this?" the Doctor stammered. He reached for his cell phone. "I'm calling the police."

Agent Bussey snatched it from the doctor's hand. "You're under arrest for conspiracy to distribute controlled substances, illegal drug prescriptions of narcotics, and failure to exercise reasonable care in the treatment of your patients."

"What are you talking about?"

"We've been sent copies of your personal and corporate computer files, along with private emails that clearly implicate your involvement in illegal activities taking place in the women's health clinics under your management."

"I've done nothing of the sort."

"What is he talking about, dad?"

"Would you like me to explain everything in front of your daughter, sir?" Agent Bussey asked.

The doctor stood frozen, as if he had turned to stone, making it easier for the Agent to snap a set of handcuffs on him.

THE PROFESSOR HAD JUST FINISHED HIS REAL ESTATE CLASS on flipping houses when one of his student's approached him.

"Have you seen this?" she asked, holding up her smart phone.

Setting his papers down, he adjusted his glasses and held the screen close. Immediately the color disappeared from his cheeks. He felt woozy. She steadied him.

Someone had posted a record of all his unpaid gambling debts amounting to over $350,000 dollars. Dates, times and the persons he owed were included.

"I thought you might want to know," she said. "The entire thing was posted on the school's website."

After thanking her, the Professor went to the men's room, and threw up in the toilet.

Then, he ran.

SPECIAL AGENT SHANTEL YIN RAISED A PAIR OF HIGH powered binoculars to her eyes. In the distance she watched an eighteen wheeler head across the desert towards a border checkpoint. She could see the words Bumble's Furniture painted in bold red letters on the trailer from over a mile away.

She knew the vehicle had crossed into Mexico two days before, and that the truck was headed back to the United States with a load of used furniture.

The driver of the truck was an undercover Special Agent who'd volunteered to make the trip. In a few minutes he would pretend that he had no idea that Special Agent Yin and her team were waiting for him.

Pulling into the checkpoint he was waved to a separate inspection area where a nonintrusive imaging machine took x-rays of his cargo. Becky, a drug sniffing K-9, assisted in the search. An hour later, six million dollars worth of meth, heroin and fentanyl was discovered hidden in hollowed out pieces of used furniture.

The driver acted shocked when Special Agent Yin told him that the Mexican National Guard had observed the entire smuggling operation from the time he dropped off his load at the Judge's pharmaceutical company, to when he loaded up their used furniture.

He screamed his innocence in two different languages when she shoved him into the back of a squad car. They both knew that when word reached the Cartel of his loyalty, his prison creds would be set.

A THOUSAND MILES AWAY, THE JUDGE RECESSED HIS COURT for lunch. He was anxious to meet some old friends at his favorite restaurant. Hanging his black robe on a wooden peg he asked his judicial assistant, "Anything more before I leave?"

"One thing your honor, Sheriff Corey is here to see you."

The Judge shrugged. "Probably related to the Smith case, send him in."

"Morning your honor."

"Morning Sheriff, I've only got a few minutes. Whose your friend?"

"This is Special Agent Chace."

"Is this about the Smith case?"

"Actually it's about drug trafficking," Chace said.

"I don't hear drug trafficking cases."

"You'll want to hear this," Chace assured him. "I'm part of an international drug task force that has been monitoring the activities at your pharmaceutical company in Mexico.

"We were sent evidence from an anonymous source that shows you have been producing illegal drugs for the Cartel. Joined by the Mexican National Guard, we surveilled your operations and watched your workers load numerous pieces of furniture into a Bumble's semi-truck.

"We stopped that truck at the border, and discovered the furniture was full of illegal drugs manufactured at your facility."

The Judge's lips curled into a scowl. "What are you talking about?"

"I'm arresting you, along with a list of others, for your role the production, distribution, trafficking, and sale of unlawful narcotics."

The Judge roared. "I'm a sworn deputy of the court. You have no authority over me."

Agent Chace yawned in the Judge's face. "Don't worry, sir. You'll be able to tell your story to a judge."

MILLIE MOCKINGBIRD LIVED FOR DAYS LIKE THIS. SHE couldn't phone the woman on her prayer team fast enough.

"Go to the church's website before they take it down. I've never seen anything like it before in my life."

The church website had been hacked, and in place of the weekly activities there was an advertisement for a rawboned woman leaning against a horse corral.

Her face was partially covered by a red bandana. She was dressed in a lacy red thong, a low cut racy red bra, leather cowboy chaps, a pink vest with fringe, black knee high stiletto boots, and a white Stetson cowboy hat. In one hand she held a bull whip.

The copy under the picture promised an intimate time of roping, tying, pole bending, and bronc riding. There was a phone number, and a phony name — Shiloh.

Even disguised in a flowing red wig and a red bandana, it was easy to recognize the protruding ears, leathery body, and the little pentagram tattooed on her wrist as belonging to Mrs. Von Heekate.

After a quick consultation, the managing editors of Von Heekate's newspapers decided that it was not in the public's best interest to learn all the details of their boss's indiscretion.

They buried the lede in a two inch column on the bottom right hand corner of page thirty in the Saturday edition. Reporters from her television stations were privately warned that their careers might be ruined if they showed up on her doorstep with their cameras and questions.

Summer Beltane was smart enough not to extend an invitation for Von Heekate to come on the show and tell her side of the story.

CHAPTER 12
THE WOLVES

"Stop worrying. We've done nothing illegal," Guile said. "We're only spiritual advisors to the board. Most importantly our names aren't connected to the corporations. Go home and get some rest. You're preaching tomorrow."

"Why shouldn't I worry?" Pendragon sulked. "They've arrested everyone on the council, and the Professor's disappeared — probably dead for all we know."

"Then get in the pulpit and place the blame where it belongs. Tell the congregation how surprised we are over this terrible situation. Tell them that we're removing everyone from the executive council. Let them know that we're as shocked as they are. Deny any knowledge of illegal activities."

Pendragon did as he was told, and used Psalm 55:12-14[1] to preach a heartbreaking sermon of betrayal and hurt by people he trusted. The congregation was moved by Pendragon's sincerity, and grieved because of the emotional pain that he and Guile felt.

After worship, the congregation gathered in the Great

The Redemption of George | 291

Hall for refreshments, and to gossip about the astonishing revelations that had come to light. There was much speculation on what had happened to the Professor.

"I was shocked to see those pictures of Mrs. Von Heekate," Guile said, from his wheelchair. "Who would have thought she was leading a double life?"

"She sure fooled me," Hal Hanks said, innocently. Although he was secretly worried if Von Heekate would keep the names of her clients confidential.

During the next hour, over strawberry mimosas and finger food, the congregation pondered the innocence or guilt of each member of the council.

"It just shows that you can never know the heart of a person," Mrs. Buttinsky said, popping a cheese puff in her mouth.

"So true," Pendragon solemnly agreed. "As Jeremiah wrote, 'The heart is deceitful above all things, and desperately wicked. Who can know it?'"

"Yes my dear friends," Guile warned. "That's why we must always be on the lookout for wolves slipping in among the sheep."

Neither Guile or Pendragon saw the wolves in black business suits slip in among the sheep until they were surrounded. Pendragon turned to one with a smile. "May I help you?"

A badge was flashed in his face. "I'm Detective Spahn, these are my partners Detectives McGriff and Ramsey. We'd like to have a word with you."

"What for?" Pendragon asked — startled.

Spahn held up a search warrant. "This morning we executed a search of your property based on expository information we received from an anonymous tip."

He showed Pendragon a thumb drive.

"We conducted a search of your computer and found hundreds of pictures and videos that allegedly show you participating in erotic rituals involving underage children."

"It's not what it looks like," Pendragon stammered. "I've done absolutely nothing wrong. Those pictures were taken at various religious fertility ceremonies that have been carried out for thousands of years. It was fully consensual, and no harm was done to the children."

"Well Pastor, in this country it's against the law to participate in erotic religious rituals with children, much less possess pictures of them.

"I'm placing you under arrest for suspicion of the sexual exploitation of children, possession of child pornography, and engaging in travel to foreign countries to engage in illicit sexual conduct with a child. Place your hands behind your back."

Pendragon quietly did as he was told, and immediately started talking. "I'm not the only one," he blubbered. "There are hundreds of others — prominent people — you've heard of them. I'll give you their names in exchange for immunity."

"What about the places they meet?" Detective Spahn asked.

"Sure, sure," Pendragon said. "Some of the places are in Europe, others are in private resorts, and some are in exclusive clubs here in the US. I can give you a list of all of them. Please don't send me to prison, I won't survive in prison."

Detective Spahn's phone buzzed. "Yes sir?"

"Have you taken Pendragon into custody?"

"He's standing right in front of me — he wants a plea deal. Says he'll swap us the names of his elite pervs for immunity."

"Bring him to me. I want to hear what he has to say."

Spahn ringed off. "That was the DA, he wants to hear what you've got to say."

"The DA?"

"One and the same."

Pendragon smiled broadly. "Mother of earth. We're old friends. He'll understand."

DETECTIVE SPAHN TOOK PENDRAGON INTO CUSTODY, AND walked him out of the Great Hall before a crowd of stunned people. Guile watched in horror as his protégé was led away in cuffs. He decided it was time to make his exit. As he began rolling his wheelchair towards the door, he was abruptly halted.

"Where are you going Pastor? The name is Detective Cruz." He leaned down and flashed his badge in the old man's face. "I'm arresting you on suspicion of embezzling the First Establishment Church Fund."

"That's preposterous," Guile sneered.

Cruz held up a search warrant. "We conducted a search of your house this morning, and discovered financial documents on your computer that show how you systematical looted, and drained the Church Fund over the past ten years."

Guile objected. "Someone planted them there. I'm a man of God, devoted to the care of my flock."

Detective Cruz was unmoved. "I have to admit that your little scheme was nearly flawless. If it weren't for a tip from someone called Vengeance, we never would have caught on to your little fraud."

"Vengeance!" Guile sputtered. His eyes went wild, and he suddenly clutched his chest, gasping for air. He slid out of the wheelchair and collapsed to the floor. "Save me, save meh, sav…," he mumbled.

Cruz watched the old man struggle for a moment before he calmly spoke into his walkie-talkie. A few minutes later the unconscious pastor was loaded into an ambulance where he was whisked to a private hospital.

Pastor Guile was jolted awake by a symphony of noises.

He heard the squeaking wheels of a cart being pushed by. The rhythmic ping of a nearby monitor. The rustle of bed sheets. The whoosh of an air duct. Someone flushing a toilet. A television playing the Summer Beltane show. A woman groaning somewhere nearby.

He tried to move but he was paralyzed, or maybe drugged. He wasn't certain. He felt loopy, sedated. He fought to open his eyes, but his lids were shut tight, as if they were taped down. He felt like he was naked, lying in a warm bed, soaking in the deep warmth of heavy blankets.

I'm in a hospital. I'm alive. Thank you great spirit.

He breathed a sigh of relief, and listened to voices speaking about their plans for the weekend. He heard them discuss politics, sports, flings, and affairs. They came and went from his bedside talking in whispers, adjusting his covers and touching his body.

"I need to replace the patient's electrode," a man's voice said. Guile felt a blanket being pulled back from his chest.

"What's this?" the man asked. "It looks like a tattoo on his left pectoral."

"Let me see," a woman's voice replied. Her fingers began exploring the skin. "It's faded over the years but it looks like a miniature star."

"It's a pentagram," the man said. "Probably the symbol of his faith."

The sound of a medical cart clattering past in the hallway broke the stillness.

"Then he should be happy to make this sacrifice," the woman's voice remarked.

Sacrifice — what sacrifice? Guile wanted to speak but he couldn't.

"We've got to move him into surgery, or we'll miss our window of opportunity," the man urged.

"Has all the paperwork been signed?" someone asked.

"Yes, we've been authorized to take whatever we need."

Confused, Guile tried to raise an arm, but he couldn't. *I didn't authorize anything, what are you talking about?*

"He's had a stroke," the man's voice said, flatly. "We're actually doing him a favor to euthanize him. He'd be incapacitated for the rest of his life, and a burden to his family."

"It will also save the taxpayers from having to pay for his ongoing medical care," the woman confided.

"The next hour will be critical," another voice injected. "If we're going to have any luck harvesting Mister X's organs he needs to be prepped right now."

"Gawd almighty! I can hear you people. I'm right here. I'm alive. I'm Pastor Guile.

It dawned on him that they couldn't hear his protests, that he was only speaking to himself. He tried to get their attention. He attempted to wiggle his fingers, nothing. He tried kicking his legs, helpless. He struggled to move his toes, useless. He was hopelessly glued to the bed, incapable of movement.

"There are still lots of parts we can salvage off the guy," the woman said. "He may be elderly, but there's still plenty of things we can sell."

"I'm especially interested in seeing his kidneys and liver," the man said. "We should be able to get at least seventy-five grand for them."

"I can get $150,000 for his lungs," another voice promised. "He didn't smoke did he?"

Guile heard someone take the aluminum chart off the foot of his bed. "No history of smoking or drinking," a woman replied."

"Perfect," the man said. "I've got a hospital in Atlanta that will take them both."

"The market is growing for these old codgers," the woman mentioned. "A memo came down saying there's a research lab up in Canada willing to pay twenty grand for his eyes."

"We need to harvest his critical organs right now," the man said. "They have to be fresh. We can store the corneas, skin, tendons, ligaments, and cartilage for use later."

"Someone call the transport company," the woman ordered.

"I already did," a younger voice replied. "They'll be here in a few minutes."

"Good," the man said. "I want his organs on ice, packed up, and shipped as soon as possible."

Guile thought he was going insane. *I'm alive! Don't you know I'm alive! I'm not old. You monsters can't tear me into pieces.*

He felt a needle stick in his arm followed by the cold rush of drugs flowing through his body. He started getting drowsy.

"Not too much of that stuff," the man ordered. "I don't want any complications."

"Alright doctor, I'll just sedate him, and keep him in twilight sleep."

The Redemption of George | 297

Guile felt his bed being wheeled out of the warm room into the cold hallway. Shadows of light passed overhead as he was rolled into the operating room. He was hoisted onto a frigid metal table, placed on his back, and preparations were made.

He felt something like a finger moving around his chest and abdomen. Horrified, he realized that someone was drawing on him, marking out surgical cut-lines.

"We'll take his brain last," the man's voice said.

Dear gawd, no! This is murder! You have no right!

Throughout the procedure Pastor Guile was completely aware as every piece was removed from his body. He wept without a sound as the scalpel sliced pieces of his body away. He screamed in silence as his organs were cut out. He shrieked mutely when they took his eyeballs. He cried in pain with each bloody amputation and dissection.

But there was nothing he could do, and even though he raged for mercy, it was only in the chamber of his own mind. The doctors and nurses couldn't hear him. They didn't want to. He had no value to them as a person. He was worth far more to them in pieces.

"Now for the piece de resistance," the man said, in a fake French accent. "Voila! We shall now remove his brain."

One of the last things that Pastor Guile heard in this life was the squeak of the operating room door as it opened, followed by footsteps walking across the floor.

"You're here just in time," the man's voice grunted. "Did you come from the transport company?"

He momentarily stopped what he was doing and his mouth dropped open under his surgical mask. Standing before him was the most perfect woman he had ever imagined. She was flawless, more woman than a woman — an artist's rendering of the feminine ideal. Every feature was idealized to perfect proportions. Her skin was luminescent, without blemish, or wrinkle. Her hair was the color of shimmering silver, styled in a pixie cut. Twin cobalt-blue eyes sparkled with the intensity of a thousand stars.

"Yes, doctor. My name is Eva. I am here for Mister X."

CHAPTER 13
AFTER ACTION REVIEW

The weather was dismally cold. A thick, drippy, early morning fog covered the spires of the First Establishment Church. George leaned against the rail of the *Sotirios* cradling a cup of scalding coffee, and listening to the periodic signals of the harbor's fog horn.

He was dressed in a heavy wool peacoat, fleece lined pants, black Irish flat cap, and insulated boots. The *Sotirios* was taking on supplies, and having some light maintenance performed. He watched as the workers use forklifts, dollies, and pure muscle to load food and equipment onboard. He wondered what new crisis the day would bring.

He missed Sarah. The only thing that brought a smile to his face was knowing that the members of executive council had troubles far greater than his own.

Peter stuck his head out the dining room's door. "George, come in here. Your breakfast is getting cold."

"It's absolutely delicious," Alisha yelled from the table.

George came inside, shed his coat, and sat down. The steward placed a large portion of scrambled eggs, hash browns, and bacon on his plate.

"I want to discuss our first mission as Vengeance," Peter said.

"SNUF's history," Kip quipped, tucking into his food. "We took out its leaders, disrupted its supply lines and dismantled its communication systems."

"All without ever having to leave the comfort of this boat," Peter boasted. "Amazing what the power of a hacker with a computer can accomplish."

Alisha played with her food. "True, but SNUF isn't the only abortion mill in America. Other monsters are still out there killing the pre-born. The law supports them, doctors make fortunes from them, and churches empower them."

"What kind of a church would sanction the massacre of babies?" Peter asked.

George looked up from his plate. "A hellish one."

"They mock the sanctity of life," Kip observed.

"I thought Jesus was the life,'" Alisha stated.

"Precisely," Kip responded. "They praise him with their mouths, but kill him with their actions."

"I realize that mothers need and deserve our support," Alisha said. "But the baby has a God-given right to life."

"We'll get the rest of the abortion mills," George pledged. "It's just a matter of time." He took a bite of food and chewed slowly.

Peter placed his fork down, and looked at George. "Have you taken a look at the stock market this morning? Bumble's is going crazy."

"I haven't gotten around to it," George admitted.

"People are buying the stock in small lots. Nothing institutional, just average folks purchasing a couple hundred shares, driving the price up. It's like every grandma in America broke her piggy bank to help you."

"Here's another thing," Kip added. "My K-9 teams found

the person who killed Cookie. It was that female cop who tried to shoot me at Lilith's service."

"How'd you figure that out?"

"It was the rope she used to kill Cookie."

"The rope?"

"She was a climbing enthusiast. Long story short, we were able to get some DNA from a strand of hair on the rope. Thanks to Peter's help we ran it through an international data base and her name popped up. Turns out she had to submit her DNA for the police job. Anyway, we traced her credit card purchases to one of the sport stores in the area. CCTV showed her buying the rope the day before. It was all the proof we needed."

"Then what??"

"We confronted her very politely."

George knew what the word "politely" meant in Kip's world.

"She confessed, and gave us Officer Smith and a couple of his buddies as her accomplices. Their careers are toast, maybe some jail time. While we questioned her, she also gave us a lead on the person who burned down Welma's house. I promise, we're going to get whoever killed her."

George cracked a smile. "I don't know how to say thanks."

"That smile on your face is all the thanks I need," Kip replied.

"It's good to see you smile," Alisha said, reaching over and patting his arm. "We know it's been tough on you with Sarah gone."

George lowered his eyes. "It'll work out, one way or another. I keep saying my prayers, hoping she'll come to her senses."

"Don't give up," Alisha encouraged.

"In other news," Peter exclaimed, changing the subject. "Letting Shantel Yin use your furniture truck was genius. That was the last nail in SNUF's coffin."

"Why did they locate the pharmaceutical company in Mexico," Alisha asked.

"So it wouldn't come under the jurisdiction of the FDA," George answered. "Who knows what kind of impure medicines they were giving the girls who came into their clinics? Shantel told me that a forensic drug analysis showed that the meds they produced contained contaminates that might have killed some of the girls."

Alisha winced.

"Same with the meth and heroin they were selling to the Cartel," Kip added. "Apparently it was so laced with fentanyl that one dose could kill the average person."

"Which explains the national epidemic of overdose deaths," Peter remarked.

"What about the workers at the church who will lose their job now that Guile stole the money," Alisha said.

"I've offered them employment at one of my hotels, or other companies," Peter replied.

"That's sweet of you," Alisha said.

"Least I could do. Guile's embezzlement wasn't their fault."

"With the theft of the fund, how will the church meet its overhead?" Kip asked. "It costs millions for payroll, insurance, utilities, maintenance, and upkeep on the buildings. Two hundred people can't afford that by themselves."

"Maybe they'll learn how to sacrifice like good Christians should," George mused.

"The wealthy never sacrifice," Peter said, wryly. "They'll leave and go over to First Establishment Church in Cozyville where they can socialize in style with other people like themselves."

"You think that the First Establishment Church in Abundance Falls will close down?"

"Most likely," Peter said.

Kip speared a couple of breakfast sausages. "Maybe you should buy the property and turn it into another one of your hotels."

George's eyes lit up. "Yeah, you could transform the sanctuary into a trendy restaurant with a micro brewery, and a bar up in the choir loft."

"Don't be profane," Alisha scolded. "If Peter buys the property the sanctuary should remain a sacred place for people to gather."

"Restaurants are sacred," George complained. "More people have probably been saved in the fellowship of a coffee shop than in a church."

"Hang on you two," Peter injected. "The First Establishment Church isn't up for sale."

"Yet," George quipped. "I'm just planning ahead."

Suddenly, something caught the corner of Alisha's eye. She pointed out the window. "Look over there. It's snowing!"

"Unbelievable," Peter muttered. "It never snows this time of year. Must be a sign from God."

"Don't know about that," George hooted. "But it's definitely a sign they'll have to cancel the golf tournament."

"I hate to say it, but I told you it would snow." Kip pushed his chair from the table, and took a modest bow. His face crinkled into a wide grin.

"So what are you going to do now, George?" Alisha asked.

George thought for a moment before speaking. "Do? I know exactly what I'll do."

CHAPTER 14
TWO YEARS LATER

The Caspar Observatory sat on the highest peak of the San Domenico Mountain range in the solitude of the Sabulous Wilderness area.

George lived in a one bedroom trailer near the base of the mountain in a mobile housing camp populated by the scientists and workers of the facility. It hadn't been easy to downsize into the small container, but he'd managed to bring the most important things in his life like his vinyl record collection, some family pictures, and a new dog.

He'd made friends, learned to play the ukulele, exercised, lost weight, and mastered the game of gin rummy. His hair was longer, his beard was full, and the angry red scar had faded under the harsh sun, and gritty arid winds.

When he wasn't working George liked to sit on his small porch listening to the sound of the wind, and think about his family. Sometimes he would watch the wildlife with a pair of binoculars, or amuse himself by observing the occasional car slowly navigate the narrow road that snaked its way up to the camp from the valley below.

At night George was never disappointed when the sky

turned into a profusion of heavenly bodies visible to the naked eye, all seemingly close enough to touch.

Although scientists are not known for their religious faith, on Sundays a few gathered with George to pray, sing hymns, and have a barbecue. He'd grown closer to God since he'd come to the mountain, and except for the fact that Sarah still didn't answer his emails, his life was at peace, the air was pure, his thoughts were clear, and he had no regrets.

IN THE ABSENCE OF GEORGE, SARAH RETURNED TO HER OLD ways, taking comfort in her wealth and the council of her friends.

For a long time she told them that George had stormed out of the house, drunk. She made it sound as if he'd picked the fight that had ruined their relationship. She painted herself as the doting wife who'd sacrificed, and suffered to help her troubled husband deal with the PTSDemons he'd gotten in the Army. She claimed her children were deeply disappointed with their father, even though that was not the case.

One day she confided to her friend, Erica. "Pastor Pendragon was right. He said that George was having a nervous breakdown, what else would explain it?"

"Poor man."

"Poor man nothing," Sarah snapped. "George doesn't deserve any sympathy."

"I'm not speaking about George," Erica said. "I'm speaking about Pastor Pendragon. I still can't believe they accused him of being a pedophile. He was such a nice person. His sermons used to make me happy."

. . .

In time, the church became an unbearable trial for Sarah. Little comments, snide remarks, and subtle rebukes became the price of attendance.

"You're blessed to be rid of him," Jackie assured her.

"I knew he was a loser," Margi comforted her.

"You don't need his abuse," Linda sympathized.

"Grab the business, the house, the bank account, and get a divorce," Pamala advised.

Sympathy calls and tenderness texts from her girl friends eventually stopped. Hal Hanks hit on her with a not so subtle suggestion that made her want to vomit.

With each passing month it became clear that George wasn't coming home to grovel. Sarah's spies reported that he'd quit Bumbles', enrolled in college, graduated with a Masters, gotten a job, and moved away.

It took her a full bottle of wine the night she finally realized that he'd left her behind. At first she was shocked, then angry, then hurt, then resentful. In time, her heart turned to poison.

With the church funds stolen, the money to hire a celebrity pastor, or pay for free social activities vanished. The denomination sent a few interim pastors to fill the gap, but the congregation decided they couldn't compare to Pendragon. People were disappearing, and the attendance was slipping.

She often thought about her fight with George. She knew she'd been rough on him, but she was convinced he deserved it. The man had threatened everything they'd worked for.

He'd offended her friends. He'd insulted Summer Beltane. He'd attacked women's rights. He'd embarrassed her by holding Welma's funeral, and his stupid dream had turned her comfortable life upside down. Yet, something bothered her.

Tonight, like most nights, she was drinking wine and talking on the phone with her friend Christy.

"Heard anything from George?"

"He emails occasionally to ask my forgiveness, but I'm not ready," she said.

"I wouldn't forgive him. He's a jerk," Christy said. "If he wants to live in the mountains like Daniel Boone then let him. You've got the house, the money, and the business. What else do you want?"

"Nothing, I suppose."

"Are you dating yet?"

"After George, who the hell would want a man?"

But that was not how she felt. She felt hollow. She felt sick with remorse. She felt an emptiness cutting into her soul like a searing scalpel. From the moment she woke up to when she uncorked her first bottle, she felt awful.

She said goodby to Christy and placed the phone on the counter. She reached for the bottle to pour herself another glass only to discover that she'd finished it. She took the empty to the recycling can and opened the lid. She was surprised to see that it was filled with empty wine bottles.

She walked back into the kitchen, found another bottle in the wine cooler, and uncorked it. After consuming a large drink, it dawned on her that it had been almost two years since George had left. It seemed like only a few months.

Millions of ugly thoughts about her ruined life swirled around in her head, until she broke down sobbing. After a good cry, she staggered up the staircase to her bedroom where she collapsed on the bed, and promptly passed out.

Sleep did not come easy. She tossed and turned in a violent slumber not knowing whether she was awake, or dreaming she was awake.

Eventually the nasty taste of sour wine in her mouth

forced her to struggle from the bed, undress, brush her teeth and collapse back under the covers.

That was when she heard the sound of a woman's voice speaking softly in the distance. She couldn't understand the words, but she knew someone was talking. It was if the person was whispering quietly to someone in the garden below her window.

She peeked at the time — three o'clock. *How could that be?*

The voice grew louder, audible. "Sarah Goodman, why do you question the work of the Lord?"

Her heart froze. She was instantly sober. She lay still, as if by being motionless she could become invisible. She squeezed her eyes tight, listening to the sounds of the old house.

She knew the fourth step of the staircase creaked when someone stepped on it, and the floorboards in the hallway gave a groan when a person approached her bedroom. Yet there was nothing — just the noise of the ceiling fan, and the occasional clunk of the refrigerator's ice maker downstairs.

Her body relaxed. She scolded herself for being so jumpy. Ever since Cookie's horrific death, she was afraid to be alone at night. Yet she lay between the sheets convinced that someone was in the room. She wished she'd allowed George to buy a gun.

"Don't be afraid Sarah," the voice said, only this time louder, with an Irish accent.

Sarah began shaking uncontrollably, tears streaming down her cheeks. She was trapped in a nightmare, unable to escape.

"Why do you cry, little one?" the voice asked. "I've been sent to collect you. My God-given name is unpronounceable to humans, so simply call me Kara."

Something unearthly squeezed her arm, and Sarah opened her eyes to see a woman's face looking at her. It was as dark and smooth as a polished stick of ebony wood. Two deep slits served as its eyes, and a Nubian nose shadowed a smiling mouth. Rivulets of gray dreadlocks cascaded down the sides of her face touching the chest of a tall stately woman. Around her neck she wore a delicate rope chain with a small golden horn attached.

"Don't hurt me," Sarah whimpered.

"Why would I do that, love?" Kara asked. "See, I've come to rescue you. Take my hand and learn, you daft little girl."

Seizing her gently, they rose through the ceiling of the house into the night sky blazing with stars. Sarah watched blankly as her world shrank into a speck, and finally disappear.

For the first time since she was a child, she took notice of the breathtaking vastness of the universe. Thousands of unimaginably immense galaxies, some with over a hundred trillion stars, and millions of complex solar systems encompassed her.

Spectacular showers of multicolored splendor streaked past them, as speeding yellow comets, and copper colored meteors whizzed by.

"It's magnificent don't ya think?" Kara asked. The question was rhetorical.

"George was right," Sarah murmured.

"Aye, he's loved the stars since he was a lad," Kara said. "The Master placed it in his heart."

"And I ridiculed him." Sarah's spirit shrank within her. "How was I to know?"

"You might have known had you ever taken a moment to look upward and inward. You were so worried about what others thought of you, your fashions, and your status that a world beyond your nose was unimaginable.

"You were a woman who craved the things of the world, and lusted for the admiration of others. It was never more apparent than when you despised your husband after he no longer shared your passion for earthy things."

Sarah hung her head like a condemned woman, for she was.

"Have you not read the Scripture that said, 'Thus says the Lord, your redeemer and the one who formed you from the womb: I, the Lord, am the maker of all things, stretching out the heavens by Myself and spreading out the earth all alone.'"[1]

She shook her head no.

"Perhaps you've read this one, 'By faith, we understand that the universe has been framed by the word of God.'"[2]

Sarah felt utterly stupid, she had no inkling what Kara was talking about.

"Holy Martyrs, girl! What did they teach you at your church?"

Sarah couldn't answer.

"Look for yourself and see the glory of the Father's creation," Kara said, extending her arms in a wide-sweeping gesture. "All of this was created to bring you closer to the Master."

"Me?"

"Who else? You and your kind are the Master's highest work of art. He formed this universe as the largest visible expression of his love that saves your world. The heavens are the Master's way of letting all people, from all times, in all stations, and from all places know that he exists, and is always near. When people look to the heavens they have a glimpse of his ordered and perfect mind. These are tangible, measurable, irrefutable works that define the depth of the Master's soul, and the complexity of his love.

"In the days before his coming these heavens were the primary way that humans came to believe in the existence of an almighty being. The writer of Psalm 73 once looked upward and confessed, "Who have I in heaven, but thee?""[3]

"This is too beautiful — too overwhelming for me to comprehend," Sarah said, beginning to weep again.

"The Master purposely made it that way. It is intended to captivate the human imagination forever."

"Is there other life out here?"

"Now there ya go," Kara scolded. "Why should there be? Yours is the only world that the Master created to dwell in. Humans are the only creatures he died to save. Why do you always search the stars looking for aliens, when the stars only exist to point to the Master?"

"We're looking for help," Sarah replied, dejectedly. "The world is hopeless."

"The Master is your world's only hope. You shouldn't go looking for creatures living in the universe to answer your questions, any more than you should go looking for intelligent life in a machine. There is only one race that he fashioned, and only one people that he chooses to live among."

Sarah felt an overpowering sense of humility. The last time she felt this way was when she gave birth to her children. "I always thought the stars were boring, just a backdrop for pool parties, or a reason for romantic songs," she said. "This is beyond expression."

"They are his gift, and a shadow of things to come," Kara said, pointing off into the distance. "Look there. That's the Bethlehem star.[4] Do you remember how the Father used it to lead the Magi to the infant Jesus?"

All Sarah could remember was sneering at George calling him the fourth Magi.

"And over there," Kara gestured. "That's the constellation Orion, called by the ancient ones the Heavenly Shepherd." [5]

Sarah had no idea that these things were mentioned in the Bible. She'd never heard Pastor Pendragon say a single word about them.

"Direct your attention to your left, and observe the seven stars of the Pleiades cluster. They represent the seven churches found in the Book of Revelation." [6]

Sarah had never made any connection between the universe, the Bible, and Jesus until now. She felt like a selfish, arrogant, ignorant cow.

"Cast your gaze upward, and you will be the first to see something very special. Your scientists have been hoping to find it."

Sarah tilted her head back. She saw nothing but an enormous dark void surrounding an even darker void.

"Your astronomers haven't discovered this, but when they do, it will reveal information that will unlock the secrets of how life was formed on earth. Someday, there will be a person who finds it and it will change the course of your world."

Ahead, a growing light emerged out of the void. Sarah saw a brilliant radiance coming from an immense circular object that looked like an enormous football stadium.

"What's that?" she gasped.

"That's heaven, love," Kara replied. "We near it. Would you like to meet Jesus?"

The Redemption of George | 313

THE DAY WAS SHORTER, THE SHADOWS LONGER, AND THE evenings were getting colder on the mountain. George stirred the bonfire and watched the sparks fly off into the heavens. He looked down into the last shadows of the valley below watching the headlights of a car begin to zig-zag up the steep mountain road to the camp.

"What should we pray for?" asked one of his friends sitting around the fire. The assembly had grown from two to twelve since George had arrived.

"We need to pray for the brave soul who's driving up the mountainside in the dark," he chuckled, poking at the logs. "That's a tough road to handle in the daytime, much less at night. Then we need to pray for our families, and our country."

"We also need to pray that our work glorifies God," said Paul Cunningham, a NASA researcher." He broke out a ukulele and began strumming the tune to Over the Rainbow.[7]

"Anyone for ribs?" asked Marina Kazakov, a Russian scientist. She placed a rack on the barbecue.

"Put me down for a plate," said Henry Ortiz, the station's climatologist.

Over the next hour the group sang, fellowshipped and prayed as the vehicle slowing traversed its way up the mountain.

The coals were dying and the group was ready to retire when the vehicle finally pulled into the campsite, its tires crunching over the gravel. Paul started strumming 'Best of My Love'[8] and the group began singing off key.

"Can anyone join in?" a woman's voice asked. George turned away from the fire to see Sarah standing in its glow.

"What the?" he asked, taking a step back.

She wavered tentatively, wondering how he would react.

"I didn't drive six hours, and all the way up this stupid hill to fight with you," she said, defensively. "I came to apologize."

She bowed her head. In the orange light of the fire George could see by the look on her face that she was suffering. Suddenly, as though a frozen water pipe burst, she broke into tears. "I'm sorry, I was wrong — so wrong. You're not stupid, you're the smartest man I know. You're not even an idiot."

George suppressed a laugh, and smiled at her.

"Can you ever forgive me?" she asked, sobbing.

"Forgive you?" he asked, taking her in his arms. "I love you, I've always loved you."

"You don't understand," she said. Then she thought twice. "What am I saying? Of course you understand."

Holding her by the shoulders he asked, "Can understand what?"

She told him in fast gasps and short bursts. "An angel named Kara took me to the stars. I saw Jesus, I saw the baby flames, I saw my place in heaven."

Paul's strumming on the ukulele changed to, 'Here comes the Sun.'[9]

"Whoa, slow down. You saw Jesus?"

"I was the stupid idiot, not you," she jabbered. "Jesus is alive, just like you tried to tell me."

"Yes, he certainly is," George agreed, wiping a tear from her cheek. "Tell me about Kara."

"She was black, she was beautiful, she was tall, her hair was in braids, she spoke with a lovely Irish accent, she wore a necklace with a golden horn, and she took me to Jesus."

George choked with emotion. There was only one person in Abundance Falls who fit that description. He was ashamed that he'd looked down on her. When would he ever learn?

Then he said, "I can't resist asking. Where was your seat in heaven?"

She snuffled, wiped her nose, and chuckled, "Right next to yours."

George clapped his hands together, and laughed. "Then we better get to work. We need to get a lot closer to Jesus."

"Let's start right now," she said, her eyes intently looking at him. "I want to pray with you — all of you." She looked around at the others.

The ukulele stopped, they joined hands, and the group bowed their heads. She began praying like she had done it all her life.

When she'd finished, she kissed George as if they were on their honeymoon. The group teased them, and they blushed.

"What's next?" George asked.

"Lets go follow a star," she answered.

And that's exactly what they did.

AFTERWORD

Another year passed. Spring transformed Abundance Falls into a city with as many colors as the sprinkles covering the donut I held in my hand. Charlie and I sat in a booth at the Starflyer Diner nursing our mugs of coffee. We'd become close friends, and we were ready to take on another church project.

Kara no longer worked here. The Great Angel had assigned her to float among a variety of coffee shops and restaurants throughout the region, where she continues to help people through their difficult times. Which is why you should always be nice to the person who serves you. For you never know when you will entertain an angel.[1]

Peter went on to expand his computer empire, became an avid student of the Bible, and is now an outspoken critic of abortion. He and George took Welma's money and established the *Welma Forthwright Foundation* to help rescue and support women and girls considering abortion.

And Kip? In addition to running his private military corporation, he is now the head of Vengeance. Together with George and Peter, he works to destroy the dragons of darkness controlling the citizens of Abundance Falls, and your community.

As Peter predicted, the congregation of the First Establishment Church drifted away when the money was gone. Today the church no longer exists, except as a memory.

However, if you ever wish to experience the glory that was once the First Establishment Church, you can make a reservation at *The First Church Bar & Grill* where, you can sit in its old sanctuary under the priceless stained glass windows, and reflect on the days when the elite ruled the world of Christianity. For this once sacred domain of worship is now a stunning restaurant complete with an outdoor patio, and a trendy bar up in the choir loft, where the only spirit you'll find is captured in a bottle.

And what of Mal'ak the reaping angel? He still serves the Master by bringing souls like yours to their eternal judgement. One day, you will meet him face to face, and I pray that you are ready.

If you're looking for a glimmer of light at the end of this tale, you'll be pleased to learn that there is an exciting new entry into the catalog of recognized astronomic phenomenon.

The entry was made after a person searching through the night sky stumbled upon a dark star that had never been found. The astounding information it revealed, caused astronomers and scientists from all over the world to readjust their thinking about the origins of the universe, time, space, physics, and humanity.

As recognition for his significant contribution to the field of astronomy, the International Astronomical Society allowed the person to name the star. He did not hesitate for an instant when telling them that it should be called, "The Sarah Star."

ABOUT THE AUTHOR

Steve lives in the Texas Hill Country with his family, and their two dogs. He was born, educated, and grew up in the heart of Southern California. He has been an ordained minister for most of his adult life.

ALSO BY STEVE WALSH

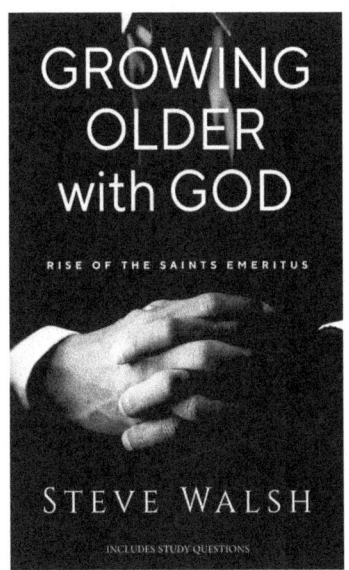

The Field Manual for aging spiritually.

Growing Older with God presents a bold, biblical approach to help you navigate the stormy waters of aging, at a time when many people feel old, tired, discouraged, or may even wonder if they should just end their life.

Growing Older with God is available in the Amazon Bookstore.

NOTES

Chapter 1

1. Paraphrased from an American Spiritual by J.W. Johnson and J.R. Johnson, 1925. https://www.negrospirituals.com
2. Doxxing is to publicly reveal personal and private information about an individual with the intent to harm them. Normally done on the internet through social media platforms.

Chapter 2

1. Matthew 18:20

Chapter 3

1. 1 John 2:15
2. Daniel 5:27
3. The expression Edge of Life, is taken from: Rybicki EP (1990). "The classification of organisms at the edge of life, or problems with virus systematics." South African Journal of Science. 86: 182–86.
4. Matthew 23:33: "Ye serpents, ye generation of vipers, how can ye escape the damnation of hell?" - Jesus.
5. Colossians 1:13-14
6. Leviticus 19:28
7. A material that is resistant to decomposition by heat.
8. 1 Peter 3:19
9. Isaiah 43:25
10. 1 John 1:9
11. 1 Peter 1:15-16, "But just as he who called you is holy, you yourselves also be holy in all of your behavior; because it is written, 'You shall be holy; for I am holy.'" (Leviticus 11:44-45)
12. Matthew 19:14
13. Daniel 12:2-3
14. Romans 10:9 — "If you will confess with your mouth that Jesus is Lord, and believe in your heart that God raised him from the dead, you

will be saved. For with the heart, one believes resulting in righteousness; and with the mouth confession is made resulting in salvation."
15. Matthew 23:14
16. Revelation 2:17 — "To him who overcomes, to him I will give of the hidden manna, and I will give him a white stone, and on the stone a new name written, which no one knows but he who receives it."
17. Psalm 22:6 — "But I am a worm, and no man; a reproach of men, and despised by the people."
18. James 4:8
19. John 6:53-56
20. https://www.weforum.org/agenda/2018/09/the-hidden-cost-of-the-electric-car-boom-child-labour/
21. Job 38:1-7
22. Based on $2.10 per meal. https://centralusa.salvationarmy.org/milwaukee/feed-the-kids/
23. Matthew 24:35
24. Psalm 19:1-4
25. John 14:2

Chapter 4

1. Jeremiah 1:5
2. Psalm 139:13-16
3. Acts 2:16-17; Joel 2:28

Chapter 5

1. Radicle, far left, revolutionary Marxists. Founded by Vladimer Lenin.
2. An act that causes the death of a fetus.
3. Intentional killing of an infant.
4. Black women are four times more likely and Hispanic women are 2.5 times more likely to have abortions than white women. https://www.thoughtco.com/abortion-facts-and-statistics-3534189
5. 2 Timothy 1:9

Chapter 6

1. An official reprimand leading to excommunication or loss of church membership.

2. 2 Corinthians 1:8-11
3. Ephesians 6:12
4. I Corinthians 1:18
5. J.R.R.Tolkien, The Fellowship of the Ring.

Chapter 7

1. George was requoting Doctor Weatherly in Rudyard Kipling's the "Phantom Rickshaw."
2. Revelation 3:20

Chapter 8

1. Ephesians 2:8 — "For it is by grace you have been saved, through faith —and this is not from yourselves, it is the gift of God." God is the embodiment and originator of grace. It is from him alone that we experience, and then reflect his grace.
2. The killing of an infant.
3. Few insults in the military are lower than being called a REMF. It usually identifies a cowardly soldier who has worked hard to avoid combat by politicking for a job in the rear.

Chapter 9

1. http://www.johnstonsarchive.net/policy/abortion/usa_abortion_by_race.html
2. Following WWII, war crimes trials were held in the city of Nuremberg, Germany for crimes against humanity. During the "Judges' Trial" sixteen jurists and lawyers were tried for their part in abusing the penal process to change the laws to further the "racial purity" program, resulting in the death of millions of Jews. All of them pleaded not guilty.
3. "Encourage the exhausted, and strengthen the feeble. Say to those with anxious heart, 'Take courage, fear not. Behold, your God will come with **vengeance**; The recompense of God will come, and He will save you." Isaiah 35:3

Chapter 10

1. https://thefederalist.com/2021/04/15/federal-government-caught-buying-fresh-flesh-of-aborted-babies-who-could-have-survived-as-preemies/

    https://www.breitbart.com/politics/2021/04/16/biden-harris-administration-to-ramp-up-experiments-using-aborted-baby-body-parts/

Chapter 12

1. "For it was not an enemy who betrayed me. . . but it was you . . . my companion, and my familiar friend. We took sweet fellowship together. We walked in God's house together."

Chapter 14

1. Isaiah 44:24
2. Hebrews 11:3
3. Psalm 73:25
4. Matthew 2:2
5. Job 9:9, 38:31; Amos 5:8
6. Job 9:9, 38:31; Amos 5:8
7. Composed by Harold Arlen with lyrics by Yip Harburg. Sung by Judy Garland in the movie The Wizard of Oz; 1939
8. Written by Don Henley, Glenn Frey, and J. D. Souther; The Eagles, On the Border; 1974
9. Written by George Harrison, The Beatles. 1969, Abby Road album.

Afterword

1. Hebrews 13:2